OPERATION BLAZO

"From what you all told me," said Admiral Gifford, "I have to assume there's a terrorist on TOA Flight 805 with the last vial of virus. As I see it, there are two threats to the world from this venom-producing virus—Flight 805 and us." He looked directly at Yael. She nodded.

"So?" Maddox bristled. "What does that mean?"

"With refueling we can catch them before they land in Honolulu."

"And then what?" Maddox didn't really want to know.

"Pray you and Doctor Ivanov—and Owen with his crippled computer—come up with a solution by then."

"But what if we don't?" Christopher protested. He watched the others look away.

"Operation Blazo," Jackson answered.

"What the hell is Blazo?"

"Our contingency plan, if all else fails."

Maddox fought against comprehension. He refused to believe.

Jackson shrugged. "Simple, Doc. We kamikaze them."

Books by Richard Parry

Ice Warrior
Venom Virus

Published by POCKET BOOKS

VENOM VIRUS

RICHARD PARRY

POCKET BOOKS

New York   London   Toronto   Sydney   Tokyo   Singapore

An *Original* Publication of POCKET BOOKS

POCKET BOOKS, a division of Simon & Schuster Inc.
1230 Avenue of the Americas, New York, NY 10020

ISBN: 0-671-74037-7

First Pocket Books printing April 1992

10 9 8 7 6 5 4 3 2 1

POCKET and colophon are registered trademarks of
Simon & Schuster Inc.

Cover art by Lee MacLeod

Printed in the U.S.A.

To my sons, David and Matthew:

*Rest satisfied with doing well,
and leave others to talk of you
as they please.*

—PYTHAGORAS

Acknowledgments

No book arises from a vacuum.

Doug Grad, Associate Editor at Pocket Books, holds my undying gratitude for his direction and support of this work. Thanks again to Sharon Coulter and Ann Marlin for their encouragement and helpful suggestions, Ron Kovalik for technical assistance, and Al Paulson for the sea snake pictures. A special thanks to Stephen D. Thomas for his lucid presentation of Micronesian culture and sailing skills in his book, *The Last Navigator*. And to my wife, Kathie, my own polar star.

VENOM
VIRUS

CHAPTER

1

Honolulu International Airport

The pain hit Malmoud at 10:27 A.M. He was walking toward the D concourse. A spasm stopped him in midstride and forced him to lean against a cement column for support. Pressing his head to the stone, the courier fought wave after wave of nausea, followed by violent muscle twitching of his lower legs. Perspiration erupted across his forehead and down the center of his back. His nails dug into the column as a second cramp twisted within his stomach. He rolled his face across the cool cement, producing a damp smear.

His eyes rested on a crumpled newspaper by his feet. The day's date, Friday, August 17, wavered in and out of focus. Crimping his eyelids, he prayed for strength. Allah, he said silently, help the faithful.

The agony abated. Malmoud eased his hold on the column and wiped his face with a shaking hand. Curiously, his throat felt thick. He had difficulty swallowing the saliva that welled in his mouth following the attack.

He noticed a heavyset Hawaiian woman in a flowered muumuu watching him. Malmoud released his hold but found that his legs were still quivering. The woman approached. He tried to will himself into invisibility, as he had been taught in his training as a recruit for the Front for Liberation outside of Beirut.

"Are you okay?" the woman asked with concern.

"Yes, yes." He searched in his rumpled pants and withdrew a soiled handkerchief, which he pressed to his lips.

"You don't look so good."

Malmoud braced against another stab of pain. The woman's perfume, a cheap derivative of pikake flowers, added to his mounting nausea. He tried to wave her away.

"I'm gonna call security. You need help."

Malmoud focused on the plastic name tag nestled between her ample breasts. The letters blurred. He blinked to keep them in focus. "You work here?" His voice was strained.

"Over in the sandwich shop. I'll go call."

"Please, don't. I . . . I don't wish to be any trouble. I'm feeling better."

"Are you sure?"

"Yes, yes. A long flight. Some stomach trouble. I'm not used to traveling, you understand? I'm already taking medication." He smiled lamely. "Too much new food!"

"Yeah, I know what you mean." The woman relaxed. "Got sick when I visited my sister in San Diego. Look, why don't you sit down in the garden?" She pointed over the edge of the ramp to a miniature Japanese garden below. Moist, fragrant breezes drifted up from the landscaped terrace. That oasis seemed out of place amid the concrete arches and frenzied travelers of Honolulu's busy airport.

"Thank you, I will."

The woman backed away, smiling. She turned and waved over her shoulder.

Malmoud waved back. Then he saw the man. Off to one side, near a portable flower stand, stood a small man in a light suit, wearing a white shirt open at the collar. The man sneezed. That sneeze caught Malmoud's attention.

2

He recognized him! It was the man from his flight from Tokyo—the same man he had seen in Beirut.

Malmoud panicked. He spun on unsteady legs, knocking into a passing girl. The girl sprawled across the cement floor with a scream. Her lei broke, spilling plastic flowers across the tiled floor. People stopped to look. The man in the light suit stepped from behind the cart.

Malmoud ran down the D concourse.

Leaping over the rope dividers, he encountered a mass of people clustered at the entrance to the metal detectors. Malmoud glanced back to see airport police helping the girl up. People were pointing at him. One officer was calling into his walkie-talkie. The short man in the light suit was walking rapidly in his direction.

Malmoud jumped onto the metal table to the left of the detector arch as a security guard grabbed at his legs. The pants fabric tore, and the guard fell, spinning under the X-ray machine. Malmoud kicked at the other guard and clambered over the wall of equipment. More people were pointing and screaming at him. His head spun. One police officer drew his revolver.

The Palestinian sprinted for the clearing between the conveyor belt and a pile of luggage abandoned by frightened travelers. His foot snagged on a loop of wire cable, and he fell heavily onto his side. In an instant he regained his feet to race down the corridor amid screaming and pushing people. Malmoud yelled to increase their confusion.

A shot clipped the wall over his head, then ricocheted into a pane of glass. The bullet and the breaking window fueled the panic in the terminal. Passengers now huddled in clusters on the floor. Adrenaline pumped through Malmoud. His heart rate tripled. His eyes focused on an emergency door that opened onto the tarmac. Escape and safety lay just beyond one last clump of people. Malmoud issued a wordless prayer of thanks and ran for the door.

He never reached the exit. Halfway there a convulsion knotted his body. Twitching in midstride like a marionette in the hands of a mad puppeteer, Malmoud jerked about, suspended in the air. His head swung around, revealing lips pulled into a tight rictus and wide, wild eyes. Flecks of foam spewed from his mouth. The seizure drew Malmoud's back into a bow until only his toes touched the ground. Then the bow snapped, and he fell to the floor. Shudders rippled over his limbs as he died.

The police officer approached while keeping the body covered with his revolver.

"My God, what is it?" A middle-aged traveler in the obligatory flowered shirt peered over his shoulder.

"Stand back." The gun stayed centered on the crumpled body.

"What is that?" The tourist pointed to the darkened blood that seeped from Malmoud's eyes and nostrils. "What *is* that? What did you shoot him with?"

The officer blanched. "I didn't hit him." Both men retreated from the corpse. The circle of curious bystanders widened about the form. "Keep back!"

"Look out! He's got some kind of disease. Look out! It's AIDS!"

"Stand back." The officer's voice was lost in a new series of shouts and screams as the terminal emptied in a broiling mass of humanity fleeing the concourse. Only a man in a light-colored suit hung at the periphery.

Downtown Honolulu

Kenzo Harii slumped into the worn leather chair behind his cluttered desk and moved to wipe the perspiration from his forehead. The battered clock on his desk read four o'clock in the afternoon. Friday afternoon, and he had hours of work left. His hand stopped in midair.

He was still wearing latex surgical gloves from his last autopsy. Kenzo turned the blood-covered gloves over, stripped them off, and tossed them into a wastepaper basket. Blood stained his right index finger and filled the groove around his nail. Another hole in his glove, he mused. At least he hadn't stuck himself this time. Life was becoming more uncertain.

As assistant coroner for the city of Honolulu he was exposed to an increasing number of autopsy cases of AIDS, hepatitis, and God knew what. He was beginning to feel like Henry Gray, the brilliant eighteenth-century anatomist who had died of smallpox. It was only a matter of time. Perhaps he should have gone into banking as his father had wanted. *Shi kata ga nai,* it cannot be helped. He shrugged with a sense of oriental fatalism.

The door to his office slammed open. Harii looked up, but he already knew who it was: Marlin Pearl, the mayor's special counsel, a gofer who did the dirty work of trying to gloss over the fact that Honolulu was a big city with rats and garbage. Hiding rapes and shark attacks was Marlin's specialty. Anything to protect tourism.

"One of these days you'll break that door, Marlin."

"Fuck the door. Harry, we got big problems."

"You always have big problems. I only have little ones, like this broken air conditioner and these unfinished autopsies." The bloodied finger waved across the piles on the desk.

"Aah! Christ, Harry, look at your finger! It's all bloody." Pearl halted in midstride, keeping his Gucci sharkskin suit a good two yards from possible contact with the contaminated digit.

"This is a bloody business."

"Well, wash it off or something. I don't like the way it looks."

"The sink in this office is broken. Don't you remember? That happened six weeks ago." The finger aimed at the attorney.

"Okay, okay, you made your point. I'll try to get it fixed."

Pearl avoided the fingertip as if it were the barrel of a gun. He checked his Ferragamo shoes for possible drips. "Did you get that new body? The airport case?"

"The one your boys blasted in front of all the haoles?"

"Not my boys, Harry. Oh, no. Not my boys. Besides, he wasn't shot."

"Yeah, well, he's downstairs in the morgue. The deaners are preparing him for autopsy now."

"They think he died of AIDS. He just went crazy and had these seizures. God, it was in front of an incoming planeload of Shriners from Chicago." Pearl winced as he watched Harii wipe his finger on his trousers. He needed a smoke.

"Doesn't sound like AIDS to me."

"Well, what do you think then? Drugs?"

"Maybe the Black Death."

"Don't say that!" Pearl searched for a cigarette.

"Don't light that in here. Formaldehyde is explosive," Harii lied.

Marlin dropped the pack atop Kenzo's desk without thinking. It landed near a jar containing slices from the liver of a man poisoned by his wife.

Marlin realized his mistake. In his office he could toss his smokes anywhere, but this pathologist's desk was covered with disease. He dreaded coming down to this hole. One never knew what might be growing on the walls. Pearl gingerly extracted his pack using two fingers. Those fingers held the cigarettes as he would hold a drowned rat while the lawyer calculated their cost versus the risk of some dreaded illness. Frugality won, and he dropped them into his coat pocket. He made a mental note to wipe off the cellophane wrapper.

"I've got the tox screen here." Harii scanned the computer printout of Malmoud's blood tests. His eyebrows rose. "Wow! This guy's full of camphorated tincture of opium."

"Opium! I knew it! A doper! That's great, a drug overdose. I'll drop the quarantine right now." Marlin chuckled with glee. Now he could remove the fake construction signs

6

he had placed around the sealed concourse. Drawn in the shape of the Menehune—the Hawaiian version of a leprechaun—the work signs sported hard hats, work belts, and apologetic placards. The airlines hated them. Removing them would get the airlines off his back. They could have their damn terminal back.

"Hold on, Marlin. Nobody overdoses on paregoric."

"Paregoric?"

"Yeah, this stiff's so full of paregoric he wouldn't be able to crap until Christmas." Kenzo turned to the folder containing the dead man's X rays. He held them up to his desk lamp. "It would be nice to have a real view box," he lamented.

"Please, Harry, I'll put it in the next budget."

"Look at this! See that? Now *that's* strange." Harii pointed to an opaque image on the abdominal film.

"Looks like a bottle."

"It is. There's a vial in the splenic flexure."

Pearl's face took on a blank look.

"The large intestine. The corpse has a vial inside his colon. It's too big to swallow accidentally. He must have done it on purpose."

"A drug carrier!" Marlin was familiar with people swallowing condoms stuffed with cocaine who died of overdoses when the condoms broke while still in their intestines.

"I don't think so. The vial is too small to make it worth his while. He's clean for all other drugs, and that bottle isn't large enough to hold all the paregoric in his system. Besides, no one smuggles paregoric. Nobody uses that stuff anymore, except in Third World countries."

"His passport says he came from Frankfurt. Frankfurt to Rome to Tokyo to here." Marlin watched his solution fade as Harii shook his head.

"All modern cities, Marlin. They don't use paregoric. It doesn't add up. My guess is that he used the paregoric to slow the transit time of his GI tract so the vial would stay inside him until he reached his destination."

"Well, what's the answer? I need to get that concourse open as soon as possible. The mayor's on my ass, and I can't keep those Menehune signs up forever. This is costing the city. Come on, I need an answer."

Harii rose from his desk. The pathologist noticed the perspiration on Pearl's forehead. "Let's do the autopsy. The answer's in that vial."

Pearl blanched. "I was afraid you'd say that."

Kenzo led the way down the back stairs to the basement that held the examining rooms while Pearl followed. Glancing over his shoulder to make sure Marlin had not escaped, Harii remarked: "Remember, Marlin, a pathologist knows everything and does everything, but one day too late."

Ten minutes later the two men stood looking at the naked body atop the stainless steel table. The body looked small, flattened, and pale, like a collapsed balloon. A violaceous hue covered the dependent side of the skin and ran along the underside of the rigid limbs. Marlin tried not to touch anything.

"Okay, Lou." The pathologist nodded to his assistant, "You do the head while I open the chest and abdomen."

Marlin Pearl swallowed hard as Kenzo selected a number ten scalpel blade and drew an exaggerated Y across the chest of the cadaver. The lower limb of the cut extended onto the abdomen, dividing the skin and muscle in the midline. The skin parted beneath the pressure of the knife to expose pale fat and ribs. No blood entered the wound. The blade bounced over the ribs. Harii dropped the scalpel on the metal table and selected a curved instrument that reminded Pearl of a linoleum knife. Leaning over the body, the pathologist deftly cut through the ribs on both sides of the sternum and lifted the anterior rib cage off.

"Bloodless surgery, Marlin," Harii remarked.

The mayor's assistant jumped as the dead man's head thumped onto the metal while Lou peeled the scalp and hair forward over the expressionless face. The deaner flicked on a circular bone saw and proceeded to cut off the top of the skull. Marlin dodged a spray of blood and bone chips that spattered their plastic aprons. The two men seemed to him to be racing, each trying to beat the other with his part of the autopsy.

Lou pried open the cranium, dropped his saw, and held up his arms like a champion. "Ta-da! I win again." Wiping his gloves on his apron, he reached over to touch a button of the stereo nestled on the wall. Music filled the autopsy room.

"This is sick, Harry, really sick," protested Marlin.

Harii laughed. "No, it's Vivaldi . . . the only way to go! Actually, Marlin, we put on that show for you. A little levity is needed once in a while. It's just hard work from here on." He opened the peritoneal cavity and ran loops of mottled bowel between his fingers. "Strange, lots of hemorrhage . . . lots of internal bleeding. Now where is that vial?"

Marlin Pearl gagged as the warm stench of decaying flesh assailed him. He staggered to the sink.

"Got it!" Kenzo exclaimed. He withdrew a loop of intestine and carefully milked it with his hands until the outline of a small cylinder bulged against the translucent wall. Then he incised the bowel wall and delivered the vial. Behind him Lou was removing the brain.

"What is it?" Marlin struggled with his nausea.

"Doesn't look like much. Looks like a standard medicine vial containing a couple of cc's of clear fluid." He held up the bottle with its black screw cap and turned it between his two fingers. The fluid reflected dully in the light. "I don't see any markings. Wait, there may be some sort of mark on the bottom of the glass!" Harii held the container up to the light, tipping his head back to peer over his half glasses. He turned the vial over. "It looks like the letter V . . . Yeah, it's a V."

Absentmindedly Kenzo shook the glass. The cap was loose. A drop of liquid fell into his eye. He screamed. The pathologist whirled, tearing at his right eye with gloved hands. The eye swelled into an inflamed mass in seconds. Harii ran blindly, knocking over instrument trays and specimen jars. Lou pinned him over the cadaver and dragged him to the sink, forcing Harii's face under the tap while the panicked physician fought him. The bulging lid covered the injured eye.

"Hold the doc!" Lou yelled at Pearl. The lawyer helped while trying to maintain as little contact as possible. Lou snatched a pair of bent paper clips that were taped to the faucet. The clips were bent in wide loops and made especially for such an emergency. Keeping Kenzo's twisting face beneath the stream of water, he hooked the wires under the bloated lid, lifting it off the steamy globe. The victim shrieked in agony as the water flushed his eye. Moments passed until the struggling ceased. Lou helped the shaking doctor to a chair.

"Thanks, Lou," Harii mumbled. "God! What was that stuff? Burns like hell." He pressed his handkerchief to the stinging area. "It's better now."

"Better get that looked at right away, Doc."

"Yeah, Harry, it looks bad."

"I think I'll sit here for a minute. Get my sea legs back." He tried to recover his composure. "Okay, feel better now. I'll get it checked. These things happen once in a while." But he knew this was his worst encounter. Banking looked better and better. He would call his father in the morning.

Kenzo Harii struggled to rise. The seizure struck without warning, arching his back and limbs so he flexed above the chair. The metal chair clattered to the floor. Spasms rocked his body. His head bobbed on an extended neck to climb along the wall. This grisly dance continued as tetany clamped Kenzo's jaws and drew back his lips. Blood spewed from his nose and mouth.

Pearl froze as he watched his acquaintance seizing. The spasms seemed endless. Caught by the suddenness and the violence of the attack, the two men could only stand and watch. In seconds that seemed like eons, Kenzo Harii died with the deadly vial locked in his hand.

"Holy shit!" Marlin tripped over the chair in his haste to escape. "Let's get out of here!" The mayor's assistant skidded across the floor on his knees, mindless of the blood and grease that now stained his trousers. His only thought was to flee.

"What about the doc?"

"Don't touch him! He's dead. Something in that bottle got him." Marlin spun toward the door. "Let's go."

Blocking his exit was a short man in a light tropical suit. "No one leaves this room," the man commanded.

"You're not allowed in here," Marlin started to protest. Then he remembered the madness he had just witnessed. "Get out of my way! We've got to get out of here before we all catch this thing! It's deadly."

"No one leaves."

"Move the fuck away from the door! Get him, Lou!" The two rushed the little man.

The man at the door produced a pistol that he leveled at Pearl's chest. The charge halted.

"Wait!" Marlin's hands jumped over his head. "Don't shoot! Look"—he tried a different approach—"that thing . . . this whole room . . . it's dangerous to be in here. Let us out, please."

The pistol remained pointed at Marlin's chest. The man shook his head as he reached behind to lock the door. "Sit over there." His eyes stayed fastened on them as he motioned to the corner farthest from the body on the floor. A sneeze jostled his gun arm.

Marlin leapt forward.

A 9mm bullet cut through Pearl's Gucci shoulder pad. "Don't shoot!" The attorney retreated to his assigned corner.

"Sit down. Otherwise I'll shoot you dead." The man moved closer to the body of the dead pathologist and knelt by the outstretched hand. The vial caught his attention.

"Don't touch that bottle!" Marlin yelled from the corner. "You'll get us all killed. It's some kind of poison."

"I won't. Now we wait for instructions." Inching around the body and the autopsy table, the man with the pistol lifted the wall phone and dialed a number. He whispered into the receiver in a foreign language.

"You can't keep us in here indefinitely. Someone's going to be looking for us."

The man with the gun wasn't listening. He settled against the door. His dark eyes searched the two men and then the dead bodies, resting on the dried blood about Malmoud's mouth and the fresh blood issuing from Harii.

"Like the others," he said to himself. "Just like the others. . . ."

CHAPTER

2

Washington, D.C.

"Why do we always seem to spend the evenings handling crises? Can't they happen, just for once, in the morning, when everyone is fresh and well rested?" The gray-haired man paced past the window. Lights from the Capitol shone through the sheer curtains. He paused imperceptibly to analyze the tinted windows. "New windows, Mort?"

"Ah, you noticed, Henry. Yes. The latest in anti-electronic surveillance coatings—marvelous new technology. Prevents monitoring of sound and electromagnetic transmissions through the glass. Also, they're said to be energy efficient. Helps keep the embassy's heating bills down. I wondered how long it would take you. That's one reason I invited you over for this evening. After all that has been said, I want you to know, my dear friend, that I have no doubts about your abilities. I can think of no one more qualified to run your government's counterintelligence section."

Henry Clay Gifford's face clouded. "You heard about my run-in with the honorable congressman from New Jersey. Amazing how porous that closed session was!"

Mordecai Lod, head of intelligence at Israel's Washington embassy, spread his hands in supplication. "My friend, this is Washington. And you Americans so pride yourselves in the openness of democracy that you fall over one another in your willingness to divulge even secret meetings." Lod smiled. "It certainly makes my job an easy one."

"I can say that the meeting wasn't . . . dull."

"Henry, I wish I could have been there to see the gentleman's face when you called him—what was the word? Neofascist, I believe?"

"I am unable to confirm or deny anything relating to such a meeting—if, indeed, such a meeting even took place."

"To be sure. Well, in fairness, my government is learning the hard way about openness, too. All the media coverage of the Palestinian unrest is hurting us."

Admiral Gifford accepted a tumbler from his host. "Bless you, Mort, you always remember my Wild Turkey." As he sipped the amber liquid, Gifford paused before the fireplace and lifted a framed photograph of a young man in Israeli Defense Force uniform. "This is your son, right? Is he still a tank commander?"

"No, Henry. Last I heard, he had decided to become an architect. But he's still in the reserves. Everyone is in the reserves." The consul shook his head sadly. "We are a nation besieged. In spite of all our gains in technology, Israel is held prisoner to the politics of the region. I don't believe our founders ever thought we would be beleaguered for the entire life of our country. It's almost too much to ask of our people. Do you know, Henry, my son has never known peace?"

"But progress is being made, Mort. Look at the recent discussions. And the possibility of elections in the West Bank."

"That is all threatened now," Lod answered flatly.

"What?"

"Yes. I have something to show you. I received it this morning."

Gifford smiled grimly. "I was waiting for the other shoe to drop. We've never had a get-together that was truly social, have we?"

"Are we so predictable, my friend? Yes, I suspect we are. We are also the products of our time. . . ."

"And we don't have the luxury of being in the reserves."

The Israeli led the admiral into a room that contained a large-screen TV. "Al Bakaar is up to something."

"That fanatic! Surely no one would listen to him."

"Khalid Al Bakaar is indeed a fanatic—and a dangerous one. I would agree with you, Henry. He's too extreme for either side. But someone's been sending him money."

"None of the big players, Mort. His Front for Liberation-Special Action Group is the laughingstock of the terrorists since they blew themselves up along with their entire supply of high explosives in Athens."

"Yes. I'm still indebted to you for those instant-acting detonators you supplied to our people."

"It was an ingenious twist—detonators that fired on insertion into plastic explosives. But you need to thank Jackson. It was his idea. And it aborted an attack on the U.S. Sixth Fleet in Falaron Bay."

"Jackson, your dependable assistant. I'm surprised he's not here."

"He's downstairs."

"Ah, yes. My men wouldn't let him up with his weapon."

"I convinced him I would be safe," Gifford chuckled. "But what of Al Bakaar?"

Lod clicked the remote control of the TV. "My men monitored this."

The screen filled with burning eyes framed by an unkempt beard and a tattered burnoose. The eyes held them captive as the lips moved, forming words in Arabic.

"I'll translate for you. He's quoting passages from the Koran that prove, he says, that he is the next prophet: how he came out of the desert, his lineage back to Mohammed, his visions—"

15

"All the usual stuff."

"Right. But this is the new part that has us worried. He says to prove to all his skeptics that this is true, he will call down a plague upon the cities of the infidels. A scourge worse than the world has ever seen, and one that the unbelievers will spread among themselves . . . until they are all destroyed."

The image dissolved in electronic snow. Mordecai clicked off the screen.

Gifford's face twitched involuntarily. "Mad as a March hare." He rubbed the prickling hairs on the back of his neck.

"And as a madman, he's always spoken directly. Henry, the man's always tried to do what he's said."

"Could this be just theatrics?"

"I doubt it. Look, after his fiasco in Greece another blunder would finish him. Even his few followers would desert him. He can't afford to make idle threats or promises he can't keep."

"A plague . . ." Gifford was already thinking.

"One spread among ourselves."

"That rules out nuclear weapons, thank God. Doesn't sound like chemical agents or like nerve gas, either."

"We don't think so. Moving canisters of those agents requires more help than Khalid can provide at this time. He's only got a handful of followers. Libya, Syria, and Iran aren't in at this time. Apparently they don't believe him."

"Let's hope they stay that way. What about the Soviets?"

"Nothing to link them in any way."

"I agree, Mort. We're not noticing any new Russian activity. Well, what's left? Biologicals?"

"I'm afraid so. That makes me worry about Iraq."

"Yeah, the Iraqis love germs. Shit! I wish the fucking scientists would stop playing around with those things. Bullets and bombs are bad enough, but how can we protect the world from a poison that's small enough to be carried in your pocket before it's dumped into some city's water supply? Botulism would be my guess."

"I agree, Henry. My men are already watching biological production centers in the Middle East, India, and Europe."

"I'll check our contacts in Japan and make a few discreet inquiries."

"Thank you, Admiral. Please excuse me. I am a poor host. Dinner has been waiting while I burdened you with my—"

The red phone on Mordecai's desk rang.

"Do you want me to leave?" Henry Clay knew that phone was a secret, secured line. His men had placed a tap on it only weeks before, but they were still struggling with the scrambling codes.

Lod shook his head. He lifted the receiver. "Yes? What? Asher, where are you? My God. But that's impossible. . . ." The Israeli listened intently, then continued an animated conversation in Hebrew.

Gifford noticed a vein swelling in the middle of his forehead. Bad news, the admiral thought. Gifford marked his watch. The time was 9:55 P.M.

Visibly shaken, Lod replaced the receiver. He slumped into the padded leather chair behind the desk. "We may be too late, Henry. One of our agents feels Khalid has already introduced his plague into the U.S."

"Where?"

"Hawaii."

"How reliable is this information, Mordecai?"

"I believe our man Asher. He just called from Honolulu."

"But do you trust this Asher?"

"I would trust him with my life. He's my son."

CHAPTER

3

Taongi Atoll, Republic of the Marshall Islands,
Micronesia

Tangaroa reefed in the crabclaw sail as the wind swirled leeward. The outrigger canoe groaned, then creaked as the mast pulled against the coconut rope lashings. Tangaroa held the lines, and the boat swung to, recognizing it would lose this battle of wills. The canoe cleared the shallow reef with the next swell and ran aground onto the white sand beach. The old man squinted into the sun.

Above him a shimmering dart drew a pale contrail across the cloudless sky. The old man had never seen a Boeing 747, except as something that left its track in his dreams. Soon, too soon, these silver birds would intrude into his world. His dreams told him so. Shaking his head, his gaze returned to his sea and its islands.

Up the beach a group of small boys was running toward the boat. He turned back to coil the husk ropes between his callused hands. Years of sun and salt water had transformed the skin into hide resembling that of the green sea turtle. Moving with a mind of their own, the hands knotted and coiled the lines, stretching their scarred and furrowed skin over joints grown large from arthritis. As the hands worked his mind searched the endless seam that joined the sea with the sky.

"Tangaroa, Tangaroa!" The boys arrived with a scattering of sand and water to leap about the canoe.

"Do I hear Uliso, the disrespectful frigate bird, calling my name?"

The youngsters collected themselves, trying hard to achieve some semblance of decorum. "No, master. Attiru." They bent politely at the waist in respect for this ancient navigator of their island.

"Good. I do not teach the old ways to frigate birds who steal my fish when my back is turned. I teach the *etu*, the secrets of navigation, and the ancient ways of our people only to men. Only to those who will be the leaders of our people."

The boys stood tall and tried to look their most serious. They clustered about the old man, jostling for position and trying not to break any of the numerous taboos, such as that against stepping over the anchor rope.

Hanging back at the fringe of the group, a boy watched the others. He was smaller than the rest and wore a threadbare T-shirt and tattered cotton shorts with the pockets torn away. His serious eyes collected the scene while his fingers ran over the sun-bleached lettering of his shirt that had once proclaimed Live and Dive in Hawaii. Thorns from the *kiawe* tree had torn out the D in Dive. The boy balanced awkwardly on his right leg, hiding his deformed left foot in the sand.

A blast from a steam whistle shattered the air. The children's heads snapped to the entrance to the harbor. The freighter from Ponape announced its arrival with another toot, and the boys were gone, scampering away to the harbor.

Tangaroa pretended not to notice or to care. The new world continued to rob his old world. The rope coiled in his hands. He laid it carefully in the canoe. When he looked up he saw the small boy still standing at a distance. The boy's dark eyes met Tangaroa's.

"Boy, come here." The navigator motioned. He watched the child approach, self-consciously dragging his clubfoot. "What is your name?"

"I'm called Mau. Because of my foot."

Tangaroa nodded. *Mau,* the hawksbill sea turtle, clumsy on land. The streaks made in the sand by the crippled limb resembled the tracks of the turtle.

"I swim well," the boy added defensively. "And Reverend Castle says I'm a good student."

Castle! The name irritated Tangaroa. Castle, who taught them that only God could provide for them, so the people forgot the ancient rituals. Soon the secret chants for calling the floating logs and calling the breadfruit and the coconut would be no more. Then if Castle's God turned his face from them, the people would die.

"What does Castle teach you about the calling?"

"That we must be good, and God will feed and clothe us." The boy mouthed the words he had learned by rote.

"What does that mean to you?" Tangaroa's eyes blazed with a fierceness that glowed through the cataracts that clouded them.

Confused, the boy shook his head.

The navigator smiled. "Does Castle believe in the calling?"

"No. He says only God can call for us, I think."

"Do you believe in the calling?"

"I don't know."

"Do you know I can call the sharks and the turtles? Perhaps I called you, Mau. Is that why you're here?"

Magic! The boy stepped back, tripping on the anchor rope.

Good, thought Tangaroa. He still fears the old ways. He still believes in magic. Where there's fear, there can be love.

"No . . . I wish to be a navigator."

"A *palu* is many things. He must be strong and fierce and he must be wise. He must believe the old ways. I don't think you believe. And your foot is not strong."

The boy flinched but recovered. *"Mau,* the turtle, was made for the sea. No one laughs at the way he swims. No one laughs at the way I swim. I can dive deep. When I am a navigator the wind will be my strength and carry me to Guam and Hawaii so I can look for my father."

The old man nodded. All the island knew of Mau's father, who had left for the University of Hawaii. A package arrived afterward with presents for his family. Mau's T-shirt was his gift. Nothing followed after that. That was five years ago. Tangaroa knew Mau wore the shirt to remind him of his father. The rest of the island had given him up for dead. No one spoke of him.

The church school bell rang. The sound tore the boy from the past into the future of TVs and aluminum cans. He bowed to Tangaroa and limped off to school.

Kaneoe Naval Air Base, Hawaii

"Okay, let me get this straight. This stuff kills on contact, and it produces seizures?" Admiral Gifford gazed at the clear fluid resting in its glass container. Three layers of metal and glass shielding protected him as he pressed his face against the viewing port. Beside him a technician, manipulating servo arms, continued the exhaustive series of tests. The liquid sparkled menacingly, as if it resented the attention.

"I guess I'd better set my watch." Gifford smiled at Jackson as he fumbled with the tiny settings on his wristwatch. "Twenty hours since the airport death, and fourteen hours since the autopsy."

"Chronometer, sir," the Marine corrected, beaming as his skipper adjusted the heavy metal-cased timepiece.

The watch was a gift from Jackson. Last winter he had

found his boss working late at his desk, nibbling on a stale bagel. It was Gifford's birthday, the Marine suddenly remembered. How Jackson had produced the watch, all carefully wrapped in Kleenex, with the stores long closed was still a mystery to Gifford. Proudly, Jackson had pointed out the many features, including four separate timers and the ability to measure tenths of a second.

"Countdown . . . to God knows what." Gifford grimly pressed the watch buttons.

Since the phone call to the Israeli embassy in Washington Gifford had slept little. After midnight the admiral, his personal team, and a group of scientists had left Andrews Air Force Base aboard a specially equipped Boeing 707, code-named *Aesop,* for an uncomfortable nonstop flight to Kaneoe. Jammed in among the myriad pieces of biological testing equipment and computers, the group sweated through a midair refueling with a KC-135 tanker, sipped cold coffee from thermoses, and reviewed all the data on the seizures. There was precious little to assess.

"And that guy carried it in his gut?" Gifford swiveled to view the partly dissected body of Malmoud. It lay on a metal operating table within the quarantine chamber built into the bowels of the plane. Because of space limitations, the naked body of Dr. Kenzo Harii, late assistant pathologist for the city of Honolulu, lay on the floor beside the operating table. Both bodies resided within arm's length of the observation port. At their heads a metal table supported the vial as the robot arms played across a series of flasks and Petri dishes. A scanning microscope descended from the ceiling of the plane, motors buzzing as it focused on slides with various stains of the fluid. The chamber lights switched to ultraviolet as the tech looked for fluorescence.

A scream within the darkened chamber preceded a string of curses. "Goddamnit, I want my lawyer! I'll sue the pants off you sons of bitches. I know my rights. Let me out! I am a lawyer!"

The lights returned.

"Ought to shoot that one. It'd save some time and trouble." Jackson, the admiral's trusty aide, rubbed his hand over his regulation Marine Corps haircut as he gestured through his port at the far corner of the isolation chamber. Marlin Pearl, Lou, and Asher Lod huddled naked against the bulkhead. Pearl's face alternated between crimson rage and ashen fear. Lou accepted his condition stoically while Asher remained alert and in control.

Gifford grinned. "Naw. That guy provides the comic relief. Jackson, have you found Owen yet?" Curtis Owen, the admiral's computer expert, had been visiting his family in Iowa when this disaster struck. Great timing, Gifford mused sourly. Well, I can't expect all my men to live in a monastery just because I'm a widower and Jackson's married to the Corps. Owen has a family. Still, why does the phone always ring when you're in the head? Without Owen, his electronic eyes were half blind.

"Still looking for him, sir. He left last night in his motor home. Fishing trip. The state troopers are tracking him."

Gifford sighed. He flicked on the microphone to the chamber. "Sorry for this inconvenience, but for obvious reasons we have to isolate all of you until this agent is identified. I'm acting in your best interests, believe me."

"By what authority, mister?" Only the dead bodies and the deadlier fluid kept Pearl in his corner; otherwise, his face would have been pressed to the portals.

"The Hawaiian Department of Public Health, the Food and Drug Administration, the U.S. Department of Public Health, and the National Institutes of Health," Gifford lied. He switched off the mike. He was racing against the clock. No one other than a handful in Washington and those here knew about this. He needed a breakthrough fast, before the leaks started.

"It's not a bacteria or rickettsia," the technician blurted.

Jackson leaned forward. "A what?"

"A rickettsia, an infective organism smaller than bacteria but larger than a virus . . . sort of in between." The scientist pointed to a screen that glowed eerily in the artificial light. "No. This stuff is smaller than both. Beyond the range of the conventional light microscope. And both the gas chromatographic analysis and the spectrograph show no known military chemical or biological agents. Looks like two distinct fractions, sir." His finger stabbed at two peaks on the screen. "Both biochemical materials."

"Are you sure?"

"Yessir. Carbon, nitrogen, hydrogen, and oxygen, and a few traces of sulfur and iron. It's definitely organic."

"It'd be a lot easier if it were a pillbox or a gun emplacement," said Jackson, sighing. His fingers drifted absentmindedly over a wall of knobs and dials.

"So it's not a fungus or bacteria like the plague?"

"No, Admiral. *Listeria pestis,* the plague of the Middle Ages, is a bacterium. Let me finish the electron microphotographs. It'll take a few more minutes. Sorry, but it's slow going working with the servo arms."

"That's okay, son. You're doing just fine."

"I could enjoy taking out a pillbox about now," Jackson said to no one in particular.

The men sat in silence as the scientist twirled the tiny joysticks that manipulated the articulated steel and aluminum arms. Delicately, the pincers that could crush a half-inch steel plate removed the glass slides plated with osmium oxide from the vacuum chamber and placed them inside the scanning compartment of the electron microscope. Flipping switches, the operator powered up the big scope. Lights dimmed as the instrument robbed electricity from the plane's power supply. The machine's cooling fans siphoned off more of the stale, hot air. The scope's screen lit up, painting the faces of the sweating men.

"Enlarging to 300,000 diameters on the scanning electron microscope," the man said. "Well, I'll be damned."

"What is it?" Gifford squinted through his half glasses at a greenish landscape littered with dozens of six-sided polyhedrons attached to narrow cylinders resembling coiled tubes of rope. The far ends of several scattered tubes sprouted threadlike filaments. The objects reminded Gifford of sperm.

"Heads and tails, sir. Heads and tails." The man at the instrument pointed out the polyhedrons as heads and the cylinders as tails.

"Heads and tails of what?"

"Viruses. And they look like influenza viruses to me."

"Nobody dies like that from the flu!"

"See those threads?" the technician persisted. "Those are DNA fibers. These influenza viruses are releasing DNA into the host cells."

"DNA?" This time it was the Marine.

"Yessir. Deoxyribonucleic acid, the basic building block of all life. You know, the stuff genes and chromosomes are made of. My guess is these viruses are introducing some new genes into the victim's cells. This is pretty advanced stuff, way over my head, sir. But that's what it looks like to me."

"Let me get this straight, son. Are you saying that the stuff in the vial—the stuff that killed these two men—is a virus? And that it killed them by messing with their chromosomes?"

"Not exactly, sir. This virus is doing what most of them do. It's transferring its own blueprint into the victim's cells. That way it uses the cell's building machinery to make more viruses. Sort of a free ride."

"But that would take days. Surely that wasn't what killed Doctor Harii."

The scientist was on the verge of crying, pressed to the limit of his expertise. "No . . . no . . . I don't know what killed him."

Gifford turned away in frustration and stomped down the narrow corridor. He needed Owen.

Jackson leaned forward and clamped the back of the scientist's neck with his hand in a viselike grip. "You're doing fucking A-OK, Doc. Like I said, pillboxes are easier."

The man nodded in appreciation, then turned back to his work.

Light flared into the darkened interior of the plane. The men inside spun to face the blinding glare. Fresh air bearing the smells of salt and frangipani rushed into the metal passageway.

"Am I too late for dessert?" A slight man wearing rumpled slacks and thick glasses stumbled through the door, pushed by the Marine guard outside, who quickly shut the hatch.

"Owen! By God, am I glad to see you! How did you get here so quickly?"

"Thank you, Admiral. Well, sir, I made the mistake of driving back to pick up an extra fishing pole. Ran right into the state troopers. They hustled me off while my family sat in the motor home. You know, Admiral, since I've been working with you—with all the odd hours and such—my mother-in-law thinks I'm selling drugs. Now she's sure of it. Anyway, I just missed your plane at Andrews, so I hopped a ride on a Tomcat."

"Good for you. Sit over here." The admiral ushered Curtis Owen to a seat in front of a computer terminal. Owen checked the display. His fingers ranged over the keys, bringing up all the available information from the ongoing tests within the flying laboratory. After fifteen minutes he leaned back in the chair. Jackson brought the nerve-racked scientist over to the terminal. Over cups of overstrong navy coffee the men shared information.

"Admiral, this poison material breaks down into two fractions: one that appears to be some sort of virus and another component that is faster acting. I'm going to establish a link with the mainframe computers at the National Institutes of Health and the Centers for Disease Control in Atlanta. Then I'll link them with that Cray supercomputer in Los Angeles that belongs to the Rand Corporation. The Cray can match the information patterns of these fractions with similar patterns in their data banks."

"Owen, I don't want this information available outside of this plane. No leaks until we know what we're dealing with."

"No problem, sir. I'll encode the data with an encrypting algorithm. The Cray can match the structures without knowing what they really are. This plane's computer will be the only one with the code. Then I'll erase all files so nothing can be deciphered. It may take a little longer, but not much."

"How much longer?"

"With the Cray . . . maybe fifteen, twenty minutes more."

Gifford looked at Jackson, who raised his eyebrows and murmured about pillboxes and one good grenade. Gifford had to agree with the Marine. He was getting too old for all this scientific mumbo jumbo. He was a sailor, not a slide-rule jockey. And his recent skirmish with the representative from New Jersey still rankled him. That damn fool wanted to slash his budget again. All the man saw was *perestroika*. If that was true, it only reduced the Russian threat. Hadn't the congressman heard of Iraq or Libya or half a dozen flea-bitten countries that could assault the U.S. with deadly weapons like this thing in the plane?

The admiral returned to the viewing port.

Asher sneezed and wiped a runny nose with his bare forearm. Two hours later the other two men inside the chamber were coughing and dabbing at their watery eyes.

Thirty-six hours later Curtis Owen still struggled with his computer. He punched the side of his video terminal. "Shit! Another blank! I don't believe this, Admiral. Nobody knows what this second fraction is."

"Second fraction?" Gifford rubbed his eyes. He envied Jackson, who was sleeping facedown over the gas chromatography machine. The admiral grimaced at the way the machine's dials were embedded in the Marine's face. Only a

Marine could sleep anywhere, he thought. "What about the first?"

"Easy. Influenza B virus. Your common, run-of-the-mill flu virus."

"The flu." Gifford shook his head.

"Yessir, but NIH and CDC can't match the second thing other than to suggest it's some sort of toxin. I'm sorry, sir. I'm trying the databases of other countries now. So far France and England are zip." Owen knew he had let the old man down. It was the last thing he wanted to do. Since his transfer to the admiral's staff, Gifford had become the father that Owen had lost ten years before.

Not really a father, Curtis conceded. More like father and idol rolled into one. Sometimes he had trouble separating the two. He'd been with the admiral for nine years, give or take special assignments and advanced computer courses. Still he held the old man in awe. He envied Jackson's easy interface with the admiral. Curtis made a mental note to try harder.

Gifford tasted the stale air inside the plane. The air conditioning had been diverted to save the precious instruments and computers. Body odors and water vapor from their breath hung in the air, mixed with a haze of oil and JP5 jet fuel that permeated the bowels of *Aesop*. The mess coated the metal walls. He felt like Jonah in the belly of the whale. And the whale had bad indigestion.

Gifford checked the dials on his watch. Forty-eight hours had passed since they'd transferred the bodies and the three men. Time was running out. Did the carrier's contacts know he had died? Did they miss him? His ticket said Los Angeles was his final destination. Final destination, Henry Clay grunted. His final destination was here—inside a flying coffin.

The man on the metal table inside the sealed chamber was booked on Hawaiian Air's Flight 83 to L.A. It had taken some doing, but the admiral had arranged for Flight 83 to be delayed eleven hours, a few hours at a time, until those passengers had missed all possible alternate flights to L.A. Then he canceled Flight 83 and rescheduled it as Flight 87, to depart twenty-four hours later. All the passengers were pissed . . . all except Malmoud.

The third page of the *Honolulu Times* carried a story of a tourist being struck and killed by a car while jaywalking. No names were mentioned, only a description of Malmoud. Gifford doubted anyone would step into that trap. He figured he had twelve more hours. . . .

An hour later Marlin Pearl and Lou started to seize.

Asher's yell called attention to the two as their convulsions ripped off EKG leads and severed the probes that connected all three to banks of monitoring devices. Warning lights flashed and sirens wailed within the aircraft. Bloody froth spewed from their mouths to speckle the glass windows. The lawyer and the deaner performed their grisly dance with death along the floor of the chamber for only a few minutes. Asher watched in horror, clutching his knees to his chest and staying pressed against the chamber wall.

"Jeeesus Christ!" Gifford flattened his face into the port. Jackson, Owen, and the scientist shared the second window.

"They're dead meat now," the Marine added as the seizures stopped.

The scientist shut down the alarms on the dead men as a pressing silence added to the stench outside the chamber.

"May I have a blanket to cover them?" Asher asked after a while.

"Sorry, son. I'd like to, but we can't open the chamber."

"I understand." Another lull followed. "You know my father?"

"Yes."

"He speaks very highly of you in his letters. I was happy when he said on the phone that you were coming."

"Look . . ." Gifford dreaded what would come next.

"I'm not asking for any special treatment. You're doing all the right things. It's just that . . . when I die, will you see that my father gets my body for burial? Those things are important to a Jew."

The technician shook his head.

"I'm afraid everybo . . . everything will have to be cremated, Asher. I wish to God I could help you, but . . ."

"Yes, of course. Perhaps my ashes?"

The technician shook his head again.

Asher saw him. He sighed. "Well, then could you arrange for a rabbi to say the kaddish for me?"

"Yes, son. I will."

"My father said you have a son also, Admiral."

"Had, Asher. He was killed in Vietnam."

"Then he died a hero."

"He was killed by friendly artillery."

"Friendly?"

Gifford's teeth ground with the rekindling of old pains, but he felt he owed the son of his friend an explanation. "He was killed by fire from our own side." Gifford suspected that the fire support team had been high on marijuana, but he could never prove it.

"I'm sorry, Admiral." The Israeli straightened his back. "Whatever this thing is, it seems to strike in the same way."

"You've seen this before?"

"Yes, we have penetrated Khalid's cell. . . ."

"The Front for Liberation?"

"Yes. Khalid Al Bakaar. I followed this man from Beirut to Frankfurt. We lost him there but picked him up again when he left for Rome. He had a companion who flew from Lebanon with him. They separated in Frankfurt. This man, Malmoud Rhashid, disappeared, and his partner rented a car. The partner had a similar seizure and crashed his car on the autobahn. We knew they were carrying something deadly, something that they got in Frankfurt. Malmoud didn't know about his associate's death."

"What happened to the body in Germany?"

"I poured gasoline on it and set the car afire." Asher

paused to consider his impending fate. Ironic, he thought, to share the same treatment. "Everything was burned up."

"Good work."

"Yes. This thing is deadly. If it spreads as Al Bakaar plans, it will devastate the world. You've got to stop it."

"Stop it!" Jackson blurted. "Shit! We don't even know what it is. How in a rusty fuck are we gonna stop it?"

Asher and the admiral smiled at the Marine's phraseology. "Your assistant has an interesting way of expressing the situation, Admiral."

"He does sum it up in a nutshell."

Curtis Owen shrieked and bounded out of his chair. Excitedly he jabbed at his CRT. Then he clapped the Marine on the back.

"Damn! Don't do that!" Jackson snarled. "For a moment I thought you had it, too. I damn near pissed my pants."

"Cobra venom!" Owen was shouting. "It's cobra venom! The second fraction is cobra venom!"

CHAPTER

4

Kaneoe Naval Air Base, Hawaii

"Cobra venom? Why would these rag heads mix that with the flu? Are you sure about that reading, Owen?"

"Yes, sir. It looks a lot like cobra venom."

"Looks like? Is it or isn't it?"

"Well, sir, it's not a perfect match, but it's damn close. The database from the Royal Australian Zoological Society comes the closest to matching. I've also got a lead on the Instituto Butantan in Brazil. It's the world's only hospital specializing in the treatment of poisonous bites, but they don't have a direct computer link."

"Who would know about this? We need an expert. Someone who specializes in snake venoms."

"We're in luck there, Admiral. I did a computer search on the words *virus, influenza,* and *venom.* One name pops out all over the literature, a guy named Christopher Maddox. Did most of the basic work in this field. Guy's brilliant. Has a Ph.D. in virology as well as an M.D. He worked at MIT, Woods Hole Oceanographic Institute, and CDC in Atlanta. Also did a stint in the navy with the germ warfare boys."

"Sounds like our man. Get him."

"I don't have a current address. He dropped out of sight two years ago. Seems his wife was killed in a plane accident, and he fell apart. Started drinking heavily, lost his security clearance, and disappeared."

"If he's still alive, I want him." Gifford glared at his watch. The forthright instrument continued to measure his helplessness: sixteen forty-five, Sunday, August 19. Day three since Malmoud died in the airport. "Find him. By God, we've got to find him."

Hanauma Bay, Hawaii

Christopher Maddox hung from the wall of coral as another surge tore at his fingers, threatening to break their hold. About him sergeant major fish fluttered in the current like yellow and black butterflies. Just beyond, where the azure of the Pacific swallowed the light and turned a deep indigo, ran the riptide known as the Molokai Express, traversing the mouth of the half-sunken volcano. Each year the Express carried careless swimmers out to sea.

Maddox checked his gauges out of habit rather than interest. Less than 800 psi in his scuba tank. His wrist-mounted Beuchat dive computer faithfully declared on its LCD face that he was allowed only ten more minutes at his current depth of sixty feet. Longer would require a decompression stop to allow the nitrogen bubbles forced into his body by the water pressure to safely outgas. Failure to decompress flew in the face of all diving safety and carried the hazard of decompression sickness, along with paralysis and death. The dive computer had tracked and calculated his diving that day. It allowed him only ten more minutes. Besides, he was almost out of air.

"Who gives a rat's ass?" Maddox railed into his regulator.

He yanked the dump valve to his buoyancy control vest and dropped like a stone into the darkness.

Kaneoe Naval Air Base, Hawaii

"I found him, Admiral." Curtis Owen spun his chair away from his monitor. His search had taken over an hour. Finally a computerized Mastercard bill produced an address. From there Owen coaxed his quarry into his electronic snare.

"Maddox?"

"Yes, sir, Dr. Christopher Maddox. He's here in Hawaii."

"Get me the phone."

Hanauma Bay, Hawaii

Maddox watched the wall of coral and volcanic rock slide past as he experienced feelings of falling down an elevator shaft in slow motion. Water pressure hammered against his lungs. The dry compressed air in his tank burned his throat. His dive computer beeped in alarm and flashed a warning to ascend. Maddox arched his back and dropped faster. One hundred. One hundred ten. One hundred twenty. At one hundred forty feet a volcanic ledge stopped his fall. The needle on his air pressure gauge slipped into the red. He was out of air.

Maddox glanced about casually, already feeling the euphoria of nitrogen narcosis and lack of oxygen. An alarmed hermit crab scuttled along the shelf with its cowrie shell abode on its back. Christopher turned into the grinning face of a tiny snowflake moray eel. Maddox grinned back. The eel mouthed water and appeared to be singing. Chris tried to sing back. He sucked hard on his regulator to extract the last quantity of air. Sadly, he waved good-bye to the eel. His finger pressed the fill valve on his BC, and the last bubble of air inflated his vest.

Slowly at first his body lifted off the ledge and rose toward the surface, leaving a swirl of sand to cover the crab. Maddox continued to suck on the empty mouthpiece. His lungs burned. Every cell in his body screamed for oxygen. His sight blurred and his head pounded. His field of vision narrowed into a tunnel with blackened walls.

Abruptly his oxygen-starved brain began to relive the nightmare that haunted his every waking hour. He was no longer inside his scuba mask looking out. He was outside looking in—looking through the Plexiglas of the crashed airplane—at the unconscious face of his wife. Unconscious, or was she already dead? In his recurring nightmares she awoke and begged him to help her as the locked cockpit leisurely filled with smoke while it ignored his pounding on the windows. It would be to no avail. The glass never gave, and flames replaced the fumes.

A blast of icy water pulled Maddox away from his dream, but he lapsed back into torment. His hands beat themselves bloody on the cowling. Inches from his dying wife, the barrier held him back. This time her eyes opened for a moment as her hair ignited. Tongues of flame licked at her flesh, rasping the skin into blackened crusts. Maddox screamed until his ears burst and his soul splintered with the sound. At that instant the fuel tank of the airplane exploded.

Christopher Maddox's head broke the surface of Hanauma Bay. His lungs gulped air as he pulled himself onto the rough coral. Scraping across the rock, he rolled onto his back. The fiery conflagration in his mind focused into the overhead sun. A depressing thought weighed on him as he started to seize. He would live another day.

Maddox rolled onto his side as he awakened. He vomited the expanded air in his belly. Bile mixed with last night's Blue Hawaiis and mai tais filled his mouth. He choked at its bitterness and flopped onto his back. The tropical sun shed its warmth impartially on his shivering body.

A shadow moved across the sun. Chris focused on the shape.

"Dr. Maddox, I presume?"

Maddox responded with a groan. The bad taste was enough. Bad jokes were too much. His vision cleared. Over him stood a tall man with close-cropped graying hair. The ridiculous flowered "Magnum P.I." shirt failed to hide a military bearing. Two policemen flanked him.

"Are you Dr. Christopher Maddox?"

"Look." Chris struggled to raise his head. "If this has anything to do with that coed last night, she told me she was twenty-one. . . ."

The gray-haired man looked at another with a crew cut and a similar patterned aloha shirt. The designs made Maddox ill. Crew-cut raised his eyebrows. Both men wore sunglasses. The older man knelt, and Chris watched his reflection in the mirrored lenses. The image of himself made him more nauseous.

"Do you do this sort of thing . . . often?" Gifford asked as the officers bundled off the doctor.

Kaneoe Naval Base, Hawaii

Three cups of steaming coffee, navy style, and half a quart of fortified tomato juice brought Christopher Maddox back to the world of reality, a world for which he cared little since the death of his wife. Nevertheless, his immediate tormentors persisted. He learned that the name of the crew-cut man was Jackson; Jackson had held him under a cold shower until both nearly froze. But his chief nemesis was the steely-willed Admiral Gifford. The man was most persuasive.

"The answer is still no, whoever you are. I'm not interested."

"All you're interested in is teaching beginning biology to pampered girls at Queen Liliolani's Finishing School! Is that it?"

"Yes. . . ."

Gifford tossed a pile of scientific articles at Maddox and gazed out the gunmetal-gray-framed window of the military building at the green-drab plane parked at the end of the runway. A circle of Marine guards surrounded the isolated 707. Gifford watched the doctor fumble with the falling papers. Time, he thought. I'm wasting precious time with this asshole.

"Wrong, mister," Gifford exploded. "You used to be a top scientist in genetic-viral research. One of the bright minds of the world. You're not interested in teaching shit! You're only interest is wallowing in guilt, wallowing in self-pity."

Henry Clay spit out the last phrase inches from the other man's face.

Maddox's eyes flared.

Good, good, thought Gifford. There's some life in you yet. "You're hiding here in this backwater with only three thoughts on your mind: feeling sorry for yourself, getting your next drink, and . . . getting into your students' pants."

The blaze in Christopher's eyes dimmed.

No, you don't, Gifford reflected. You don't slip out from under me that easily. He played his trump card. "What would your wife think of you now? I bet she'd be damn proud."

"Goddamn you!" Maddox launched from his chair, fists swinging at the old man.

Gifford blocked the punch, and in a blur Maddox was pinned with his right arm held behind him in a viselike grip, his face smashed into the wall. Jackson smiled appreciatively. He'd taught the old man that aikido trick only months ago.

"Damn you to hell! You've got no right—" Maddox rasped out amid the burning tears.

"I've got every right. See that plane out there?" He dragged the doctor to the window and pressed his face to the glass. "I've got the right to try to save the son of a friend on that plane. I've got the right—and the responsibility—to try to save millions of innocent people from what's in that plane. That's my goddamn right. And my duty. And it's your responsibility, too. Your wife would be the first to tell you so." He released the physician to slide down the window, leaving a bloody streak across the glass.

Owen knelt by Maddox and offered a Kleenex to stop the bleeding. Christopher looked up into the first set of sympathetic eyes he had seen in the group. "Dr. Maddox, we're facing a threat to the safety of the entire world. That's a rather abstract concept. But I've got a daughter who's going to have a birthday in five days, and I want to see her blow out those thirteen candles. That's sort of silly, but it's very important to my wife and me."

Maddox nodded. He and Sara had wanted a girl. "Okay, what do you want?"

Owen helped him to a chair as Gifford and Jackson dumped piles of computer printouts on the table. Maddox gulped more coffee as he studied the reports. They watched him shake his head.

"You guys are making this up, right? This is some kind of war-game exercise."

"I wish that were the case, Doctor. Let me make it crystal clear. As director of counterintelligence for the United States government, I am conducting an official investigation into what we believe is a threat to the security of our country and possibly the world."

"This shit'll eat up the fan when it hits," Jackson added.

"Okay. I don't see the analysis of this fluid in these reports."

"That's on board the plane, Doctor. It's on the computer. Admiral Gifford didn't want it printed out for security reasons. If you're ready, I'll take you out there." Owen looked to Gifford for approval.

The admiral nodded.

Jackson watched Owen and Maddox drive to the end of the tarmac. "Fucking-A, Skipper. It worked just like you said. The old good guy-bad guy routine." He swiveled to follow the jeep. "I thought Owen played his part well."

Gifford nodded. "You do what it takes. Unfortunately, we need this guy. We don't have time to find an alternate. I hope he doesn't fold on us when he finds out what's involved."

"Yeah, I read that part where he's afraid to fly. What a wimp!"

"You've never crashed in a small plane—a crash that killed your wife."

"Naw, Admiral. What woman would want to marry me? All I've ever known was the Corps." Jackson wished he hadn't brought up the subject. He knew the old man was thinking about his own wife, who had been killed by a drunk driver outside Washington, D.C. Jackson had stood beside his boss when the old man identified her remains. God, he loved his C.O.

The fact that Gifford had saved his life during the fall of Saigon only added to his loyalty. Jackson rubbed the ragged scar tissue on his chest. Burning buildings, smoke, and the pain from the AK-47 bullet returned as he relived that day when Gifford carried him to safety. And now he'd reopened one of the admiral's wounds. He wished he hadn't caused that painful memory.

"Everyone's married to something, Jackson. Owen's got his computers, Maddox has his guilt, and you've got the Corps." Gifford clapped his sergeant on the back.

"Semper Fi, Admiral. Semper Fi," the Marine barked,

happy for the change. "Does the good doctor know about the drop yet?"

"One step at a time, sergeant. We don't want to spook the fish until we set the hook."

Christopher Maddox settled into the padded chair in front of the array of computer screens. At the far end of the tube the scientist was running more tests. Christopher whistled as he glanced about the cramped fuselage. It's on the ground, he told himself. It's okay. "Wow. Now I know where the federal budget goes."

Owen grinned. "Nice, isn't it? I just found out about this myself. This plane is code-named *Aesop*. It's part of the president's COG."

"COG?"

"Continuity of government. All part of the Doomsday Project. You know, in case of nuclear attack. This is like one of the Kneecap aircraft—National Emergency Airborne Command Post. Mount Weather in Virginia and the Kneecap aircraft are designed for nuclear attacks. But this plane is built for germ warfare. The Kneecaps are Boeing 747s. This is an older 707."

"Why is that?"

"Two reasons, as far as I can tell. One, it uses a different pressurization system that makes it easier to modify for biological protection. And second, the air force already had it, so they didn't have to go to Congress for the appropriation. *Aesop* is real hush-hush. Never appeared as a line item in the budget. The various computers and scientific equipment came from requests scattered across all the services. Primarily it was designed to protect the president and a small staff from a biological warfare attack."

"The sort of thing people dismiss as a fable."

"Right, hence its name. *Aesop*. Except it got upgraded after all those reports of yellow rain in Afghanistan and Cambodia. The fables became reality. Now Aesop has the facilities to handle an infected person and hopefully treat him." Owen pointed to the viewing ports.

"Jesus Christ," Maddox whispered as he viewed the carnage within the chamber. "You weren't kidding."

Asher Lod pointed to his ear.

Owen switched on the intercom. "Yes?"

"May I have some water? I'm thirsty."

"Sure." Owen snapped off the microphone as the technician manipulated the servo arms to open a series of stopcocks that let fresh water run into a row of Pyrex cups fitted within a recess in the chamber.

Asher drank gratefully.

"We can't figure out why he's still alive." Owen pointed to Asher. "He was exposed at the same time as all the rest."

Unhearing, Asher sneezed and wiped his nose on his forearm. He looked truly miserable.

"Well, let's see what this stuff looks like." Christopher typed out his request on the keyboard. As he read and searched through the databanks he failed to notice the hook gently setting in his mouth. He even failed to notice Gifford and Jackson come on board. Soon Maddox and Owen were excitedly jabbering to each other. Then Maddox pushed back his chair and rubbed his eyes.

"Whoever did this is a genius, but a fucking twisted one. He's got to be mad."

"What is it?" Gifford spoke first.

"It's not a mix of cobra venom and virus like you thought. No. It's just the virus."

"Well, where does the venom come from?"

"It comes from them." Owen pointed to the bodies. "From us."

Gifford frowned. "Are you saying they took some venom?"

"No. No, Admiral. They made it!"

"What are you saying?"

"Their bodies produced the venom just the way their

41

bodies make other things, like . . . like insulin. And it's not cobra venom. It's sea snake venom. *Pelamis platuris*—the yellow-bellied sea snake, to be precise—quite deadly. Much more so than the cobra."

"How the hell do you know that?" Jackson asked.

"Because, Mr. Jackson," said Maddox, looking very despondent, "I invented this process."

CHAPTER

5

Taongi Atoll, Marshall Islands

Piles of black lava spilled into the sea, frozen in time by the cooling air and the jealous hand of the sea that refused to relinquish even an inch of its realm. Arrested in its march, the molten stone had puddled into ebony swirls and heaps that stared enviously at the freedom of the water. Razor-edged boulders topped this geologic confection. Here and there the monotonous, flat black rock sported rust-colored patches of algae lining the tidal pools and water-filled crevices. The ceaseless struggle continued at the water line, where the sea battered the immobile stone. Weakened by this attack, the lava paled into colors of pink and tan with tatters of sea lettuce waving in the surge like banners on besieged ramparts. The smell of salt spray was heavy in the air, and the thunderous surge completed the battle scene.

The old navigator sat atop the lava and watched the rain slanting along the horizon. The first glow of morning struggled through gaps in the clouds. All life was a struggle, the old man sighed. Sea and land, old and new.

The pain in his chest caught his breath. The squeeze grew directly beneath the sea snake tattoo that writhed across his breast. As before, it moved into his left side. Annoyed with his weakness, he straightened and massaged his left arm to remove the ache that ran down the limb. A footstep in the sand alerted him. He ceased rubbing.

"*Atirro,* Navigator." The boy bowed.

"The turtle is up early."

"I've been thinking about what you said. I would like to learn the *etak* of navigation from you, and with the Christian schooling I can live in both worlds. I've given it much thought, and that seems the best way to me," the boy added brightly.

"Look at your tracks in the sand," Tangaroa commanded.

The boy looked over his shoulder. "Yes?"

"What do you see?"

"The water washes over my tracks?"

"Yes. No navigator has figured a course between the *etak* and the *itang,* the talk of light, and the world of the westerners. One is like the sea, and one is like the land. One will wash over the other."

"It doesn't have to be that way!" the boy protested.

"If you know that, you're wiser than me. No, Mau, one rubs out the other. Mine is a spirit world where the fish and gods of the sea guide the pilot. Castle's world has its spirit caught on paper, in the black book. His chants come from that book. Mine come from my heart. Mine were taught to me by my father. . . ." Tangaroa stopped, regretting his unfortunate slip.

"My father is not here to teach me." Mau struggled with tear-filled eyes.

"Yes."

"Your son is not here, either!"

"Yes." Tangaroa contemplated what might have been if his son had become a navigator rather than a dock worker in Truk. Old anguish added to the pain in his heart. He wished Mau would go so he could massage the growing pain that ran down into his left arm.

Don't be foolish, a voice inside him whispered. Your time

is short. This boy may be the answer to your prayers. When you are gone who will carry on the *etak?*

"I'm sorry for my harsh words, Navigator." The boy placed a *ti* leaf containing three cigarettes on the sand in front of Tangaroa.

The old man nodded. Three cigarettes were a small fortune to this boy. "To be a navigator you must believe in the old ways." He shook his head sadly. "Otherwise you'll learn nothing, only the words. If the words come from your lips and not from your heart, the gods will not listen."

Mau twisted his clubfoot deeper into the sand. "Reverend Castle's world has TV and VCRs. I can believe what I see. I see his TV pictures. I see the ship that brings cigarettes and candy from Ponape. But no one sees the old gods. No one sees the old ways, only the new things."

"Castle's TV makes pictures that come from his world. That much is clear. His power comes from the West. My power comes from the sea snake." Tangaroa's finger jabbed at the coiled serpent tattoo. "His poison bite gives me my power."

Mau nodded. Everyone on the island knew of the connection between this *palu* and sea snakes.

"Would you believe if you saw something from my world?"

"Yes."

"Good. Come with me." The old man descended to the water's edge. The rays of the rising sun broke through the clouds and painted the water as Tangaroa took a cowrie shell and bamboo frame rattle from his canoe and waded into the surf. He stopped to call over his shoulder. "Is the turtle afraid of the water?"

Hastily the boy followed the old man until both stood in water up to their waists.

"Now you'll have something for your eyes to see." The navigator grasped the rattle above his head and began the ancient chant he had learned from his father, a chant as old as the history of his people. The morning breezes swirled around the figures, riffling the water and stinging their eyes with salt spray.

The chant intensified, and sweat glistened on Tangaroa's brow and arms. The pain within his chest returned, but he paid it no mind. He thrust the cowrie rattle into the water. The wind ceased. A heavy silence blanketed the water. The old man struck the rattle against his thigh. The dried shells clattered against the bamboo framework. Instantly the chant heightened. The rattle thrashed the water. Again and again the instrument beat the waves into froth that covered the two. Then he stopped, and silence rolled over them like thunder during the spring rains, threatening to squash these tiny interlopers for trespassing, for meddling. The sun hid.

Two dark fins broke the glassy surface a hundred yards to sea.

The boy stiffened. Sharks never crossed the reef to enter this lagoon! The ebony sickles moved unerringly for them. Mau's eyes widened. Oceanic whalers! The sleek, deep water hunters with long pectorals that followed the whales and blackfish. Not the harmless white-tipped reef sharks. Man-eaters!

Tangaroa resumed his calling. The sharks sped to his side with sinuous, fluid movements. Separating, the whalers passed along both sides of the old man. The tips of their pectoral fins caressed his legs as they glided past. The navigator called them by their ancient names, and they responded. Swimming back in tight circles, the fish slid through the sea in flickering patterns of indigo. Closer they came until their narrow snouts broke the water. Black, soulless eyes rolled to inspect man and boy.

The navigator stroked the sharks' blue skin and talked softly to them. Mau remained frozen in fear. Gently the old man grasped the boy's rigid hand and directed it to one blue whaler. Like friendly dogs the man-eaters rolled under the touch.

The sun reappeared and lit the sky and sea with matching patterns of crimson and lavender.

Mau's face lit with an intensity to match the sunrise. "I will be a *palu!*" he said, laughing.

Tangaroa smiled through the pain. That vision of the silver airplane returned.

Kaneoe Naval Air Base, Hawaii

"It was four years ago when I was at Woods Hole. I was involved in genetic research. It's been known for some time that some viruses can insert their DNA into the DNA of a host cell, any cell that will accept them. That way the virus's DNA becomes a semipermanent part of the infected cell's chromosome. It retains the options of living happily ever after, so to speak, as part of the cell, or turning to the lytic pathway."

"Lytic pathway?" Gifford shifted in his seat. What he was hearing made him more uncomfortable than the chair.

"Yes. In the lytic pathway the virus separates its DNA so that it links to itself and forms a circle. This rolling circle acts like an assembly line and rolls off multiple copies of the viral genes like so many sausage links. These virus genes direct the synthesis and production of the head and tail proteins of the virus particles. The parts assemble themselves, and the cell bursts, releasing hundreds of new viruses. See, these are the heads and tails." Maddox pointed to the polygons and coiled cylinders in the electron microphotograph. "Bingo, you come down with a cold or the flu. It happens every day."

"That's all very interesting, Doctor. But what has that got to do with cobra—I mean sea snake—venom?"

"Normally, this process only takes place with DNA that is similar or closely related. But with techniques of cleaving and splicing DNA onto a carrier molecule you can transfer

47

unrelated genetic material into an organism. Genetic engineering.

"As a project, I spliced the gene for making the venom from the yellow-bellied sea snake into the influenza B virus."

"And what does that do?" Gifford had to ask, but his mind already knew.

"The virus carries the gene into the cell's chromosomes . . . and within forty-eight hours the animal's cells begin producing sea snake venom. The effect was uniformly fatal for the hosts."

"God in heaven! You did this with people?"

"Death from within." Jackson whistled through his teeth.

"No! I used rhesus monkeys."

"Goddamn you crackpot scientists! Do you know what you've done?"

"I did it, Admiral, with a grant from the Defense Department! Don't get high and mighty with me. You're the one who's in the business of killing. This was purely an experiment."

Gifford's narrowed eyes flickered dangerously. "When I kill, it's for a purpose, and it's directed at a specific foe. I usually know who he is. I have to live with it, and I have to justify it to myself. I don't unleash random destruction and try to hide behind a cloak of scientific experimentation."

"Great! You're infected with a dose of hoplite mentality, Admiral. Grecian warriors one on one! It's acceptable to spill a man's guts onto the sand as long as you look him in the eyes. That makes it all right. But pity the poor researcher who comes up with something that might be dangerous in the wrong hands, because he's a mass murderer. Anyway, the idea wasn't mine alone."

"What do you mean?"

"Half the governments in the so-called civilized world have been working for years to produce the same thing. The Italians gassed the Ethiopians. The Japanese launched a mere eight hundred poison gas attacks on the Chinese in

Manchuria. And only recently the Vietnamese used their 'yellow rain' on the Hmong.

"And surely, Admiral, you know about the Iraqi Kurds!" Maddox was livid now. "You must have seen those pictures in *Time*. And yet the CDC sent three shipments of West Nile Fever virus in 1985 to Iraq . . . to . . . to . . . a government that poisoned its own people."

"That was against my advice." Gifford frowned.

"But we did it anyway, didn't we? And we didn't balk when the Germans sold Iraq T-2 and TH-2, both deadly mycotoxins."

The admiral could only shake his head.

"Well, our governments wanted more, something more deadly, so they initiated research on linking cobra venom to the influenza virus. For Christ's sake, the *Wall Street Journal* even ran a series about it."

Gifford nodded. "But it didn't work. . . ."

"No! Because it took a brilliant mind like mine to realize that the venom-producing gene in the sea snake was just the thing. Poor *Pelamis platurus*, one of the most docile and at the same time most deadly creatures on earth. Its venom is a hundred times more powerful than the cobra's, yet it avoids contact with man and lives at sea—the last refuge that creatures have from man."

"And your tests worked?"

"Like a charm! But I'm not stupid, Admiral. When I saw what it could be used for, I destroyed my records. I falsified logbooks and reported my experiments a failure. It wasn't hard for them to believe me; after all, everyone else had failed. The government withdrew its grant; I lost a lot of money. A small price to pay for saving the world, don't you think, Admiral?" Maddox slumped into his seat, exhausted from his revelation.

"Did anyone else have access to your notes?"

"No."

"And you're sure all the evidence was destroyed?"

"I burned it myself. . . ." A terrible image flashed in the

mind of Christopher Maddox. "Wait! Wait! The last day I noticed some of the papers were out of sequence . . . as if they had been looked at. I didn't think much of it, because the last step—a crucial one—I kept in another place."

"Who else was in that lab?" The old terrier smelled a rat.

"Nobody. Except the janitor, a German fellow."

"What happened to him?"

"I don't know. He left several days later."

Gifford glanced at his watch: day four. A drop of perspiration slid from his forehead to spatter over the watch crystal. He wiped it away. He was out of time. The rescheduled Hawaiian flight was landing in Los Angeles. Malmoud's contacts would be there.

Inside the isolation chamber, Asher Lod coughed and sneezed continuously. Maddox had drawn his blood for tests using the servo arms and had examined him by way of a pair of reinforced rubber arms with gloves fitted to them that were built into one side of the chamber.

"Why isn't he dead?" Jackson asked the obvious question. "He looks like he's just got a cold."

"You may have hit the nail on the head. The tests show that he had a good case of influenza-B virus, similar to the venom virus, but of a different strain. You see, the influenza virus can mutate—change slightly—after several passages through different people."

"Is that why there's a new flu season every winter?" Curtis Owen asked as he fumbled with a stack of computer papers.

"Right. The virus changes its surface configuration slightly so the body's defenses don't recognize it. The venom virus kills its host rapidly, so it never gets a chance to mutate. It looks like this man got a fortuitous dose of the current, most popular flu just before he was exposed to the sea snake venom-producing one."

"How did that help him?" Gifford saw a possible method of treatment.

"Well, the first virus infection sneaks through the cell

walls. But the body realizes, so to speak, that it's been had, so it activates its complement."

"Complement?" Now Jackson was lost.

"Yes. Complement is a series of surface antibodies that the body produces for protection. The 'normal' influenza that got in first activated the body's complement. Presto, along comes the second, deadly influenza. The body is ready with its defenses, and the venom virus gets destroyed. Ta-da! This man survives, but with a miserable cold."

"Doctor! Why couldn't we inoculate everyone against this thing? Or simply dose 'em all with the 'normal' influenza?"

"Wouldn't work, Admiral. First, there's not enough influenza vaccine to treat the world's population. To produce that much would take too long. It looks like these fanatics are ready to dump it now. Secondly, to protect someone by infection, you'd have to infect them at precisely the right time, just before they came in contact with this deadly strain. It would be impossible unless you knew when they were going to be attacked."

"Admiral." Owen pressed the earpiece of his headset against his ear. "I just got a call from the city morgue. Two men are there to claim Malmoud's body. They say they're his cousins."

"Here in Honolulu? Nothing from L.A.?"

"No, sir. They're here in Hawaii. Our men ran a check on them. They're both operating under Lebanese passports. Arrived here last month on student visas."

"Maddox, could they be carriers?"

"Doubtful. Why would you cluster your carriers together? One vial of this stuff goes a hell of a long way."

Henry Clay bobbed his head. "I agree. This is a support team. We're still in luck! Malmoud never planned on going to Los Angeles. The pickup is here in Honolulu. Okay, Jackson, implement our little surprise."

"Aye, aye, sir!" Jackson grabbed Owen's headset and barked a string of commands to those on the other end.

"Surprise, Admiral?" Owen tried to recover his poise and smooth the few strands of hair that covered his balding head.

"Yes, Curtis." Gifford rubbed his hands together. He loved killing rats. "I can't take any chances with those two reporting back. And I sure can't give 'em that raghead in there. So they get a sealed coffin—for immigration and customs reasons. My guess is they have orders to get his body somewhere and remove the bottle. But the coffin doesn't have a body—it has one of Jackson's specials. Our men follow in an unmarked car, and as they pass a remote spot my men trigger the good Marine's surprise. There's enough explosives and incendiaries in the coffin to reduce everything—car, cousins, even the tires—to nice, safe cinders."

"What happened to your 'look 'em in the eye' credo, Admiral?"

"I'd love to be there, Doctor. Unfortunately, I have this social engagement with you. Now, what do you suggest we do with the articles in the isolation chamber? Our time has run out."

"Disinfect Asher with Betadine and hose him down. Then let him out."

"And the rest?"

"Burn it all."

"My father never knew I was recruited in the Shin Beth—the secret branch of the Mossad—until I called him from Honolulu. He thought I was only an architect. But I didn't know what else to do. I foolishly let Malmoud see me in the airport—you see, I'm still an architect at heart." Asher Lod gratefully accepted the cup of steaming coffee and cradled it in his hands. In spite of the hundred-degree interior temperature, he shivered with fever.

"So you think he picked up his vial in Frankfurt?"

"Yes, Admiral. My team followed Malmoud and his partner from Beirut. We'd been watching the FFL ever since these crazy videotapes started appearing. I guess they're not so crazy. When we got a tip from our contact—"

"You have a mole in Khalid's organization? God, what I wouldn't give for one!"

"Yes, sir. Strangely, he came forward on his own."

"Do you trust him? You don't think he's a double agent?"

"Of course we worry, but his information has been correct. We gave him a chance to expose some of our lesser contacts in the PLO to . . . to . . . what is the phrase you Americans use?"

"Smoke him out."

"Precisely. Thank you, Mr. Jackson. Yes, we tried to smoke him out, and nothing happened."

"Which means he may be smart and playing for higher stakes."

"Yes, Admiral." Lod wiped at his nose.

"All right." Gifford sighed. Too many loose ends, too many variables. This was like looking for a needle in a haystack the size of the world. Worse, the needle was small, only a few microns long. "Maddox, what do I do with the goddamned airport? Burn that to the ground, too?"

"No, I think it's safe."

"What makes you so sure?"

Maddox held up a sheaf of computer printouts. "The guy on the autopsy table died from direct contact with residual venom that leaked out of the bottle—the same way Dr. Harii died when a drop hit him in the eye. Sea snake venom is rapidly absorbed across mucous membranes like the lining of the intestine and the conjunctival lining of the eye. I suspect the same thing happened to the other terrorist that Lod described seizing in Germany. As smart as the mastermind is, he overlooked the fact that the body's digestive juices would dissolve the seals on the vial caps. The other two were infected by the gene-carrying virus in the autopsy room, probably from an aerosol created by Harii during his seizures. They died forty-eight hours later from sea snake venom produced by their own bodies—the way this Khalid intended. If Asher hadn't kept everybody in the autopsy room, my guess is that the islands of Hawaii would be filled with corpses rotting in the sun, and infected tourists would be spreading this plague around the world."

"Thank you, Doctor, for that graphic narration. Since we are all aware of the consequences of failure, I suggest we get cracking and stop this thing."

"If that is possible."

"You, for one, Dr. Maddox, ought to pray we're not too late. Otherwise you will have a special place of infamy in whatever history mankind has left. I needn't remind you that the Manhattan Project that produced the atomic bomb, which you are so willing to make the total responsibility of the military, consisted of thousands of scientists. Here you have singlehandedly exceeded their wildest expectations."

"I already have enough guilt, Admiral. Your speech wasn't necessary." Maddox ached for a drink. He covered his shaking hands.

"In the words of one of my former commanders, I want to make it perfectly clear. Owen, what have you found out?"

Curtis Owen adjusted his glasses and leafed through the product of his computer searches. "Admiral, besides Dr. Maddox, only two experts stand out in this field. A. J. Yetsin in Moscow and Y. M. Ivanov in Tel Aviv. Ivanov apparently emigrated to Israel from Russia."

Maddox nodded. "Yetsin died several months ago. Ivanov must be in his eighties. I can't believe he'd be working with terrorists."

"Well, Doctor, that just leaves you and possibly another mad scientist."

"What are you implying?" Tension filled the closed space.

Gifford rubbed his chin. His jaw muscles knotted. He had seen Maddox's twitching hands. "I'm inclined to go with the other mad scientist for the time being. Your priorities seem to be campus carousing and bar-hopping."

"Fuck you . . . sir!"

"Good, Doctor. Very original. By the way, Owen found

out something else about you in his inquiry. You were in the naval reserve, weren't you?"

"That was years ago."

Gifford's face spread into a Cheshire cat grin. "Yes, but you never resigned your commission. And you're still under thirty-five."

"I served my time!"

"By the power invested in me, I am now activating your commission—with, of course, an increase in rank. Welcome aboard, Commander Maddox."

"Shit! I'm not happy to be aboard."

Hours later Jackson entered through the triple-sealed plane door with a deformed bag of sandwiches. Behind him night filled the sky, punctuated only by the scattered lights of the security fence along the runway. The musky aroma of frangipani and hibiscus spilled into the stale air of the aircraft. The Marine looked wistfully at the sultry night. The door clanged shut, and he was once more entombed. He joined a conference in progress.

"Commander Maddox will fly with you, Asher, to the Chaim air base on the outskirts of Beirut. Arrangements have been made to meet Y. M. Ivanov. From there you'll have to get into Beirut to meet with your mole. It's risky, but we have no choice."

"I agree, Admiral."

"Wait! Wait just a minute. I don't fly."

"There's no other option, Commander. After all, you got to Hawaii by flying."

"Yeah, that was with a lot of Valium."

"That's out of the question. You need to arrive with all your faculties intact."

"Believe me, Admiral Gifford, without some help during the flight none of my faculties will be intact."

"No Valium. Sorry."

"No help, no fly."

"Excuse me, Admiral." Curtis Owen moved to resolve the

impasse. "Regulations would allow something for medicinal purposes."

"What did you have in mind?"

"Wild Turkey. Your favorite."

"By God, you're beginning to worry me, Owen. You're starting to think like a politician." Gifford patted his aide on the back. A moment of levity broke the tension, and laughter filled the ship. In that moment no one saw Christopher Maddox slip a small vial into his pocket.

Tinges of mauve and rose colored the predawn violet sky along the tropical green mountain range behind Kaneoe field. The light touched the blackened runway and stopped short of following the strip to the sea. Within the shadows a plane waited at the end of the tarmac like some feral animal ready to pounce.

A fortified Christopher Maddox wobbled toward that shadow within the steady grip of Jackson and Owen. Admiral Gifford and Asher Lod brought up the rear. As the aircraft loomed from the shadows Maddox stumbled to a halt.

"Hey, guys," he slobbered with the profound affection a drunk holds for his comrades, "where's the TWA?"

"Oh, we have a private plane for you, Commander," Gifford answered sarcastically, angered because he had walked into the back of Maddox.

"Gee, that's nice of you guys. Where is it?"

"Straight ahead." Jackson hoisted the physician.

"But that looks like a . . . a . . . whatchamacallit."

"A Vigilante, Commander. Very good."

Over the doctor's feeble protests Jackson and the flight crew loaded Maddox into the belly of the supersonic bomber. Asher followed. The undersurface hatch slammed shut, abruptly stifling the protests from inside. A blanched face passed momentarily by the eight-inch-square window reserved for the bombardier. Silence returned to the base. The ground crew worked efficiently.

"I love this early morning tranquillity," Gifford mused as he walked back.

"I suppose shore leave is out of the question," the Marine said hopefully.

"Afraid so."

An ear-splitting rumble destroyed the stillness. The three remaining men covered their ears. White-hot gasses flared from the jet engines. The Vigilante leapt from the shadows to race down the blackened strip. Searing exhaust carrying the odor of JP-5 jet fuel swirled around the men as the plane streaked past in a blur of olive and green. The blue-white ball of the afterburners rose from the ground and climbed sharply to penetrate the clouds. Rolling thunder trailed to the end of the runway.

"We'll have to call him 'Supersonic Maddox' after this, eh, Admiral?" Owen wiped the lava dust from his face.

Gifford sighed.

Jackson read the signs. "You think he's going to FUBAR this thing." He used the Marine acronym for Fuck Up Beyond All Repair.

"If this guy isn't the biggest cluster fuck I've ever seen, then I don't know what is. Goddamn, but he's all we've got. Everything's riding on that rummy who may be suicidal—I read your psych profile, Owen. I got a bad feeling about this whole operation. If he screws up, our shit's in the wind."

"Did you tell him about Operation Blazo, Admiral?"

"Hell, no! I may be an ignorant old sailor, but I'm not stupid." Henry Clay Gifford stared into the sunrise, then at the illuminated dials of his timepiece. "Day five."

CHAPTER

——— 6 ———

Taongi Atoll, Marshall Islands

"This is Cu, the month of the dolphin. The storm star that fights with the phases of the moon is Uliul. There!" Tangaroa pointed to the Belt of Orion. "Storms will come when Uliul fights with the waning moon, but they won't be bad storms. Next month will be the month of the turtles." The old man grinned and nudged the boy. "You'll have little brothers then, eh?"

Mau hopped to the prow of the outrigger canoe and peered into the night. *"Auren Mangar!* Light of the Flying Fish!" He waved excitedly at Venus.

"Paugh! Even a blind woman can find the Flying Fish," the navigator chided. "Recite for me the *wofanu* for Satawal. Then I'll know that a woman has not crept onto my canoe while I wasn't looking."

"I sit on Satawal, I go rising Mailap to Truk, I sit on Truk, I go setting Mailap on Satawal. . . ." The boy puffed out his chest as he held onto the gaff. Words of the primeval litany of star courses and islands spilled from him. This "gaze at the islands" allowed a *palu* to chart a course to any island for which he could recite the *wofanu*.

"Good! Good!" Tangaroa clapped his hands. Instinctively he adjusted the tiller for the falling wind.

"Now I'm a navigator, too!"

"You wear a *thu,* but it's too big for you!" Tangaroa roared with laughter as he pointed at the twisted loincloth that hung precariously on the boy's bony hips.

Indian Ocean, Midair

"Shit, he's puking again! How can he do that? He's got to be empty by now." The copilot of the A-3 Vigilante twisted in his seat to peer down the narrow crawlway of the fuselage.

Designed as a supersonic nuclear attack bomber, the slender plane was built to fly low and fast below enemy radar while carrying a single hydrogen bomb within its belly. Over target it was to climb steeply and eject the nuclear weapon out the back of the ship. Planners expected the pilot to be momentarily blinded by the nuclear explosion, so the navigator was to fly the Vigilante to safety from his windowless position. Under testing, the navigators suffered from such extreme vertigo that a small window with a shutter was cut into the fuselage. Christopher Maddox now suffered with his face pressed to the navigator's viewing port.

The advent of nuclear missiles had led to the Vigilante's current role as a reconnaissance ship. Cameras and sensitive listening devices filled the bay formerly reserved for weapons of mass destruction. This special plane carried a different modification. Its belly held a pod designed to carry sensitive equipment, even people if necessary. This pod carried one newly commissioned naval commander and one Israeli agent. Streaking through the atmosphere at three times the speed of sound, the A-3 crossed the Pacific, pausing twice to refuel in midair from an A-2 tanker that found them in the blue sky. The A-2 satisfied the Vigilante's thirst with fuel pumped through a metal umbilical cord.

Below, the waters of the Gulf of Arabia slipped past, flickering intermittently through gaps in the clouds. The pilot and his navigator checked their Heads Up Display, scanning the digital readouts and computer images that the microcircuits fed to their screens. No missile tracking warning lights appeared as they skirted the edges of the Persian Gulf and the hostile zones of Iran and Iraq. Flying high and fast, the Vigilante passed with comparative immunity.

Golden orange lights flooded the cockpit from the sun chasing the aircraft along the curve of the globe. Except for the roar of the engines, the scene lent itself to thoughts of creation and meditation. Water, earth, and sky blended together in harmony.

Harmony was far from Christopher Maddox. Wedged against the wall of a cold cylinder, he struggled to retain his sanity. Control of his stomach and bladder was lost from the onset in his battle of nerves. The scorn of the pilots and the stoic reserve of Asher meant nothing to him.

Why am I afraid? he asked himself. Not afraid to die, surely. That would be a welcome relief compared to the hell he'd suffered daily since that terrible plane crash. He prayed for sweet oblivion. Anything that might set him free—a mechanical flaw, a loose fitting, a sensitive warhead under the wing—anything that would obliterate him and turn this titanium-alloy torture chamber into dust and flaming metal.

Perhaps it would not be quick and painless. No matter. He had been there before. It would not be new: the fleeting disbelief that comes from mechanical failure, Icarus watching his melting wax, the price of divine aspirations.

He, Christopher Allen Maddox, had paid for his grasp at immortality, hiring that private Piper Cherokee so he and his wife could speed to his new appointment as director of the Institute for Viral Studies. He had reached for the sun, and the gods had burned him.

"No, no!" he said out loud, causing Asher to open his eyes and regard him suspiciously. No, the gods hadn't burned him. They preferred to play with him, to let him live, to let him gnaw at his liver like some variant of Prometheus. He hadn't burned. Only cuts and bruises resulted from the crash. The gods were careful.

Maddox forced his face against the navigator's viewing port. Bile and vomit coated the inside of his oxygen mask, sliding down his neck inside his flight suit. Rancid fumes of sour mash whiskey racked his nostrils. The suit, bathed in now-cold urine, chafed with every movement. Why was he afraid? A dazzling beam of sunlight burned his eyes. And he knew. He was afraid of the memory.

Deep within him the fear gave way to the agony that he lived with every day—the dread that had bonded to his very chromosomes like his precious viruses. Maddox started to hyperventilate. His face mask fogged. The gods thrust him back into his private hell and returned him to the crash that had killed his love.

As his lungs blew off carbon dioxide his brain responded to the chemical imbalance. The Vigilante dissolved about him. His mind flew back in time as his body hurtled forward. He was clutching his wife, listening to the curses of their pilot, praying as the Cherokee spiraled toward the mountaintop.

It was all there, enshrined in his mind. The growing landscape, each rock and shrub, each stunted tree growing as the ground neared. The shriek of metal over stone and gravel overriding his wife's cry as they hit. He had never lost consciousness. It was all there.

Somehow the impact flung him out of the cockpit as the plane continued on to wedge between two boulders, jamming the doors closed. He hobbled to the plane. Inside his wife rested as if asleep. Was she already dead? He prayed so. Beside her the pilot slumped over bloodied controls.

Then came the smoke, tiny tendrils at first, caressing her body. The doors were stuck. He pounded on the windows. He shouted until his voice cracked. He seized a rock and pounded at the barrier. The smoke grew and called its brothers, the flames. Mocking him, they danced about the trapped bodies. Did she move? Was she alive? He battered at the millimeters that separated them until his bloodied hands streaked the Plexiglas. The flames increased until the metal of the cockpit glowed. Maddox hammered harder. The ends of the broken bones in his forearm grated together and threatened to puncture his skin. He felt no pain, only weakness. The fumes separated to torture him with glimpses of his sweetheart. Her hair smoked and shriveled in the heat. The tip of her nose and her ears, still bearing the diamond earrings she loved, blackened and withered. Her face blistered and scorched. Her lips shrank to reveal her teeth. He was powerless to help.

Christopher Maddox raised the stone to smash his own head, to join his wife, but the weakened arm dropped it. He screamed, and his soul broke to rush out with his wail. Then the plane exploded.

"Can you hear me?" the voice hissed. The drawn face of Asher materialized from the black oblivion that cloaked Maddox. "Dr. Maddox?" Urgency filled the voice, but it was also restrained, muffled as the Israeli hid his companion from the view of the flight crew. Lod glanced over his shoulder. The crew continued to fly the plane. Lod shook the doctor, his fingers digging into Maddox's arms.

"Yes . . ." Maddox focused on the piercing eyes. He forced himself into a sitting position against the metal wall of the pod. Bile bathed his lips. Alloy barriers, braided hoses, and wire harnesses defined his current world. He was back in the plane, condemned to live. He groaned.

"You had a seizure! Do you have the virus?" The grip moved to his throat. Lod's eyes held the weird light of a religious fanatic.

"No, this happens to me a lot . . . when I hyperventilate.

Something to do with an irritable focus on the cortex of my brain. From an old injury. I don't have the virus."

"Don't lie!" The grip tightened. "I'll kill you and wreck this plane. I'll have to . . ."

"Go ahead. Make my day! You'd do me a big favor."

The stranglehold relaxed. Asher dropped back on his heels. He searched Christopher's face. "What sort of a man asks for death?" he asked. Aversion filled his face. "How can you help the world? You don't even wish to save yourself!" His words were heavy with bitterness. "Oy, I'll never see my unborn child or my wife. All our fates rest with you, and you don't care."

"Everything okay back there?" the navigator shouted.

"Yes, he's still sick," Asher answered.

"Goddamn." The navigator scuttled back out of the crawlway like a crab. "Keep that puke in there."

Now Maddox grabbed the Israeli. "Do you love your wife?" Lod started at the intensity that burst from the ashes he had stirred.

"More than anything!"

"Fine. Then you know how I felt. Only I was unable to save my wife. And every day it haunts me."

Heavy moments of silence passed as the two men explored each other's faces. Asher saw only the truth. He nodded.

In the cockpit the pilot and copilot were issuing coded signals to Israeli tracking stations as they passed into the territory of Israel. An American AWACS watched all this from just over the horizon and passed the signals on to relays that sent the messages to Admiral Gifford in *Aesop*.

"Shit!" the pilot cursed after receiving instructions from the ground. "The IDF says our designated airfield is under artillery and rocket attack from the Christian sectors."

"Lebanon?" The copilot had voiced bad vibes about this whole spook operation from the start. "I told you so, didn't I? This isn't good."

"Yeah, yeah. Save it, will you?"

"Well, what do we do now?"

"Get home base on the horn." The pilot used the code name for *Aesop*.

AWACS dutifully relayed the scrambled transmissions. The Vigilante began a slow descent as it circled the desert. Dropping through the cloud layers, the craft registered as a momentary blip on the radar screens of the Israelis and their surrounding enemies before it leveled off below the track of the radar.

"Okay, guys! Drop time. Strap in!" The copilot crawled to the mouth of the pod. He placed his hands and knees cautiously while avoiding traces of Maddox's airsickness.

"What do you mean? Jump?" Maddox was beyond caring, but Asher answered the obvious question. "We're not trained to parachute."

"Didn't think so. Neither of you boys look like airborne to me. Look, the airfield where we planned to land is under rocket attack. The admiral was afraid of this, so he made contingency plans."

"Bless him, he is a caring soul," Maddox mumbled.

"He knew you guys had no jump experience. Am I right, Commander?"

"Black shoe myself, Lieutenant." Maddox referred to the age-old separation between the black-shoe sailors who sailed the fleet and the brown shoes of naval aviation.

"Right," the copilot continued. "And no time to train you, so you guys get a pod shot."

"A pod shot?" Maddox could only guess.

"Yessir. This capsule can be dropped out the back. It has its own chute. Nifty, huh? It'll be a piece of cake. So you better strap in. We'll be over the drop zone in ten minutes." With a parting grin the aviator checked the restraining harnesses of the astonished men and slammed the hatch to the pod.

Maddox and Asher clutched at the nylon webbing that held them on the padded frames and listened to the clanging and thumping as the copilot readied the canister. Pressurized aeroquip hoses hissed as they were disconnected. The copilot's face appeared at a tiny viewing port. His thumb waggled in a thumbs-up salute, then he disappeared. The two men exchanged looks as they waited.

"God! I love this maneuver," the pilot exclaimed after his partner returned to his seat and buckled in. "Did you clue them in?"

"Naw, some things are best left unsaid. Twelve seconds to drop zone."

"Okay, here we go!"

The copilot checked their ground contour radar as the afterburners fired, boosting the thrust by ten thousand pounds. The radar's map of greenish phosphors painted the visor of his helmet.

The Vigilante surged forward. This was what it had been built for, a racing thoroughbred among already refined stock. G-forces pressed the men into their padded chairs. Like a darting needle the plane shot by, a silver blur four hundred feet above the desert floor. The setting sun glinted off its wings. Ahead, plumes of dirty smoke lifted in twisted columns over the besieged airfield.

The Vigilante split the smoke. The pilot pulled back hard on the control stick, and the plane climbed at ninety degrees. The desert floor dropped sharply away. At twenty-five thousand feet the copilot yanked the pod release, and the metal cylinder slid backward out of the belly of the accelerating plane.

"Bombs away," the pilot shouted, in reference to the long-replaced function of the Vigilante. Cutting across its own contrails, the plane vanished at MaCH 2.8.

Inside the ejected pod the American and the Israeli flattened from the developing G-forces of the run across the field topped off with the gut-wrenching climb. Spinning with the released cylinder, they noticed the sharp deceleration as their container reached the peak of its height before it began to fall under the pull of gravity. Suddenly they were tumbling backward, plunging earthward with increasing speed. Both men screamed.

The parachute opened, and the drop ended with a bone-jarring snap. Relief flooded their minds as they descended in gentle, wavering arcs below the opened chute. The feeling was almost pleasant.

Any gratification ended with the impact on the desert floor.

Swirling winds whipped the parachute silk to drag the pod over the dunes. The hatch opened. Sand and light poured into the interior, followed by the head of an Israeli soldier. A shell exploded nearby. The face at the hatch disappeared. Shrapnel fragments pinged the sides of the pod.

Asher and Maddox scrambled out. They followed the running soldier. Ahead, a series of sandbagged trenches beckoned. They vaulted the barrier as another blast showered them with sand and fingerlike streamers of smoking cordite.

Maddox tumbled, coughing and retching, into the trench. Raising his head, he looked about. It was dusk. Horizontal rays dropped below the low hills as the moon rose. The shelling continued.

Explosions tore deep holes in the sand, but the desert swallowed this latest insult from mankind without comment. The sands had seen Saracens, Hittites, Ottomans and their modern offspring as well, and cared little for any of them. The shells did little damage with the metal fragments muffled by the surrounding grit. The firing abated with the diminishing light.

Maddox uncoiled from his pocket in the slit trench and peered over the rim. Darkness fell quickly as the sun dropped below the vast sea of sand. The undulating dunes reminded Christopher of ocean swells. He felt almost at home, almost in Hawaii. He rose unsteadily. Silence pressed upon the trench.

Instantly a three-shot salvo exploded about him. He

pitched forward onto his face. Sand choked his nostrils. Sputtering and swearing, he looked up as a shadow fell over him.

She was standing in the moonlight. Swirling dust and sand enveloped her like a surrealistic cloak that the moon backlit into a turbulent glow. No movie director could have created a more dramatic entrance. This apparition stood over him and looked down.

She was beautiful, and he hated her for it. The light illuminated her pale skin, imparting a ghostly radiance to her that seemed to be his wife calling from beyond the grave. But the girl's hair was raven black, and her eyes a pale violet such as he had never seen before. She wore a shirt and khaki shorts that failed to hide her long legs. Her beauty stirred feelings in him that he had tried to kill with the death of his wife. For that he hated her all the more . . . that and the poise and self-assurance she radiated while he groveled in the dirt.

He rose unsteadily, despising her with every fiber of his body. She walked to him and extended her hand.

"Hello, Dr. Maddox. I'm Y. M. Ivanov."

"You're a woman!" he blurted out. The thought slipped out as words. He saw the first imperfections in her face as two tiny frown lines formed at her eyebrows.

She recovered swiftly. "Yes, last time I looked I was." Her face resumed its placid veneer, but her forceful grip indicated that she also had claws.

"Sorry." He hoped the darkness hid his blush. "It's just that . . . your name, Y. M. Ivanov. I assumed that . . ."

"Yes, I know. That Y. M. Ivanov was a man."

They stood holding hands amid the dust storms of biting sand that came with the night wind.

Lod looked at them in amazement. "Come on! Let's get out of here," he yelled impatiently.

Ivanov smiled and bundled the amazed physician off to the sandbagged command post. Maddox allowed himself to be guided by her firm pressure on his arm. A waft of her perfume, an exotic blend of lime and cinnamon, cut through his bile-soaked smell. He glanced at his soiled jumpsuit. Globs of dried vomit clung to the fabric like decorations of cowardice. He winced.

"Are you hurt?"

"No," he lied. But he hurt inside.

The steaming mug of coffee infused life into Christopher Maddox. Warmth radiated from his fingertips to the pit of his stomach, and the nutty aroma cleansed his mouth of all aftertaste from his airsickness. In the far corner Asher munched happily on handfuls of dried dates while talking to the airfield commander.

Maddox ran his hand through his hair in a lame attempt to appear presentable. Ivanov watched him. She seemed unconcerned with his disreputable appearance. The harsh light of the naked light bulb failed to diminish her beauty. Beauty and the beast, Maddox reflected.

"I thought Y. Ivanov was a man in his eighties. In fact, I wrote to him several years ago."

"You're right. That Y. Ivanov is my grandfather."

"Your grandfather?"

"Yes, Yitsak Ivanov, Professor Maddox. Unfortunately, he is recovering from a mild stroke, and we felt this journey would be too strenuous for him. He thinks very highly of your work. He told me he wanted to meet you. When he knew he couldn't come, he told me about you."

"Oh! What did he say?"

"That you were a great mind in modern genetic engineering. But you don't look the way I expected."

Maddox glanced down at his soiled jumpsuit. "What did you expect?" he asked defensively.

"Someone shorter and older . . ."

"And cleaner."

Her laughter was warm and unpretentious. "Yes. He didn't say anything about your stomach."

"It's a recent affliction since my wife died," Maddox replied darkly.

"Yes."

Asher and the post commander approached. The officer was obviously unhappy about his orders. Shaking his florid face, he threw up his hands in exasperation and stomped off. "We're to meet with my intelligence group in three hours. Something's come up."

"Can I walk there? I've had enough flying."

"We can drive there. It's not far. Nothing's far away in Israel," the girl added.

"We?" Maddox studied her. "You're more than just the welcoming committee?"

She bristled. "I hold my doctorate in marine biology. My specialty is sea snakes."

Nearby the commander's ears perked up at this new information. Asher shot her a warning look.

She continued in a whisper, but her anger was obvious. "When it seemed the Soviets wouldn't allow my grandfather to emigrate, he taught me everything he knew about gene splicing with the influenza virus. I speak Hebrew, Russian, Arabic, German, and English. So, Dr. Maddox, I am qualified to be part of this team. I'm not the welcoming committee, as you so crudely put it! Nor am I one of your fawning college students who sleeps with you to get an A!"

"Ouch! Low blow. You've been talking to my mentor, Admiral Gifford."

"I'm also a reserve captain in the Israeli Defense Force. With marksmanship training! So I can shoot off anything you might have between your legs!"

"It's not a big thing," he replied deadpan.

She snorted in derision, spun on her heel, and stormed off.

Asher punched him, aiming for a clean area of fabric. "I think she likes you. Let's go."

Maddox followed lamely. Asher and the officer jumped into a battered jeep and sped away. The doctor stumbled through their dust to find Ivanov waiting in a small white Toyota with a cracked windshield. Numerous dents decorated the fenders. The girl steamed behind the steering wheel. He slipped into the passenger seat. Before he could close the door she took off with a neck-snapping burst of speed. The battered car streaked along the winding road, skimming edges of precipitous dropoffs as they descended into the valley. Sparkling lights marked a populated area ahead. Maddox marveled at the normal appearance so close to his recent shelling.

"Look, I'm sorry for what I said."

She shot him a withering look.

"I am sorry, and I apologize. There was no excuse for that."

Silence followed.

He squirmed in the cramped seat. "What's that place?" He pointed to the lights.

"Nahariya," she answered flatly.

"Shit," he mumbled to himself.

"What?"

"Nothing." If she's stupid enough to want to go in with us, who am I to complain? he debated silently. But he didn't want her to go. The thought of another exquisite creature like her—so like his wife in many ways, yet totally different —being destroyed was unbearable. He tried to erase that possibility by concentrating on the black arc of the Red Sea as they raced along the coast. He caught her looking at him.

"You stink." She wrinkled her nose. "And you're dirty. Don't you have any clean clothing?"

"The airline lost my luggage."

She couldn't help laughing, although she tried not to.

"See, I made you laugh." He shrugged. "Waste not fresh tears over old griefs."

"Euripides." Her reply caught him by surprise. Now they were both laughing.

"What's Y.M. stand for if Yitzak is your grandfather?"

"Yael."

"Yale, like the enemy of Harvard?"

"No, Y-a-e-l." She pursed her lips and accentuated the

70

syllables. "It's a good Hebrew name. My friends call me
Yanni sometimes, Dr. Maddox."

"Call me Chris. That's short for Christopher. It's a good
Christian name. We can't go about calling each other
Doctor. Doctor. Doctor. Sounds like hospital grand rounds.
God! I wonder if I'll ever attend another grand rounds, or if
there'll even be grand rounds. How do people live here with
this constant war?"

"We live every minute. To dwell on the past or wait for the
future is foolish." She looked at him knowingly.

He nodded. But how do you pry the past out of your
mind? he wondered.

They drove into Nahariya. The evening traffic resembled
any town's, but Christopher noticed many of the men
carried Uzi submachine pistols. The jeep slipped through a
traffic stop and disappeared into the traffic. Yael made a
sharp right turn off the main thoroughfare onto a back street
that ran parallel to the harbor. White stucco apartments and
duplexes dotted the terraced streets. She stopped in front of
a small split-level.

"Is this it?"

"No. This is my home. Come inside. We have time before
the meeting." She skipped up the stairs, leaving him admiring her legs. He followed, confused. Inside, she took his
hand and pushed him into a tiny bathroom. "Shower," she
commanded as she shut the door.

The scalding water blasted away the layers of grime.
Maddox closed his eyes and imagined a world of hot water
and soap without artillery shells. He sampled her shampoo
and lathered his head. Steam clouded the shower and the
small room.

A blast of cold air startled him. He forced protesting eyes
open through the stinging soap. The shower curtain opened
on clattering metal rings.

Yael stood in the steam, watching him. Maddox froze,
clutching a bar of soap. Her eyes ran over his naked body,
appraising him. Their gaze traveled down to rest between

his legs. The corners of her mouth twitched. Then she was gone, and another draft of evening air hit him.

Christopher stood blinking in the shower. What the hell, he wondered. Are we playing mind games? He dropped the soap and turned off the shower.

Folded neatly by the sink was a clean set of clothes. His jumpsuit lay piled on the floor where he had tossed it. Hurriedly he rummaged through the flight outfit and withdrew the black-capped vial. He slipped it into the pocket of the clean pants as he dressed. The worn tan shirt and slacks were loose on his thin frame, and the legs of the trousers ended three inches above his ankles. He laced on the canvas-and-rubber boots. No socks or underwear, he noted.

The smell of olive oil and cloves filled the hallway. He followed the sound of something sizzling into a small kitchen. Plates of salad, figs, and oranges covered a table set for two. Yael continued her operations at the stove, although he noticed her stiffen as he entered. A desk filled the room's remaining space. Books and papers, all neatly ordered, covered the desktop. Christopher noticed framed photographs of Yael and a square-set man with dark, curling hair. The man was dressed in clothes similar to what Maddox now wore. The doctor's stomach growled.

"Sit down. The fish is almost ready."

He picked a chair and unfolded his napkin. She turned with a platter of braised fish that made his mouth water. She served him and returned with a bottle of white wine.

"Ah . . . I'll just have water." He covered the wineglass with his hand. "I guess I'm on duty. The U.S. Navy is dry, you know—no drinking on duty." He hoped she bought his lame excuse and didn't see his hand trembling. His body was screaming for a drink.

The fish was delicious. She sipped her wine, nibbled salad, and watched as he demolished the meal. Soon the uncomfortable feeling he got from her scrutiny outweighed his hunger.

"When does your husband come home?" he asked. It sounded awkward to him the minute the words passed his lips, like 'How about an evening quickie while hubby's away?' But the words were out. Suave, Chris, very suave, he groaned inwardly.

"He was killed a year ago."

The words cut into Maddox. He felt more depressed. That wine bottle called. "I'm sorry. I know how you feel." His response was spontaneous and from his heart. She seemed to note that.

"He was killed by Palestinians, terrorists."

"You don't have to explain."

"I don't mind anymore. At first it was very painful. I cried a lot. My grandfather helped. He's a very wise and practical man. Now I have my work. Nahum was killed while doing his reserve time. I tried to find out the details, but it was all classified. It was in Lebanon, I discovered. On some mission. It's ironic. Nahum was a political scientist. He spoke strongly for the Palestinians, for giving them back their land. And they killed him."

"That sucks."

"Sucks?" The tiny frown lines appeared.

"Bad figure of speech. The world is crazy. On the brink of destruction. I find life makes little sense. It's best not to care. You only get hurt."

"No, that's wrong! I feel sorry for you if that's how you are. If you don't care, you're as good as dead. Grandfather taught me that life, any life, no matter how desperate or bad, is worth living because of the infinite possibilities for something good happening. 'Think of all the genetic potential,' he says, 'if not now, then in the future through the offspring.'" She leaned forward on her hands and smiled. "He says he's an incurable scientist, but I think he's an incurable optimist."

"I'd like to meet him . . . when we get back."

The violet eyes hypnotized him. He could swim in their

depths forever. But the eyes saw through him, probed into his hidden places with gentle fingers that held him fast. The eyes widened in surprise and understanding.

"You don't think we'll get back! That's it! That's why you don't want me to go! And I thought you didn't think I was qualified!" She laughed as she leaned over the table and hugged him. Glasses spilled. She sat back, beaming happily. Maddox savored the tingling warmth on his cheek and the smell of her perfume. She made him feel alive, and he felt uncomfortable in that role.

"I don't think we will."

"Yes, we will." She glanced at her watch. "We've got to go."

Maps covered the walls of the office of the Northern District Intelligence Section. Men in opened-necked shirts and tan uniforms knotted about a large map of Beirut. Asher separated from the group to greet them. Yael left them and joined the group at the map.

"I told you she likes you." He winked. "Did you guys . . . you know?"

"I got a shower and a meal. That's all! You need some saltpeter, Asher."

The Israeli grinned. "Yes. You're right. I've been away from my wife too long. Just the same, Maddox, you'd better watch your step. Israeli women are extremely direct."

"I thought she was Russian," Maddox countered.

"She is," Asher persisted as his smile widened. "But now she's become an Israeli, too. In making up for those lost years as a Jew in Russia, she may be overzealous." His finger waggled in front of Christopher's nose. "She may be overdoing it, sort of a super-Israeli. I've seen it before. They're really dangerous."

The district commander, a tired-looking man with fringes of gray hair decorating the sides of his bald head, cleared the room of everyone except Maddox, Asher, and Yael. He tapped his finger nervously as he waited for the room to empty. Nicotine stains colored the two fingers on his right hand that held a battered cigarette. He drew in a tight puff and squinted through the smoke.

"I don't like this, Asher. Not at all. Al Bakaar's group are known for their loyalty. They're religious fanatics. We've never been able to crack their cell, then all of a sudden this 'Sparrow' comes to us! It smells like a trap. I need more time to develop this contact. And now we think Al Bakaar is getting money from the Iraqis."

"Levi, he did give us the Athens operation."

"Worthless pieces of shit! It could be that was simply bait for us. For a bigger prize."

"What prize, Levi?"

"You, for example, Asher. The son of a director of counterintelligence. This could be an elaborate hoax to get you! What would I tell your father then, eh, Asher? That I let the son of my old friend walk into a trap?"

"I agree," Maddox piped up. "And I don't think Dr. Ivanov should go either." He grunted as Yael's elbow savagely struck his rib.

The commander eyed them suspiciously. "Are you two lovers?"

"Hell, no!" Christopher protested as Yael steamed. "Is that all you guys think about? It's just that . . . it's risky, and . . ." His plea fizzled out.

The commander puffed furiously. "They have to go, American! If I could send you alone, it would make me very happy. To my way of thinking, there are more Americans than Israelis. I would rather we lose one of you than one of us, especially one like you!"

"Do you know Admiral Gifford?" Maddox quipped. "He's turning into my Boswell."

"You don't even speak Arabic," the commander continued, "let alone know Beirut. You wouldn't last two minutes. Do you even know how to shoot a gun?"

"All Americans do," Christopher replied sourly. "Just ask the Indians."

"Most amusing. I hope your sense of humor continues. Asher has to go because they asked for him. Dr. Ivanov goes because of her qualifications. In Israel the women fight alongside the men. I trust them implicitly. You're the weak link, Dr. Maddox. I don't understand the details of this new threat from Al Bakaar, but if it is true, our survival as a nation depends on this mission. That is too important to trust to a drunk."

"Thanks for the vote of confidence."

"You have a smart mouth, American. I hope to God your mind is also smart."

CHAPTER

7

Beirut, Southern Suburbs

A predawn crimson glow lit the western sky behind the mountains that rimmed the Bekaa Valley. Centuries of strife had drenched the soil with human blood, and still the deadly irrigation persisted. Tonight everything was still except for the sporadic crackle of small-arms fire among the rubble of this once-beautiful city. Not content with ravishing and murdering Beirut, her tormentors continued to squabble amid her bones.

The black-painted Westland Lynx 3 helicopter roared across the undulating sands at its top speed of 190 miles per hour. Ahead, the stacked rubble of squared stucco houses rose as moon-splashed shards among blackened date palms. Mortar and plaster rubble filled the narrow streets. No lights emanated from these sand castles crafted by the hand of a demented giant.

Twin Rolls-Royce Gem 60 turboshafts powered the craft as it hugged the terrain at sixty feet to avoid Syrian radar. Peering through his night-vision goggles at his Night Vision/Heads Up Display, the pilot concentrated on the greenish landscape with its superimposed red numbers and symbols as his feet and arms danced over the controls. Beside him the copilot hunched over the projected map display that painted contour lines over the flat-panel head-down TV display. Evading the hills and rocks, the Lynx rolled and drifted between disasters. The two men spoke softly in Hebrew as they shared information from the infrared high-definition TV and the NV/HUD.

Bathed in crimson from the night lights, Christopher Maddox struggled again with old ghosts. His fish dinner tormented him with instant resurrection. Only pride and force of will kept his meal down. Across from him, strapped into her seat, Yael watched him with widened eyes and taut lips. Yet she managed a smile. He wished her gone so he could slip into his familiar gutter. Without her present he could have collapsed, babbling and incoherent, before the yawning door of the helicopter. Instead he pulled off a lamentable imitation of John Wayne and clambered aboard.

He glanced at his watch. Thirty minutes. The commander was wrong; he had lasted more than two minutes. Fuck that old bald guy. Seated beside him, Asher read his thoughts and flashed a thumbs-up sign. Maddox nodded. Fuck him, too. And the girl most of all.

The winchman came aft and crouched by Asher. The night-vision goggles affixed to his helmet gave him the appearance of a praying mantis. Asher shouted into Christopher's ear.

"Ten more minutes!" He squeezed the doctor's leg. "No parachutes this time, my friend."

Asher and Yael pulled back the bolts on their Uzis and let them snap forward, chambering a low-velocity 9mm round into the silenced chamber. Maddox fumbled with his. The bolt stuck open. He cursed. Yael reached over and slapped the cocking knob, and the bolt clacked shut. She beamed at him.

The Lynx banked abruptly, then dropped into a small

square. The pilot rotated the helicopter in a full circle as he scanned the buildings with infrared and night vision. Nothing moved. The rotors whipped dust and scattered papers into the air. The craft hovered four feet above the debris. Only the chop of the rotors disturbed the air.

"Looks clear," the winchman shouted. He popped the starboard hatch and stepped to one side to man the machine gun. Asher, the girl, and Maddox hurried to the door.

The square exploded. A hand-held RPG fired from the second story of a seemingly deserted building streaked into the nose of the Lynx. Muzzle flashes of automatic weapons fire danced around the courtyard like twinkling stars. Green tracers floated about the helicopter.

The self-propelled grenade gutted the cockpit, killing the pilot and copilot. The Lynx rolled to the starboard side as it pitched back on its tail pylon, sparks flying as the titanium tail rotor struck the paving stones. The pylon snapped.

The fire into the square intensified. As the helicopter's main blade snapped against a building with an ear-bursting shriek of tortured alloys the Lynx jumped in midair and slammed to the ground.

The spin threw Maddox and the girl out into the darkness that filled the square while the dying Lynx thrashed at its tormentors. Maddox landed across a pile of bricks and rubble with Yael at his side. His Uzi spun away into the night. The girl crouched and fired at the figures that now darted into the clearing. Her efforts were rewarded with return fire in their direction.

"Get your ass down!"

"Shut up!" She aimed and fired another three-shot burst at a shadowy figure that crumpled near the fire of the burning helicopter. Bullets snapped through the air, and chips of masonry ricocheted inches from their heads.

Maddox's hand stabbed at the glowing helicopter. "It's going to blow!" Without waiting for her reply he hefted her over his shoulder, and they tumbled down the scree into the darkness. A second later an RPG shattered their last position.

"Shit!" Christopher cursed as he propelled himself over the rocks with arms and legs flailing away like a crocodile heading for water. He dragged the protesting girl behind. He paused in a dust-filled crater to peer over the rim.

Lurid shadows from the flames fluttered over the wreckage. Maddox watched as a figure stopped over a wounded Israeli to fire a burst into the downed man's face. Yael snarled and raised her weapon.

"No, you don't! We can't help them. We've got to get away!" Maddox yelled.

"You coward!"

He clamped one hand over her mouth, stripping the Uzi from her grasp as he dragged her deeper into the shadows. She bit his hand, but he held on. Then the Lynx exploded, sending a fireball coursing into the air. Stark images of black and white, life and death, good and evil froze for that instant in the flash. The blast ignited two terrorists who stumbled a few paces before crumpling into flaming heaps. The flames died out, and darkness returned to the square.

Light from the morning sun crept through a rent in the shattered walls and into the bombed-out cellar where the two of them hid. The light seared into the eye that Maddox kept pressed to the crack as he watched the square. Nothing moved. Only the blackened carcass of the helicopter and the fly-covered bodies bore witness to the events that night. The heat-shimmering air pressed down into the rubble that filled their hole. It would soon get hotter.

He swallowed, and his parched tongue rasped over dust-caked lips. His night vigil was ended. The shouting, jubilant terrorists had not found them. Now they were gone, and the heat of the day replaced them as tormentor. He forced his brain to think, but the blazing light confused him. He fought for a reference. What day was it? Wednesday, it was

Wednesday, August 22. Three days ago he was happily drunk.

Amazingly, the girl slept atop his left arm. Christopher flexed the numb limb. Instantly she was awake, her Uzi held in both hands. He watched comprehension rush into her eyes. His slight movement wafted a blistering mix of alkali dust and hot air through the crack. He could hardly breathe.

"Don't touch me!" The ferocity startled him.

"Hey, look. I'm not the enemy. . . ." His words grated out. More dust filled his nostrils.

"You're a coward. I should shoot you."

"Go ahead. See if I care. It'd be faster than baking in this hole. Go on, if it makes you feel better." The dark dog of his depression had kept vigil with him all night. He was prepared. Just one last dig, though. "Shoot, but the fact remains that I saved your life."

She pushed the snub-nosed muzzle hard into his neck, under his jaw. It hurt, but he didn't care. His dry throat betrayed him, and he coughed. Maddox cursed at his weakness. She pushed harder. "You ran. I could have saved Asher."

"You couldn't save shit with that tiny popgun!"

"I could have killed some!" Her protest carried less conviction.

"And gotten yourself killed! Those guys were playing with bigger toys, in case you didn't notice."

"Better that than running. Asher was your friend. How could you leave him?"

"I have no friends." His response was spontaneous and genuine.

She withdrew the gun. A flicker of sadness filled her face. "I'm sorry for you," she said. "But every Israeli is worth fighting for . . . we are so few, everyone counts. We don't leave our wounded, and we don't leave our dead."

"Save me the patriotic speeches. If we fail, there'll be a hell of a lot more dead than those in the square."

"You're right. What do you suggest we do now?" Her change caught him off guard.

"We've got to get out of this cellar before we bake. We also need to get water. After that, I don't know what to do. Maybe try to contact this Sparrow? But he may be the one who set us up. I can't think that far in advance." His body ached for the blanket of alcohol. Even though he knew it would burn in his throat, he longed to pull that cloth over his head and sink into oblivion. Shot down in a Moslem state where alcohol was forbidden. The thought struck him as funny. Just my luck, he chuckled.

She stared at him, half expecting him to leap up and tear off his clothing in some mad fit. "What's so funny?" she demanded.

"Nothing. I was just wishing for a drink."

"Of water?"

"No. Actually, a mai tai."

"A coward hides behind liquor."

"You better believe it, babe. But right now I'd settle for water—shows how low I've sunk." With that he backed away from her Uzi and started to crawl over the shards of masonry. His movement filled the pit with dust. She followed.

He slid over the rocks, trying to ignore the sharp corners and splinters that jabbed at his skin. Arriving at the opening, he stopped and listened. No sounds. He inched forward into the light.

A small boy with saucer-sized dark eyes stood watching Maddox emerge from his hole. The physician froze. The child smiled. Maddox returned the smile. The boy dropped the stones he was holding and ran screaming away.

"Shit!"

"What did you do?"

"I smiled, goddamnit! Is everybody in this part of the world fucking crazy?" He was on his feet now, running low to the ground. Yael ran behind in a similar crouch. Shouts came from around the corner . . . ahead. Maddox skidded as he reversed direction, heading for the skeleton of a four-story building. More shouts behind. Laughter, too. The FFL was enjoying the chase. Christopher hurtled through the door frame of the only standing wall and fell headlong over a twisted bed frame. The wire springs sang out in protest, announcing their location. Yael helped him to his feet, and the two darted down a bombed-out side street. Arabic posters and slogans in splashed white swaths covered the remaining walls. A tattered curtain flew from a lower window. The waving cloth caught Christopher's attention.

"In here!" he yelled.

"No! Wait!"

"Yes!" He grabbed her wrist and pulled her after him. Then he saw them, but it was too late.

The six men looked up from a map that rested beneath four stones that held it neatly in place across a splintered table. A part of Maddox's mind noted that incongruous bit of order in the surrounding chaos of the war-torn district. The men all wore astonished looks and green-and-white checkered burnooses—the symbol of the FFL.

Beside the table, guarded by a terrorist with an AK-47, knelt Asher Lod. That terrorist reacted first. The guard's weapon jumped to Christopher's chest. Asher sprang at his guard as he fired. The burst splintered the wood of the door frame level with Christopher's chest. The other FFL awoke from their trance in a wild scramble for their weapons. The table upended and the map fluttered to the debris-laden floor.

Maddox stepped to the inside of the rising muzzle of the closest Palestinian and snapped a vicious chop to the man's neck with the flat of his hand. A blurred picture of rotted teeth and a dense black beard filled his vision as the man collapsed into him. A three-shot burst struck the Arab in the back as Maddox wrenched away the man's AK-47.

"Run!" Chris yelled at the astonished Yael. "Get the hell

out of here!" He punctuated his words with a full burst from his captured automatic that dissolved the room in splintered wood and plaster chips. Terrorists flew in all directions. His right foot caught another man as he dived for Maddox's legs. Dropping like a poleaxed ox, that man tumbled between Chris and Yael, forcing them apart. Out of the corner of his eye Maddox saw Yael firing the Uzi braced against her hip. Grim determination marked the set of her jaw.

"Goddamnit! Run!"

Maddox fired point-blank into a green-and-white-covered head, turning it into a bloody, shapeless mass. Blood and bone fragments spattered his face, but he didn't care. The girl wouldn't leave!

The Kalashnikov bucked in his hands, firing with its own selective eye turned to the swirling melee boxed in the gutted building. Bodies snapped and jerked as his rounds reached them. Crimson gouts and streaks painted the chalky walls. Maddox was out of control now, yelling as he killed. Without hope, he found the work easy.

More terrorists entered through the shattered windows. Maddox fired at them. Screams and curses followed his shots. He would kill every one of them. He wouldn't let them harm her.

Yael went down. A pile of terrorists overwhelmed her and pulled her kicking to the floor.

Bellowing in rage, Maddox waded to her side, feet slipping on the carnage. He almost made it. Something exploded against his head. Lights blazed briefly before a megavoltage of pain toppled him onto his back.

Still he clawed to reach her. Yael cried out and struggled for his groping hand. Things slowed and blurred as he watched a rifle butt descend toward his face. The metal recoil plate grew to fill his vision. A spectacular starburst announced its arrival.

Blackness followed.

Kaneoe Marine Air Station, Hawaii

"Six hours! Jeeesus Christ, Jackson! Six hours and still no word of them!" Admiral Gifford hopped about beside the parked *Aesop*. The Marine watched the admiral's balled fist looking for something to strike. The hands dropped to the officer's side. The tensed body relaxed. Suddenly the right fist flicked up in a blinding flash to hammer the metal side of the plane.

"Goddamnit!" A string of profanity that would blister the ears of a bosun's mate followed.

Jackson smiled.

"What are you grinning at?" Henry Clay snapped.

"Your vocabulary, sir. I detected a few new phrases that I'd somehow missed in my twenty in the Corps. I'm proud to serve under so eloquent a skipper."

"What a cluster fuck, Sergeant! No sign of Mr. Wonder Boy for six hours. I'm too old for this crap! Never could sit around much with my thumb up my ass. I'd give my pension for SEAL teams two and four and the go-ahead to go over there and give those ragheads a KaBar butt fuck."

"Aye, aye, sir!" The Marine slapped the honed and oiled knife at his side. All Marines trusted their KaBars implicitly. In a lightning move he whipped out the fighting knife and presented it, butt first, to his boss. "You can use mine, sir!"

A twinkle returned to Gifford's eyes. The fists unclenched. "Ah! Wouldn't that be grand?" Gifford's eyes glazed into that faraway land of imagination, of an older, simpler time of action. He enjoyed the thought for a moment before allowing reality to pull him back. The glow faded. "Back to the options, Jackson. What are our alternatives?"

"One. Maddox is dead.

"If he is, we're FUBAR. That would leave us with no leads and God knows how many FFLs carrying bottles of venom-producing virus into the States. There'd be no way to stop them."

"Could we cancel all visas for Arabs?"

"No. They'd simply get someone else. Like a Japanese Red Guard. Besides, the carriers may already be inside the U.S. No, if that is the case, we'll be facing a national—worldwide—catastrophe worse than a nuclear attack. I'd have to recommend to the president that he activate COG and scramble onto his Kneecap aircraft." Gifford pictured the frenzied exodus of the President, his cabinet, and top bureaucrats to Mount Washington and the sealed bomb shelters tunneled deep beneath the mountain. He saw the frantic efforts of the molelike government struggling with a dying nation. Cities choked with dead and dying. Chaos shredding the fabric of American society into tattered patches of survivors killing themselves in their efforts to remain unpolluted. He shut his eyes, but the images persisted. He looked at his watch. "I'll give the Israelis four more hours. If Maddox comes up dead or still missing by then, I'll call the president. What's option two?"

"Two. He's still alive and on course."

"Do you believe that?"

The Marine shrugged.

"I know what you mean, Jackson. No way in hell. But the guy's such a mess he just might make it. He goes against all plans. God knows he's operating by his own set of rules, and that might be the edge we need. He's unpredictable. No one knows how he'll react in a situation. But I'm counting on one thing."

"What's that, Skipper?"

"He feels responsible for some of this mess. After all, that piece of gene splicing was his brainchild."

"You think that's enough?"

"I hope so. I hope to God it is." Gifford looked away to

hide the doubt that crossed his face. "In any case, we've got four hours. . . ."

Beirut, Southern Suburbs

The stars returned. Lights swirled and coalesced into a blinding intensity that layered slabs of pain atop his head. Maddox huddled in a field of agony behind swollen eyelids. He knew he was dead. I can live with this, he thought. He giggled at the incongruity of that thought: I can live with being dead. His lids opened hesitantly to allow him to sample the afterlife. Heaven or hell looked like pubic hairs. His vision cleared. He was looking at his crotch. Maddox moaned. He was still alive. He was tied to a wooden chair with his head hanging over a rope encircling his neck. And he was naked.

Christopher raised his head. That aggravated his discomfort. His eyes met a vision both terrifying and beautiful. Facing him, tied to a similar chair and equally naked, sat Yael. Ropes held her arms behind her back and forced her legs apart. Light from a single overhead light bulb cast illumination over her lean body. He followed a drop of perspiration as it rolled unhurriedly between the cleft of her tanned breasts to trace along her stomach before it raced down between her legs.

Maybe heaven after all, he mused. He envied that drop. He felt stirrings of life again. A crooked grin caused his split lips to bleed, and he drooled blood and saliva into his lap. Smooth move, Chris. How to impress a girl on your first date. He tried to swallow, but the rope cut into his neck and he choked instead.

Their eyes met. Yael flashed a look of defiance, causing him acute sensations of embarrassment. Part of him wished to caress her, to dive into the sea of black waves that covered her shoulders, while another part wanted to cover her nakedness, to protect her. He averted his gaze. Pretending to be analyzing their prison, he craned his neck to look around. The room was windowless. Only a heavy door in one wall relieved the gray monotony. Their clothes lay in a pile on the cement floor next to a heavy-duty Caterpillar tractor battery. Sinister cables snaked from its terminals. A filthy sponge bobbed in a rust-covered bucket. Odd brown stains that reminded Chris of dried blood dappled the cement.

"So, do you come here often?" he quipped to Yael.

"What?" She regarded him uncertainly. Clearly his actions at the burning helicopter proved he was a coward, but in the bombed-out room he had fought like a tiger. She was confused.

"It's a joke." He shook his head lamely. "An American saying . . . when people . . . when a guy meets a girl at a bar. . . ."

She decided he was mad.

"What do we do now?" He tried not to look at her, but he found himself staring. The sheer beauty of her nude body glowing in the light reminded him of a work of art that turned this abyss into an Eden. She watched him proudly.

"I'm sorry I let you come."

"It was never your choice," she added with finality. The dialogue was ended.

"Well, it's time for the Seventh Cavalry to come riding to the rescue." Maddox tested the ropes. They felt tighter than a sumo wrestler's belt. The coarse hemp bit into his skin with every breath. He watched the girl's breasts move as she also struggled. Pay attention, Chris, he reminded himself. This isn't a kinky parlor game we're playing here.

"The cavalry?"

"Sure. In the movies John Wayne and the cavalry always rescue the good guys in the end. I'm ready. How about you?"

"You are very strange, Christopher Maddox." Her face brightened, and she flashed a smile. "Yes! I know . . . when the Indians are about to win. Or the . . . the bad guys. I remember. In the American movies."

The door creaked open.

"Here come the bad guys." Maddox watched as a squat man in streaked green camouflage fatigues swaggered into the room. Greasy stubble covered his face and neck, extending down through the opening of his shirt to enmesh a gold chain that hung from his neck. He carried a black rectangular box with side terminals and a rheostat knob on top. He grunted as he set the box near the battery and connected the two.

The man's eyes bulged as he spied the naked girl. He straightened, wiping his hands on his pants, and a slow grin spread across his face. Thick lips sneered to reveal an uneven row of blackened and missing teeth. An evil-looking tongue rolled over his lower lip. He spoke to Yael. She replied in venomous tones. The Arab smiled.

A shadow fell across the doorway, and the fat man stiffened. He bowed in respect, touching grimy fingers to his lips and forehead.

Both captives watched a gaunt man in flowing white robes enter. He seemed to float toward them, followed by aides in assorted combat dress. The fat man bent low, almost kneeling.

Maddox looked up and saw madness. Coal-black eyes lodged in sunken orbits burned with an unholy fire from a cadaverous face. A mask of tranquility covered the taut skin stretched across high cheekbones and a hawklike nose, but the eyes betrayed the cauldron that bubbled within.

"I am the Mahdi." The voice came from unmoving lips as if from the folds of the robe. The words carried a trace of an English accent. "To the unfaithful, I am called Khalid Al Bakaar." A murmur of approval swept from his followers. "What were you coming to do?"

"Tourists," Maddox injected.

The jailer struck him across the mouth with his beefy hand.

The Mahdi raised long, slender fingers, and the jailer dropped to his knees.

"I ask again, why did you come here?"

Maddox tasted the blood in his mouth and prepared to speak. But before he could answer, Yael spit at the man in white. Aides rushed to position their bodies in front of their leader.

"Are you spies?" A glint of recognition flashed in the black eyes, and they narrowed to fearful slits. "Did you come to find out about the plague? Did someone talk? Do you know about the pestilence that I will soon unleash upon the unfaithful?"

Yael gasped.

"We don't know about any bullshit plague!" Maddox bounced his chair on the floor. "I'm a crack assassin for the CIA!" He hoped his show of bravado would cover Yael's slip. The men looked at him doubtfully. He played his ace. "I'm here to assassinate you!"

One man spoke in rapid bursts of Arabic. He produced Yael's silenced Uzi and offered it to the Mahdi with both hands. Khalid ran his hand lightly over the weapon.

"What is your name, American?"

"John Rambo."

More hurried discussion ensued. Several men nodded.

Bakaar's eyes narrowed again. "My men say that is a movie."

"It's about me. I am the famous John Rambo. The American and Israeli governments picked me because I'm the best. That shows how much they fear your power."

The Mahdi's eyes widened.

Aha, thought Maddox, even the Chosen is subject to flattery. "They fear you will unify all the Arab nations and destroy Israel. So they paid me twenty million to kill you."

"Only twenty million? I'm worth much more."

"Things are tight. There's a recession on in the U.S."

"And you failed."

"I wouldn't have if these stupid Israelis hadn't botched their part. Especially this worthless girl. She's only an interpreter. She knows nothing. Let her go . . . let her live with her shame. She can tell her government how we failed." Christopher hoped they would buy it.

Yael blazed at him.

Khalid ignored the girl or failed to notice her. He thought for a moment, pressing his fingertips to his lips. "I believe some of what you say. What matters is if you are this John Rambo or not. Do not feel bad because you failed. It is written that I cannot die by fire or the sword. And not by the hand of man." The Mahdi spread his arms in an encircling movement and raised his voice. "This man's failure reaffirms the prophecy."

His men touched their lips and foreheads and murmured thanks to Allah. Al Bakaar spun in another whirl of white and floated out the portal.

"Holy One," the jailer called out in deferential tones. "What of the prisoners?"

The billowing sheet paused. "They are unbelievers. Interrogate them . . . then do what you will with them. I must prepare for my visit to Vibrogene." The white mist drifted away, and the door shut.

The jailer turned to Yael. He wiped his hands in growing circles on his trousers as he approached her. His movements reminded Maddox of a cat stalking a crippled bird. She tensed as he circled her chair, testing her bonds. Evidently he was aware of this bird's claws.

His hamlike hands shot out to fondle her breasts. Yael's back arched, and she held herself so rigidly that splinters from the chair dug into the skin over her shoulder blades. The jailer enjoyed her discomfort. Leisurely he caressed her, exploring her curves with filth-encrusted fingers.

She made no sound, no movement, but Chris noted the knotting of her jaw muscles and her eyes glowing like lethal weapons. He felt one touch from them would incinerate her tormentor. Still she held her head erect.

"Hey! Hey!" Maddox squirmed against his ropes. The terrorist ignored him. "Hey, pig face! She's not your type! She's not a camel or a little boy!"

The jailer delivered a vicious chop across the doctor's face. "I speak English, too, Yankee dog," he grunted. He aimed a kick at Maddox's exposed groin, but the physician twisted, and the blow caught his hipbone, driving him and his chair against the wall, where they both tilted at a precarious angle.

Maddox felt his right arm move under the shifted ropes.

The man returned to Yael. He pinched her nipples, then his hand slid down her flat belly to disappear into the black triangle of hair between her legs. She never acknowledged his existence as he played with her. He stroked harder, twisting his fingers, trying to force her to cry out.

Tears welled in her eyes. Tears of humiliation. The jailer misread them and laughed in triumph. He fumbled with his pants. He stood before her displaying his manhood.

"Now, Zionist whore, you will feel a real man. Not one of your circumcised eunuchs." He bent forward.

Yael spit in his face.

The jailer jerked backward as if hit by acid. His shoulder struck the chair, and he fell over Maddox. The two tumbled to the floor. Chris saw his chance as his arm slipped free. He aimed for the terrorist's exposed anatomy.

"Gotcha, pig fucker!" Maddox's free hand clamped onto the man's scrotum. As an added measure his hand gave a malicious twist.

The terrorist shrieked like a castrated bull. Flailing and kicking, the two rolled across the stone floor. Fists pounded into the physician's unprotected face. Bound to the chair except for his one arm, Maddox had no defense. Desperate blows rained over the doctor's body. But he held on, tightening his grip with every opportunity, focusing his entire will into the muscles of his hand. Each impact only caused his fingers to draw tighter about the terrorist's vulnerable anatomy.

Maddox was winning. The jailer's eyes bulged from a crimson face. The blows weakened, and his cries diminished until with a shudder the man fainted.

Chris used his free arm to lift his body and the chair off the ground. He bent his neck to look at an astonished Yael. Gratitude and confusion reflected down at him. He redoubled his effort to slip out of the bonds, but the ropes cleverly tightened with his movements. Finally his arm weakened, and he collapsed at her feet.

"Shit!" he gasped. Dust from the floor spiraled about his face as he fought for his breath. He twisted again, but it was no use. His body sagged. Then he started to chuckle. He choked on the dust, hawked, and spit a glob of blood-tinged phlegm. "Well," he added philosophically, "I don't think you have to worry about this camel jockey, anyway."

Yael smile bravely through the tears that flowed freely down her face. "You shouldn't have done that. Now they'll really torture you."

"It was worth it," he replied. "Did you see the look on his face?" Maddox grunted in satisfaction. He tested the cords that now threatened to cut off his air. "Goddamnit! I feel like a sea turtle on his back!"

"Thank you . . . for . . ."

"Forget it."

"No! I won't forget it! Thank you for helping me. I . . . I've been wrong about you. I thought you were a coward, but you aren't. I'm not sure exactly what you are, but you're not a coward. I don't know what you are."

"Crazy."

"No, not that either. I think you've been very badly hurt by your wife's death."

"Who told you about my wife?"

"Grandfather. You'd really like him. He's the wisest person I know."

"I'd like to meet him, but I'm glad you were at the airport

instead. God, a beautiful girl tied naked to a chair, and I can't do a damned thing about it!" he lamented.

Yael blushed, and Chris watched the color flow down her neck onto her breasts.

"This is embarrassing." She tried to recover. "Now there's nothing about me that you haven't seen."

"It all looks good to me."

"Thank you."

"Well, this has been the wildest time I've ever had on a first date." Scuffling sounds outside the door reminded him of their situation. "Look, any minute this goon's friends will be coming. We don't have much time. So I have to say this now because I may not get another chance."

"Yes, Chris?"

"I'm just happy I met you. You're the first person—the only person—I've met since my wife died that made me feel alive. You know, like something in life was worth living and fighting for."

"I know." She blew him a kiss.

"Thanks."

The heavy door grated open on rusted hinges.

Outside the building that served as headquarters for the Front for Liberation a messenger clambered over the rubble that clogged the back street. Hugging the long shadows of the afternoon sun, the man slithered to the next doorway. He paused to shift the bundle he carried and glance about. The destroyed facade ahead resembled all the rest. Few knew that the basement housed the general command's center for terrorist activities. Now the courier scanned the skeletonized buildings. Tattered posters, shards of glass, splintered doors, and blowing papers—the usual detritus of a dead community—greeted his glance. Nothing moved in the back alleys—those forced by circumstance to exist nearby avoided this area under threat of death. He glanced at the sky. Only a solitary bird drifted along in the updrafts from the simmering heat. The man nodded in satisfaction.

He adjusted his green and white *kafiya* before slipping down the cellar door.

Two hundred meters above him the bird drifted over the building tops. Also using the shadows, it floated closer on muffled wings. Silently it grew as it approached until its true shape became apparent. Gliding on fiberglass and composite wings invisible to radar, the twin-boom pusher-propeller-driven aircraft loitered in the area.

If the messenger had waited he might have recognized that his bird was a Tadiran Mastiff, a sophisticated mini Remotely Piloted Vehicle designed by the Israelis for dangerous reconnaissance. The 160-kilogram mini-RPV looked like a large model airplane, but there the resemblance ended. Powered by a pusher prop that dispelled its exhaust gases, the mini-RPV was virtually invisible to infrared detection. Nonreflective paint and composite materials minimized its radar signature. The Mastiff was built to linger in hostile areas for up to seven hours. This version carried forty kilograms of TV equipment and an advanced Forward-Looking Infrared scanner. The FLIR scanner had locked onto the furtive messenger, and the TV camera zoomed to follow him to his hideout. Already the loyal Mastiff was sending encoded infrared and TV pictures to its mobile ground control station.

Seventy miles to the south an Israeli captain peered over his glasses as encrypted data poured onto his CRT terminal. The Israeli roused himself from his nap to watch the lines fill his screen. Routinely, the material would be transferred to tape reels and sent in raw form to intelligence headquarters for the northern sector with the afternoon courier. But this morning he was bored.

Scratching an annoying mosquito bite, he rolled the trackball beneath his fingertips to select *print and decode* from his computer menu. What were a few more pieces of paper? The politicians wasted millions on their own speeches and all the damned new regulations they were forcing down everyone's throat in their effort to curb inflation. Besides, he needed more practice with the new Hewlett-Packard color laser printer. This would be a perfect excuse to use it. He hummed happily as the file transfer light on the printer glowed and the Canon print engine began the transfer.

Love those colors, the captain thought, all 256, not counting the shades. The first computer-enhanced print slid into the basket. The Israeli held it up for inspection, captivated by the laser-sharp photo of the surrealistic landscape. His eyes focused on the green and white checked *kafiya* on the head of a man with an AK-47. His mouth dropped open. The man was carrying an Israeli pilot's helmet with the latest Night Vision/Heads Up Display!

Five minutes later the laser print was speeding to sector command by special courier motorbike.

The fat man grinned evilly at Maddox. In his eagerness for revenge he moved too fast, and a stab of pain from his swollen scrotum caught him in midstride. It also reminded him of his hatred of this man trussed before him like a sacrificial lamb. This unbeliever would pay!

"Do you know what this is, my friend?" He tightened the terminals of the rheostat and dangled the two wires before Maddox. Each wire ended with an alligator clamp. "We are very modern in our methods of persuasion. It was the French, I believe, who developed this use for electricity."

Chris smiled grimly at Yael. Sweat covered his body. He wished she wasn't there. It was only a matter of time before he screamed.

The jailer leered at Yael. "Soon, my pretty Zionist, I will fix your friend. Something in return for what he did to me."

The man doused Maddox with the foul contents of the bucket, then attached one clip to the skin of the doctor's chest. An enormous grin spread across his face as he snapped the other clamp onto the inside of Christopher's thigh.

"Now. Just a taste at first. Yes. Only a little." His fat

hands adjusted the rheostat dial and flipped a switch. The resistor hummed.

A million clusters of pain blossomed inside the physician's body as the electric current surged through his muscles. The muscle fibers contracted involuntarily, jerking his head back and arching his spine until his body bent against the ropes and the wooden chair like a drawn bow. His fingers clawed at the wooden rests, digging new grooves beside older scars of previous tortures. His short-circuited chest muscles jammed in full contraction, pulling his ribs apart and cutting off his breathing. He was suffocating.

A second before the physician could pass out the jailer cut the current. Maddox flopped into the chair like a rag doll. Starved lungs sucked in air. All of Christopher's muscles burned. The impact and awareness of his agony burst upon him as oxygen relit his sensations. Then the Arab hit the switch, and another jolt struck him. The terrorist was very clever—he would push Christopher to the brink of no return, only to allow his body, with its innate will to live, to fight back from the grave. Then the torture would resume.

After minutes that lasted lifetimes Maddox fainted. His oxygen-starved brain hallucinated. He watched his fingers grasping at his wife as she stood before him. His right hand caught hold of her dress, preventing her from blowing away in the wind that swept through his mind. She smiled at him, and then he knew she was dead. Part of his mind filled with her voice, saying: "Let me rest. Let me go. I'm dead." She smiled again, his fingers loosened, and she blew away in a shower of sparks.

Tepid water poured over his head, filling his mouth and nostrils. He choked and sputtered awake. The room spun into focus. All his muscles twitched involuntarily. Maddox forced his head up. His eyes met Yael's as his head bobbed to one side. A great sadness filled her face, and he was touched by her concern. She was suffering more than he was. Maddox managed a crooked smile and a wink.

"So! Are you ready?" His torturer repositioned the lower

clamp. Maddox scarcely felt the teeth of the alligator clip bite into his scrotum. The fat man spun the rheostat dial to full power. "Few men can take the full current. If you do survive this, it won't be as a man! Better pray for death, American." The jailer bent close as he fingered the switch. "Wait." A hateful idea illuminated the man's features. "You two should be together." He laughed at this idea. "Yes. To witness this famed assassin's last moments." He slid Yael's chair forward until she and Maddox were facing each other.

Chris glanced at the girl. He decided that the last thing he wanted to see was her tear-filled face, so he looked past her at the grimy plaster wall.

"One. Two. Three." The terrorist enjoyed his count. His finger dropped to the switch.

Maddox focused tightly on the wall.

The wall erupted in a jagged loop. Maddox blinked. Plaster dust billowed from seams that appeared suddenly. Sound from the blast was followed by flying shards of plaster that spewed over him. The wall within the loop disintegrated, crashing down in a cloud of powder. Simultaneously the overhead light bulb went out, cloaking the room in darkness. A flash grenade exploded in a blinding fireball.

Two men dressed totally in black stepped through the hole in the wall. Both men carried automatic pistols in a two-handed grip, with flashlights strapped to their right forearms. The lights sliced through the clouds of plaster dust, searching the room. The beams crossed over Yael and Maddox to focus on the face of the astonished terrorist. Both pistols fired, and the jailer's head exploded from two low-velocity 149-grain 9mm bullets. He fell forward onto his knees before collapsing like a sack of rags. One man in black stepped over the body and spoke into a radio taped to the collar of his Kevlar vest.

A stream of Israeli commandos poured through the breach. The first, carrying a twelve-gauge shotgun, blew the hinges off the door while another tossed a grenade into the corridor. Shrieks and cries of pain followed its explosion.

More men fired their silenced Uzis into the confused mass of terrorists. The firefight advanced down the hall.

The men in black picked up Yael and Maddox and carried them, still tied to their chairs, out the hole.

Maddox blinked at the blazing sunlight. Dust and sand stung his face. Overhead a specially modified Sikorsky MH-53J PAVE LOW III-E swung in wide arcs above the square and the carcass of the Lynx like a vengeful dragon. Explosive shells spewed from its chain guns, tearing away at the surrounding buildings. The three 7.62mm miniguns shredded their targets with two thousand rounds per minute. From time to time the helicopter would swing to a coordinate requested by the commandos and fire a brace of Stinger missiles into a resistant pocket of terrorists.

Maddox looked up as a shadow fell across him.

"Asher!" Yael screamed.

"You two!" Asher Lod clucked, shaking his head like a disapproving Jewish mother. "I leave you alone for a moment, and you take off your clothes and have kinky sex!"

Yael blushed five shades of crimson.

Lod bent close to Maddox as he gingerly removed the electrical clamps. The Israeli winced in sympathy. "Looks like they tried to perform a *bris* on you. But it looks okay." He gestured over his shoulder at the girl. "See, Chris, I told you she likes you. You don't have a chance now she's seen you in the raw."

Before the two victims could respond, Lod shouted in Hebrew, and two medical corpsmen cut their ropes, placed them on stretchers, and jogged off in a half crouch to the waiting helicopter.

"Wait!" Maddox rolled off the stretcher and scrambled back toward the hole. "I've got to get my clothes!"

Asher ran after with his mouth agape. "Stop, Chris! You can get new clothes!"

"No! No!" Maddox dodged the restraining arms as he dived through the wall. He located the pile of garments more by memory than by sight in the gloom of the shattered basement. Seconds later Lod and one corpsman reached his side and pulled him back to safety. Bullets clipped the air as they raced to the landing site in the square. Defending commandos watched in astonishment as a naked Maddox ran by with his ball of clothing.

No one saw Maddox check his pocket for the black-capped vial.

The commandos withdrew under fire, tightening their perimeter until the rear guard shuffled up the tail ramp amid scattered bullets. Four rounds struck the MH-53, but the ceramic armor and self-sealing fuel tanks shrugged off the wounds.

A terrorist rose to the left of the aircraft to aim an RPG-7. The copilot saw him and shouted to the gunner as the MH swung to meet the threat. The Israeli pressed his electronic trigger a split second before the terrorist. A burst of fire from the Gatling gun shot the man into rags.

"I love it!" Asher pounded the back of the pilot. "This is a PAVE LOW III-E, right?"

The pilot nodded. "Yes, sir. The enhanced version. Has terrain-following radar and ring laser gyro inertial navigation."

"Yes, yes." Asher bobbed enthusiastically. "INS. And encrypted satellite communications. I read about these. But I thought only the Americans had them in England."

"Yes, sir. The U.S. Air Force 21st Special Operations Squadron in Woodbridge."

"So when did we get this?" Asher held on as the pilot banked to avoid a missile fired from about four miles away. He ejected an electronic jamming pod and launched a set of flares. The helicopter climbed steeply. Both men watched the missile's exhaust trail veer sharply toward the magnesium flares. The missile exploded in an orange ball that died into a brownish smudge to hang harmlessly below the helicopter.

"SAM," the pilot cursed. "Those fucking Syrians are giving 'em away like candy. But I got a fix on him!" The man tapped the glowing orange-and-blue screen on his electronic countermeasure module. A blinking set of red numbers covered the upper corner. He barked a set of coordinates into his headset.

Overhead, a KFIR fighter dropped like a hawk from his orbit and blanketed the missile site with napalm. The jellied gasoline incinerated the terrorists.

"Outstanding! But you didn't answer my question. When did we get this bird?"

"Officially we don't have one."

"I see." Asher chuckled. "Well, better send a coded transmission. Tell them we recovered the honeymooners."

Lod walked back past the rows of soldiers until he spotted Yael and Maddox sitting in the last two web seats. The American huddled against the metal framework behind a wadded shield of his shirt and pants. His eyes remained fixed on the gaping ramp and the spinning desert below. Visible shudders racked his frame. The surrounding Israelis watched him with growing contempt.

Maddox fought with the muscle spasms from his recent electric encounter as well as his older fears. Yael shot a fiery glance at the commandos as she wrapped a blanket around him. She spotted Asher.

"Well, did you get Al Bakaar?"

Lod shook his head. "Missed him by minutes. But we killed thirty-seven of them. With only two of ours wounded . . . that's good." He sounded unconvincing.

Yael shook her head. "Not good enough. How did you find us?"

"Ah. When they caught us in the square, I got thrown off the helicopter. That's all I remember. I woke up in that FFL outpost. They were happily beating me for information. I figured it was all over for me. But you two charged in there, and I escaped." Asher spread his hands in supplication. "Sorry. I saw you go down, and I couldn't help . . . so I ran. By the way, what were you two doing exactly?"

"Rescuing you," she lied.

"Thanks. Well, I hid in a bombed-out garage. I didn't know what else to do. While I was trying to think of something brilliant to do, this assault unit showed up in this helicopter, and then I joined them. Would you believe it? The FFL headquarters was pinpointed by one of our drones flying overhead. I guess we're all lucky."

"But no closer to stopping the virus," Yael interjected. Disappointment filled her voice.

"Vibrogene." The hoarsely spoken word was barely more than a whisper.

Asher and Yael looked at Maddox in astonishment.

"Vibrogene." His jaws rattled as he fought for control. "Khalid said he was going to Vibrogene."

"What's Vibrogene?" Asher moved to screen them from the curious stares of the troopers.

Maddox drew his lips back into a smile of triumph, but the dried lips stuck to his teeth to produce a ghastly rictus. His eyes burned intensely. "Vibrogene is a genetic laboratory in Germany."

CHAPTER

8

Kaneoe Marine Air Base, Hawaii

"GODDAMNIT! Goddamnit to hell! What timing! What fucking bad timing!"

The Marine guards patroling the perimeter of the air base glanced in the direction of the jet plane and shifted their M-16s. They were under orders to shoot anyone trying to cross the orange lines painted in a hundred-meter circle around the mysterious aircraft parked on the secondary airstrip normally reserved for Tomcats. The displaced F-18 served as the ready response fighter for the air base. Now it sat sullenly off the main strip. Satisfied that the three men standing outside the Boeing 707 were not trying anything foolish, the Marines relaxed. One lit up a smoke, silently thanking his lucky stars that he was not one of those three inside the orange "dead line."

Until he knew for certain that Maddox was correct in his diagnosis, Gifford was taking no chances. No one exposed to this deadly virus—no one living, that was—was free to leave. Even the dead were not free to leave *Aesop*.

"We should be happy he's still alive, Admiral." Owen

winced at the string of curses that followed. He kept a wary eye on the aluminum clipboard that Gifford was trying to fold into creative shapes. On occasion the admiral had thrown similar objects. Once, a field grade officer—a navy captain, to be precise—had required a trip to the infirmary for stitches to repair a nasty cut of his forehead from one of Gifford's airmail messages. The clipboard rose overhead in his clenched fist. Owen and Jackson crouched. But there it stayed, swinging in wide arcs as Henry Clay thundered.

"Why the hell didn't we get that message an hour ago, before I called the president, the National Security Council, and the Subcommittee on Security with my friend, Representative Schmittler? That prick from New Jersey! This is just what he wanted. My story had them wetting their pants. How Al Bakaar and his fanatics had an influenza virus with the gene for sea snake venom spliced into it, and they were dumping it all over the U.S. I painted them a picture of corpses piling up in all the major cities. A non-nuclear holocaust, I called it. No way to stop it. You could almost hear their bowels moving over the phone! Why, Mother Gifford must be rolling over in her grave at the eloquence of her poor Tennessean son. And then I had to tell them how our best plan to stop it got flushed down the toilet bowl when the FFL waxed our boy scout. Good God!"

"Admiral, at that time we thought Maddox was dead, that the whole mission—Lod, Dr. Ivanov, and Dr. Maddox—were killed in Beirut." Jackson repeated the obvious. "And it was past the deadline we set. . . ."

"*I* set that goddamned deadline, Owen! Whatever possessed me to pick that hour, I'll never know."

Gifford squinted into the Hawaiian sun that danced over the azure ocean. The refreshing waves sparkled tantalizingly just out of reach. A breeze carried the salty taste from the sea. So close, yet a life away. He longed to sit in some shady corner of a deserted island. Perhaps to fish. His father loved fly fishing. What did he love? Gifford asked himself. As he spent longer hours crammed in that metal funeral home, the question rose with disturbing frequency. Did he love anything now, with his wife gone? Not much, he had to admit. He was a burned-out old man.

Bullshit, a voice inside him snarled. You love the chase! You love every minute of this dirty business, and you're the goddamned best at it this side of the Soviet Union. You're a battled-scarred old terrier who kills rats. Burned out? No fucking way! You'll die with a rat in your jaws.

Fishing? Fuck the fish! That was for retirees.

Gifford winced. Six days ago this deadly virus had landed in Hawaii, and still its source eluded him. At this rate, he and a major chunk of the world's population faced permanent retirement within two to three weeks. And he was groping blindly for a way to stop the release of this twentieth-century plague. He felt poorly equipped to battle molecular killers. All his years of military experience counted for naught. A lifetime studying tactics, great battles, and great strategists like Sun Tsu and von Clausewitz was totally wasted. All his training, all the experience that held back fear and allowed him to direct men while whizzing pieces of hot metal from guns and grenades threatened to shred his flesh—all that was useless against an invisible enemy. Worse still, this cruel scientific prank turned one's own body into the enemy! He recalled Pogo's statement: "We have met the enemy and he is us."

Was this the prototype for the wars of the future? Would the generals of the future be technicians hunched over microscopes and computers? He had heard this before with the atomic age. But it always boiled down to men fighting and killing one another in hand-to-hand combat in the dark and the mud. Deep inside he knew nothing had changed. Luck and the actions of a few won battles. That much was constant.

"Well"—Henry Clay always faced the truth, no matter how painful—"we're still in business, but my credibility is shot. Especially after I called them back when Maddox turned up alive. There's no way the president and his advisors would ever activate COG now and evacuate. Not after I lied and told them I'd swallowed an elaborate hoax by the Front for Liberation that was designed to blackmail us."

"You had to, Admiral. You had no choice. Particularly when Representative Schmittler threatened to go to the news media with all this. He would have tipped off the terrorists."

Jackson nodded. "Yes, sir. That fudge packer would have blown the cover on Maddox."

"Sergeant, that's no way to refer to one of our elected officials. But you're right. We needed to protect our operation." A sly grin spread across the old man's face. "Representative Schmittler should stick to blowing things he's more familiar with."

"Aye, aye, Skipper!"

"The fact remains that we looked like bumbling fools after you called back and told them we'd just discovered it was a sham. Where does that leave us now, Admiral?"

"Up the creek, Owen. All that fancy talk from the president was just politicalese, and it boils down to this: we're on our own. He bailed us out with Schmittler only because it made *him* look bad, too. But that's as far as it goes. It's an election year, and those guys—especially the president—don't want to touch this tar baby. Everything we do from here on out will be labeled by them as unofficial. If we screw up, it's on our heads." Gifford paused to let his words sink in. Inwardly he rejoiced at the stalwart expressions on his men's faces. He grinned. "But we already knew that. If we lose this one, it won't much matter. We'll all be dead. On the other hand, how often do a scuffed-up sea dog, a jarhead, and a computer hacker get a chance to save the world? Sure, Maddox is questionable, but I couldn't ask for a better team than you two."

"Lunchtime!"

The three turned as Ames, the onboard technician, appeared at the hatch, arms cradling brown cardboard boxes and a thermos of steaming coffee. Ames had shown a penchant for housekeeping and worked hard to keep the aircraft spaces tidy. He squatted on the lower rung of the ladder and offered his wares.

"MRE's!" Owen fingered an olive-colored plastic pouch as if it contained toilet bowl cleaner. "Surrounded by millions in technology, and all we've got is this: Meals, Ready to Eat! Meals Rejected by Ethiopians is more like it!"

"Cut your grousing, Owen." Jackson was already eating his fruit slices while he inventoried his carton. "This is the staff of life." He peered over into Owen's box. "Trade you my beans and weenies for your chicken à la king?"

"No way."

Jackson shrugged. His chocolate bar vanished in one gulp. Removing a cigarette from his pocket, he lit up and inhaled a lungful of smoke.

"Those things will kill you." Owen dodged a cloud of smoke that Jackson blew at him.

"Trouble with you, Owen, is you're too hidebound."

"Hidebound?"

"Yeah. Afraid to live life to the fullest. Too inhibited. 'Course, maybe that's 'cause you're air force."

"Watch it," Ames joined in.

"Nothing personal. I like flyboys. They saved my ass several times in Nam, but you guys spend all that time up in the air, never get to experience life on its basic level. Don't get to savor the true . . . what's the word, Admiral?"

"I believe the word you want is ambience, Sergeant."

"Yes, sir, thank you. The true ambience of life. You know, mud and heat, all that shit. Why, Owen, I bet you never got the drippy dick, did you?"

"Hell, no."

"See, that's what I mean." Jackson drew slowly on his cigarette and squinted through the smoke. "When this is all over, I'm personally going to introduce you to the true ambience." He watched the admiral cradling his coffee mug. His carton of MREs was unopened. "You ought to eat something, Skipper. Gotta keep your strength up."

"Who's mothering whom, Sergeant?" Gifford snorted.

"Well, can I have your fruit slices, sir? That is, if you don't want them."

Henry Clay broke open the box and tossed the food to Jackson. Out of habit the naval officer munched on the chocolate bar as his mind sorted the thousands of permutations that faced them. He saw Jackson grinning at him as he watched his commander eat. Gifford tossed another bag at the Marine.

"Say, Owen," Ames interrupted, "how's your daughter doing? When's your next call to her?"

Owen stiffened.

Ames realized his mistake. He grimaced as the programmer looked at the admiral.

"I'm sorry, sir," Owen stammered. "It's just that Annie's birthday is in three days, and I didn't get a chance to buy her a present. You know, we left in the middle of the night and all . . . and she and her mother worry when they don't hear from me."

Gifford listened intently. "What's this about calls?"

"Oh, no verbal calls, sir! I . . . I just . . . well, I couldn't get to a pay phone, with those guys ready to shoot anyone who crossed the line."

"I offered to sneak him out, sir," Jackson volunteered. "With a little camo on our faces I could get him past those guards. I've been watching them. They're sloppy for jarheads. Not up to the usual standard of the Corps. Not like us Force Recon or, begging the admiral's pardon, the SEALs."

Henry Clay was undeterred. "What kind of calls, Owen?"

"By modem, sir."

"Modem?"

"Yessir. A modem is a telecommunications device used by one computer to talk to another computer over telephone lines. . . ."

"Can the lecture, Owen. I know what a modem is!"

"Yes, sir. Well. Annie's real good at using the Apple computer that I got her . . . so I've been sending her messages. . . ."

Gifford looked puzzled. "I didn't see any messages. I get a printout of all transmissions from *Aesop.*"

"Ah, well, I don't use the VAX 100 or the other minis."

"How in the hell do you send the messages, then?"

"I built a modem out of parts from the other computers. The transmissions bypass the log-on routine of the ship's main computer. It doesn't show up on your printout, Admiral. It's sort of a two-million-dollar modem. . . ."

"Two million! What do they usually cost?"

"About a hundred dollars."

"Are you telling me you're using over a million dollars in military parts to send electronic postcards to your family?"

"Yes, sir. That about sums it up."

Jackson nudged Owen. "Better tell him the rest, Curtis."

Curtis Owen appeared to shrink even farther into the blistering tarmac.

"Good God! There's more?"

"Ah . . . I . . . I planned on paying you back, Admiral. Next paycheck for sure."

"Paying me back? I don't have a million for you to spend. Just what did you do?"

"Well." Owen squared his shoulders, prepared to receive his punishment. "You know Annie's birthday is coming up, and I didn't get a chance to shop. I logged on to The Sharper Image and ordered one of those blue neon telephones—the kind that lights up in the dark. It's just what a thirteen-year-old girl would want. Only ninety-nine dollars."

"So?"

"I used your VISA number." Owen's voice sounded like a child's after being caught with his hand in the cookie jar.

"How did you get my VISA number?"

"Oh, it's on file at the store."

"But it's password protected."

"Yes, Admiral, but you use the same password for everything, so it wasn't hard to guess. It took us maybe twenty minutes to figure out. Right?" Owen looked at Jackson.

"So what is my password?" Gifford asked suspiciously.

"Your wife's maiden name!" the Marine blurted out.

"Jeeesus! I think I'm surrounded by the offspring of horse thieves," Gifford said, laughing.

"It's okay then, sir?"

Gifford was laughing so hard he could only nod as he wiped the tears from his eyes. When he regained control he looked at his men. "Is there anyone on this base that doesn't know my password?" Shaking his head, he boarded the aircraft.

He was still chuckling to himself as he passed the isolation chamber and saw the bodies of Pearl, Dr. Harii, the deaner, and the terrorist through the viewing port. Gifford pressed his face to the quartz glass for the longest time before he issued a heartfelt sigh. Sadly he went back out into the sunlight.

"Men." Henry Clay stopped on the last rung of the ladder. He waited as they clustered around, each still smiling with relief from the modem affair. A part of his mind, an analytical segment that he hated at times like this, noted that this was the perfect opportunity for this order. "Men, we have a problem." He remembered how Napoleon Bonaparte started similar speeches to his soldiers before battle.

"Just tell us what to do, Admiral." It was Jackson, always the Marine.

Good men hadn't changed, Gifford thought. "We have four bodies in there." His head jerked toward the open door. "And they're still dangerous. Even in death they can kill. This ship'll be taking off soon to fly to Frankfurt to coordinate with Dr. Maddox, but we can't risk flying around with those infected corpses. We need to dispose of them safely."

"How do we do that, sir?" Ames lost his smile first.

"Cremate 'em in the lab incinerator. Didn't you tell me

that its exhaust chimney is fitted with an ultraviolet flash chamber and two micropore filters that trap and destroy particles even as small as DNA or virus fragments?"

"That's true, Admiral," Ames said. "But the furnace wasn't designed for human bodies. It's too small. They wouldn't fit!"

"We'll have to cut them up." He waited for the astonished looks to fade. "I propose a schedule: one body apiece. We've got six hours. I suggest we get cracking."

Curtis Owen withdrew his sweating hands from the rubber gloves that penetrated the steel walls of the isolation chamber. Blinking, he moved to trap a bead of perspiration as it slid into his eye. He raised his hand to his glasses—and stopped. For the thousandth time he checked the silicone-rubber seals and the metal ring clamps that mated the gloves with similar gaskets belonging to the chamber. Only flimsy millimeters of silicone protected him from the killers he couldn't see, killers he found hard even to imagine. Ones that might cross the tiniest defect in the gloves to hide unseen on his hands. From there it was a small jump into his nostrils . . . and death.

Owen kept his hands from his face. The droplet flooded his right eye, obscuring his sight. He blinked until the eye cleared. Beside him Jackson operated another set of servo arms with his nose bent against his viewing port. The Marine still managed to chew his gum while whistling to himself. A crumpled cigarette sat behind one ear. His feet tapped in time to the movements of his hands.

God! He might be playing pinball or a video game instead of cutting up a human being, thought Owen. Jackson removed both hands to rub his scalp, a move that made the computer expert shudder.

Jackson caught Owen's stare out of the corner of his eye. "Hey Owen, I got two more legs to go and I'm finished. How're you doing?"

Curtis blanched.

"Aw, this ain't bad." The Marine tipped back in his chair and locked his fingers behind his head. "Not bad at all. You want bad? That was sixty-eight. During the Tet. Shit, now that was bad! Did I ever tell you about that?"

Owen shook his head to clear a wave of nausea as he looked into the startled, shriveling eyes of the dead Marlin Pearl.

"No? Well, me and my squad was pinned down on the banks of the Perfume River just below the Dong Ba Market. You know, in Hue. Outside the Imperial City. You ever hear of the Citadel? Like I said, it was during the Tet offensive. They tried to rush us. NVA all over the place. Yeah, the slopes cut us up bad. Half my men were wounded. Bodies everywhere. We piled them into barricades. There we were, up to our asses in water and crouching behind these stiffs. Well, all day long this went on. With the sun baking those bodies, they got real ripe." The Marine shifted uneasily. "I can still remember the sound of bullets hitting those bloated bodies. Goddamn! I just kept shooting and scrunching deeper into those stiffs. We were pinned down all night. And it got cold. In the morning the NVA pulled back. But those damned bodies stiffened up. Had to cut my way out of my pile. Hacking at those rotten bodies in the water with my KaBar—"

"Jesus Christ, Jackson! Just shut up!"

"Yeah, this is a piece of cake compared to that," Jackson grumbled as he returned to work.

Owen ran his fingers over the metal handgrips inside his servo arms. The claw and pincer terminal devices shifted. He swallowed, forcing his muscles to contract over a dry throat. Best get on with it. But he couldn't. Not while those opaque eyes watched him. He had to do something.

Owen directed his left servo to a polyethylene specimen bag near the foot of the table. The pincers snagged the draw cord at the mouth of the bag, and Owen eased the bag over the dead man's head. A corner of the plastic caught on

Pearl's ear, but with persistence both metal arms raised the stiffened neck and teased the bag over the face. With a sigh Owen slid the drawstring closed about the neck.

Using the foot pedals recessed beneath the operating chair, Owen activated the CO_2 laser. Warning lights accompanied the hum of the laser. He watched the panel of lights change from red to orange and then to green as the laser built up power. An impersonal beep notified him of full capacity. The sound startled him. Other than the constant hum of the straining air conditioners and the computer fans—and the whistling of Jackson—the airplane was deathly still.

He lifted the laser scalpel in a process that resembled dream sequence more than physical action. His mind played out the procession of actions, and his unseen hands moved to that script. Tiny microswitches and pressure receptors recorded the movement of his muscles and fed those coordinates to a microchip that refined Curtis Owen's trembling hands into smooth vectors of purposeful movement. The steel and plastic pincers moved to the junction of the polyethylene bag and the dead man's neck.

Owen said a prayer for Marlin Pearl and for himself. His finger clicked off the laser guard.

A pencil-thin beam of bluish-white light linked the laser with the cadaver's neck. With a puff of smoke the skin vaporized, leaving a bloodless channel. Owen traced across the anterior surface, and the neck opened into a ghastly mouth, exposing sealed muscle and whitish cervical bone. Weaving back and forth over the neck, the laser cut through until the head separated from the body and rolled to one side in the bag. Owen took a deep breath.

The servo arms lifted the cords. The bag swayed in midair with the severed head of the former legal assistant to the mayor of Honolulu. The arms directed the bag into the incinerator, where it was stacked alongside the limbs of Kenzo Harii.

Jackson's servos slammed the incinerator door and snapped on the disposal cycle. The Marine winked at Owen.

One hour and twenty minutes later the oven door closed on the last sections of the dead men.

CHAPTER
─── 9 ───

Köln, Germany

Sally Ericson absentmindedly brushed the crumbs on the tablecloth into a pile as she watched couples strolling hand in hand along the shops of the Hohe Strasse. She hadn't expected it, but Köln seemed the city of lovers. Even the ubiquitous Henckel Knife Company signs with its two figures made her realize she was alone. So she sighed and tidied up the remnants of cake she'd eaten with her afternoon coffee, the *Kaffee und Kuchen* so dear to Germans.

She finished the last of her postcards, penciling in the date: August 23. Tomorrow her whirlwind tour would be over, then it was on to Los Angeles to visit her brother before flying home to Chicago.

Chicago, the thought of her apartment in Oak Park, the muggy fall weather, and the start of another year of substitute teaching weighed on her like an anchor. Chicago was so settled, so routine. She envied these shoppers. Life had to be more exciting for them.

Köln made her restless: It was too romantic. And it was too familiar. The twin towers of the cathedral loomed over the city like pictures from the travel books she carried. They

115

watched over her as they watched over the city. The darkly Gothic crystalline spires anchored the modern glass and steel buildings that seemed to float and glide about the cathedral.

After the Allied bombing destroyed most of the city in the Second World War the *Kölners* had rebuilt with a zest for modern design. Some said it was to free them from their dark memories under Hitler. Whatever the reason, the city had blossomed into an astounding modern setting for architectural jewels that dated back to Roman and Gothic times.

Sally liked that. She never felt lost as she prowled the shops and flea markets. The cathedral spires were always there. At night the neon lights replaced the bustle while the illuminated spires watched.

But late mornings were the loneliest. So she would sit at an outside table at one of the *Konditorei* and sample the wonderful cakes and pastries while the smells of the bakeries filled the air and mixed with the eau de Cologne from the perfume shops. Watching the shoppers helped distract her. It was more colorful than the soap operas she watched at home.

A couple wended their way toward her. They stood out from the others. Neither carried parcels nor packages, and they moved with purpose. Obviously they weren't interested in shopping. Sally watched them. The girl was about her age, but strikingly beautiful. A light breeze tossed raven hair about a face containing pale violet eyes. Sally thought she might be an actress. Certainly her figure was that of a model. This girl clung to the arm of a grim-faced man. He had to be an American, with his close-cropped hair. They made a handsome pair except for the severe set of the man's face. They also made an odd couple. She walked with lightness and a bounce that spoke of an inner happiness, while he plodded straight along with determination. He seemed to carry the weight of the planet on his back.

Sally's actress flashed a smile at her as they passed. The man never noticed. The Chicagoan sensed this lady loved the man, but Sally felt he carried a great sadness. How poignant, she thought. The lady is happy to love and live in the present, while her man is caught in the future . . . or was it the past?

She watched them move on. The lady's hair danced with the swing of her head as they disappeared down Breite Strasse.

Sally sighed: Life should be lived. She felt alone.

Half an hour passed while she wallowed in self-pity. To pamper herself she ordered a Berliner Weisse, one of those delicious fruit-flavored beers she had first encountered in Berlin. The dusky brew, served in its outlandishly oversize balloon glass with a straw, arrived with her smiling waiter. The dark foam beckoned. Two Berliner Weisses later, Sally savored the warm glow inside her. Time to go. She assembled her packages and knocked over her glass.

Amber stains floated across the tablecloth. Heads turned. Dabbing at the tide only made matters worse. She wanted to cry.

A large napkin smothered the torrent as it raced over the table edge and onto Sally's dress. The girl looked up into coal-black eyes that mesmerized her.

"Permit me to help." A smile revealed white teeth set in a swarthy complexion. "I am Hadi Najem Hashim."

"Vibrogene, GmbH." Maddox stopped pacing the hotel room to peer out the window. He pushed the lace curtains aside. East along Komodien Strasse the twin spires of the Dom of Saint Peter and Mary rose from cathedral square. Beyond, metal and cement spans of the Hohenzollern-Brücke crossed the Rhine. "Two sites!" Maddox spun about. "The damned company has a factory and a research facility. That's two sites to check out. I didn't figure on that."

"Sit down." Yael patted the bed beside her. A map rested

117

across her knees. "We can handle it." Her soothing tones failed to placate him, and he returned to pacing.

"And where the hell is Asher?" Maddox recrossed the floor, keeping a wide distance between himself and the bed.

"Like I said before, Asher's checking with the Israeli embassy. To see if there's any new data on Khalid."

"Well, he should've been back by now." The circles kept their distance from her.

"Are you afraid of me, Christopher?"

"What? No, of course not!"

"Well, sit down so we can look at the map."

Maddox approached the bed like a firewalker with neither shoes nor faith. He sat beside her.

"Good," she purred. "Now, the factory is north of here. Asher will go there." Her finger pointed to the northern sector, then rested lightly on his leg.

Maddox stiffened.

"And you and I will go to Vibrogene's headquarters, here." Her hand slid along his leg.

Maddox started to say something, but Yael reached up and kissed him. The warmth of her lips poured a life into him that he was afraid to remember. Inside, his stomach churned as fire spilled over his frozen heart. Her fire melted away the ice.

He crushed her in his arms. The spice of her perfume encircled him, and her little body pressed eagerly against him. But he broke away.

"This is no good. I . . . we shouldn't start."

"Yes, we should."

"No." He was afraid. The bathroom offered sanctuary. Quickly he locked the door behind him. His flushed face stared back at him in the mirror. He was sweating profusely. A cold shower, that would help. Stripping off his clothing, he entered the shower.

Needles of ice water riveted his skin, but soon his muscles shivered from the cold. The damaged muscle fibers burned and cramped. He switched to hot and sighed as the scalding water loosened his painful tissues. Steam filled the room.

"You lied," her voice chided as he felt her satiny body slide against him. "Back in Nahariya you said you were small, but you're not."

"How did you get in? I locked the door."

"My commando training. Now you have nowhere to hide." She slipped into his arms and flicked her tongue over his lips. "Don't be afraid." She read his thoughts. "We've both lost someone close. Once in a lifetime is enough. It won't happen again, and I won't leave you."

He pressed her against the shower wall as she clasped her legs around him and they sank into the billowing steam.

"Are you a terrorist?" Sally asked innocently as her rescuer directed her through the mass of shoppers. She didn't really care, she told herself. He was so . . . so . . . continental was the word that came to mind, not at all like men she'd known in Chicago. She snuggled inside the coat he'd thrown over her sopping dress and let him direct her by the light pressure on her arm.

Startled, he laughed. "Heavens, no! I'm a pharmacist." He stopped and looked down at her. "But I am an Arab. I'm Algerian. Does that make a difference?"

She loved the way he talked. He reminded her of Omar Sharif, the movie actor. "No, no, of course not! It's just that the embassy warned us about terrorists, you know." She felt stupid. Here this man was helping her, and she was acting like a Midwest hayseed.

"A few fanatics are ruining it for all of us." Sadness inundated his face. "You don't know how terrible it is to have everyone accusing you of being one of those damn Palestinians just because your skin is dark, just because you are Arabic. It's not fair. I think I know how the American blacks feel." He resumed their pace.

"I'm sorry, I didn't mean . . ."

"Please, don't apologize. I should ask your pardon for my outburst. But it's tiresome. Look, would you feel safer with me if I told you I was a Roman Catholic?"

Sally smiled and shook her mass of curls. She was still feeling the effect of her beers. "I feel safe with you."

"Good, because I feel safe with you, too." There was that broad grin again. "You may not know it, but my mother warned me about beautiful, blond American women. That's how I knew to speak to you in English. You're wearing American clothes."

"I'm not beautiful. . . ."

"Oh, yes, you are."

"Do you really think so?" She would never have spoken this way except for the Berliner Weisses and the romantic effect of Köln.

"Yes, truthfully. You are very pretty. But I shouldn't be so forward. I don't even know your name."

"Sally. Sally Ericson from Chicago."

"Chicago! What a coincidence. I'm going there in two weeks."

"Really?"

"Yes," he answered excitedly. "I have finally obtained my visa. I have to take a course at Loyola University, and then I can be a pharmacist in Chicago. That's one reason for my unfortunate outburst. I've had to wait two years for my visa because of all this mess with the terrorists. The U.S. isn't too keen on Arabs these days."

"You poor dear. It must be awful."

"Yes, but now it's over. I'm very excited. Perhaps I could see you when I get there. I don't know anyone in Chicago except for my uncle. Why do they call it the Windy City?"

Sally shivered at the thought of Chicago's cold wind off Lake Michigan.

Hadi looked startled. "I'm sorry. Here I'm babbling, and you're cold from your wet dress. I must take you somewhere warm. Where would you like to go?"

"I'm staying at the Intercity Hotel."

"On Bahnhofsvorplatz. I know it well. Good views of the cathedral. I stayed there when I first came to Köln, before I got lodgings closer to the university. It's only a few blocks away. Here, I'll keep you warm."

Sally snuggled under his arm as they walked to her hotel. Now she fit in with the others. Even the concierge flashed her a perceptive smile when she asked for her room key. Excitement and anxiety threatened to swamp Sally as they rode the open elevator to the third floor. The passing tiers slid by the ornate gilded gratings, adding to her image of romance.

Remembering something she had read, she handed Hadi the key. He opened the door for her. Just inside she spun and impulsively kissed him. To her surprise, he kissed her back. This was like her dreams. Her head swam as his hands explored her body. She moaned as his fingers caressed her breasts and his kisses covered her neck.

Then she was helping him unbutton her dress, tearing at her stockings as he carried her to the bed. He removed her bra and panties as she fumbled with his clothes. She tried to bridle her urgency to savor these delicious moments. This was so much more romantic than the back seat of a car or her sofa bed at home. This dark man with his strange cologne was unlike any man she had known in Chicago.

He was more experienced than she. Under his tutelage their lovemaking was leisurely and prolonged beyond anything she had experienced. Eventually she closed her eyes and dreamed of princes and fairy-tale castles.

Later she awoke in his arms with a contented sigh. "In the movies they light up cigarettes."

"I don't smoke."

"Good, neither do I. Are you hungry? Suddenly I'm famished. I could order room service, if you'd like."

He hesitated.

"Don't feel like a kept man!" she scolded him gently. She bit her lip. "Look at me. Acting like a teacher again. I'm sorry, Hadi. Am I being too . . . too pushy?"

"Pushy?"

"You know, too forward. I don't know how your women act. Are they subservient?"

"You amaze me! So many questions! How can I answer them all?"

Sally pouted.

"All right." He laughed. "I'll try. First, yes, I'm hungry. But I feel I should buy lunch. I like you too much to have you think I'm a gigolo."

Sally shook her head. "If you take me out for lunch, we'll have to get dressed." She smiled knowingly. "There are better things we can do . . . here." She rubbed her thigh against him.

"Secondly, you are forward. But I like that. The women in my country live under veils. Besides being beautiful, you're very refreshing. Very American. And I'm going to be an American also."

She gazed up at him, searching. His open face mirrored her hopes. "Hadi, this is special to me. I don't know what came over me, because I don't do this with every man I see. But I really like you."

"This is special for me, too."

"Oh, good!" She threw her arms about his neck. "Let's have a special lunch served in bed. Maybe champagne?" She cradled the phone. The bulky antique receiver sat on its cradle and looked as if it belonged to a duchess. It was all so perfect.

"No champagne for me, please. It makes my head swim."

"Another wine?"

"Coffee. So I can concentrate on your beauty."

"Okay, let's try something daring from room service."

Their meal was delicious, the bellboy exhibited the right measure of continental aplomb while serving them in bed, and Sally loved her champagne. She failed to notice that Hadi Hashim avoided the *Leberkas*, a meat loaf served with crisp pretzels and sweet mustard, and made of pork.

CHAPTER

—— 10 ——

Köln, Germany

"I don't like this, Yael. Why a meeting tonight?" Christopher Maddox squinted at his wristwatch in the shadows of the parked car. The illuminated dial read nine o'clock in the evening. A light rain speckled the hood and added to his feeling of uneasiness. The canned wintergreen air freshener smell in the interior of the rental car completed his isolation. "Why not tomorrow morning, like normal?"

"Chris, his secretary explained that. Doktor Fuchs likes to work at night, or at least into the evening."

"Okay, okay. Have you got the briefcase?"

"It's under your feet," she replied patiently.

"Damn, I told you this is all new to me. Secret agent man isn't my specialty." He waved his arms for emphasis. "Ouch!" Maddox winced as his right shoulder struck the doorpost of the car.

"Oh, does it still hurt? You must be getting a reaction from your shots."

"Yeah," he said as he rubbed his swollen arm. "It ought to be sore. They used a needle the size of a bayonet." He fingered the painful bump. "Why did Gifford insist on my having those typhoid and yellow fever shots anyway?"

Yael shrugged. "Well, you were in an endemic area, and you know how bureaucrats are. He was probably just following instructions."

"He's probably a sadist who couldn't pass up the opportunity to hurt someone. It's damn stupid to worry about yellow fever when a killer virus is about to wipe out the human race."

Yael swung the rented Mercedes diesel into the evening traffic, expertly finding the exit for Vibrogene headquarters.

The glass and steel building sat amid tastefully planted maple and conifer trees. Winding amid the vegetation, Vibrogene's research center blended its three stories of mirrored glass and steel girders into the foliage. At the building's base decorative bricks seemed to anchor the structure to the manicured lawn. Lights burned on all the floors, but the reflective glass veiled any activity.

"Damn! Looks like they're home." Maddox clutched the leather briefcase as he looked inside. "Let's go over this again. I press the inside of this back panel to activate the homing device, right?" He patted the attaché case that Gifford had given him. Tiny microcircuits laced its inner lining, coursing behind the silk brocade to a transmitter linked with *Aesop*. There was also a miniature microphone with a dense crystal microchip capable of recording two hours of conversation. The briefcase was for documenting their conversations inside Vibrogene. The homing device was Curtis Owen's afterthought. No one expected any trouble. "Any smell of trouble, I press this baby, and Gifford charges in with the German equivalent of the Seventh Cavalry."

Yael beamed at her lover. She braked at the guardhouse. "Doctors Markland and Ben-Yaron, to see Herr Doktor Fuchs." It was Yael's idea to use her dead husband's name as her cover.

The guard checked his computer screen and nodded. The electronic gate slid open, and Yael drove to the main door. The parking spaces were all empty.

Two security checks later, an Aryan-looking guard ushered them into a large office on the uppermost floor. Chris and Yael sat together on a leather sofa facing a wide polished ebony desk that occupied the center of the room. Maddox set the briefcase on the floor beside the couch. Bronze and copper metallized panels covered the wall that curved behind the desk. A stylized chandelier hung from the high ceiling to gaze ominously upon them. It reminded Maddox of a guillotine blade. The entire room was without warmth.

"Look at that! Now that's weird." Maddox motioned to a futuristic sculpture placed in front of the desk. The artist had melted metal and glass fragments into a twisted amalgam that seemed to clutch at charred fragments of wood. Enormous heat had fused those materials into molten glass and dripping iron shards that scorched the wood.

A curious clicking sound like the scurrying of a crab permeated the chamber, growing in intensity while seeming to come from all sides. Abruptly a bronze panel slid open with a hiss, and Herr Doktor Fuchs entered.

The noise came from metal crutches and leg braces that scraped the polished floor as the elderly man dragged himself painfully toward them.

The two rose as the doctor worked his way into the padded chair behind the desk. As he dropped into the chair he acknowledged their presence with a deft flick of his eyes.

Yael shivered as Fuchs's gaze crossed her like a serpent's tongue.

"You were admiring my piece, eh?" The watery blue eyes gestured to the sculpture. Pinpoint pupils resided at the center of opaque irises that held little life. His eyes danced about, providing the sole animation for this stilted body, disappearing from time to time behind heavy eyelids that dropped like shutters. Stringy white hair crowned an amorphous face of pale folds of flesh that rippled around cruel, sensuous lips.

Jabba the Hutt after liposuction, Maddox reflected. How old was this man? It was impossible to tell.

"It's from Dresden. An unusual work, but one with some sentimental value to me." The eyes covered a computer screen set beneath the desk's surface. "Permit me to introduce myself. I am Erhardt Dieter Fuchs. And you are doctors Markland and Ben-Yaron? From America."

"Yes, sir." Chris spoke first. "As our letter stated, we've been hired by a major pharmaceutical house in the U.S. that wishes to license one of your genetic engineering processes. Specifically the process for producing fourth-generation cephalosporins." Gifford had supplied them with both a cover letter and background information on Vibrogene's bioengineering patents, but information on the director, Erhardt Dieter Fuchs, was strangely lacking.

"Indeed."

"We'd like to see your production facilities," Yael added. "The contracts will be handled by the legal department. Our task, Herr Doktor, is evaluation of Vibrogene's production capability."

Erhardt Fuchs nodded with a disinterested air. "I have prepared a small tour for you. Your letter didn't give us much time, but I think you will find it interesting. Perhaps even stimulating." The rubbery lips moved into a smile.

"We apologize for that, but Dr. Ben-Yaron and I were asked to make this visit on rather short notice also. I hope we haven't caused you too much inconvenience."

Fuchs spread his hands in supplication. His fingers were strangely tapered and delicate, like those of a pianist, inconsistent with his twisted form. "A little trouble, perhaps. But with trouble comes the opportunity for something new, yes?" Suddenly he struggled to his feet, fit his arms into the braces of his metal crutches with surprising ease, and vanished through an opening glass panel.

Yael and Maddox hurried after. In his haste to follow this unexpected move Maddox forgot his briefcase.

Fuchs led them down a corridor that opened into a central chamber filled with incubation vessels and computer-controlled processors. Technicians in white lab coats tended these synthetic systems. Doktor Fuchs moved past to enter an escalator that carried him to the main floor of the building. There he disappeared down a smaller hallway and through a heavy door that bore the international warning symbol for biological hazards. The door contained three sets of neoprene seals to create an airlock.

Inside, another similar but closed door led to a pristine observation chamber that contained two operating-room tables. A thick window permitted full view of this room. Incubators, vials, and Erlenmeyer flasks covered a table at the far wall.

Yael gasped.

Above the table, rows of aquariums held swimming sea snakes.

"*Laticauda laticauda,* the banded sea snake, and of course our friend, *Pelamis platuris,* the yellow-bellied sea snake. Only a few of the fifty species I've worked with. They are my tireless associates. I'm pleased you recognize them, Dr. Ben-Yaron. May I introduce you to another of my associates?"

From the shadows a man stepped into the light. Maddox had assumed he was a technician because of his white coat.

"Dr. Maddox, we meet again. Or should I call you John Rambo?" Khalid Al Bakaar chuckled as he removed his protective hood. "And your charming Zionist friend. What did you call yourself? Ben-Yaron? Ben-Yaron?" He stroked his chin. "That name is familiar. Yes, there was another Ben-Yaron, an Israeli agent we caught a year ago. In some ways he was like you, Dr. Maddox. Electricity failed to loosen his tongue. I personally cut his throat when he refused to answer my questions. But Ben-Yaron is a common name. . . ."

Yael leapt at his throat. "He was my husband, you murderer!"

Khalid fired a Taser from the folds of his robes. The tiny metal darts struck Yael in midair. Forty thousand volts coursed through the connecting wires to paralyze her voluntary muscles. Stunned, she collapsed on the floor.

"Goddamn you!" were the only words Maddox uttered before another set of darts hit him in the chest. His muscles exploded, and he crumpled next to her.

The leering faces of Fuchs and Khalid dimmed as he slipped into unconsciousness.

Giessen Army Base near Köln, Germany

Gifford and Jackson paced within the perimeter of *Aesop*, indifferent to the rain and darkness. These days the two men spent hours walking as they discussed their plans while Owen busied himself with the onboard computers.

"Admiral! Admiral!" Curtis Owen vaulted from his seat, waving his arms as he stuck his head out the airplane's hatch. "I've got a hit!"

The admiral and his Marine sprinted back to Owen.

"Trouble, sir! Look!" Owen pointed to a straight line running across a small cathode ray tube mounted above a bank of computer screens. Its green phosphors contrasted with the orange, amber, and blue CRTs. A steady-pitched beeping accompanied the straight line.

"Is that the briefcase?"

"No, sir. That's still working." Curtis's finger jabbed at the bottom of the screen where another series of well-behaved square waves followed the flat line above it. "It's the homing device we injected into Commander Maddox's arm. It's gone dead!"

"Was the briefcase activated?"

"No, sir."

"Hah! I win. I knew that pointy head couldn't keep the procedure straight. It's a good thing we tagged him." Jackson cuffed Owen in the back. "You owe me five bucks."

"Stow it," Henry Clay snapped. "What do you think happened, Owen? Equipment malfunction?"

"Don't think so, sir. That microcircuit is real rugged. Same chip as used on the astronauts. Looks like it got shorted out, like it got a big jolt of electricity."

"Is he still at Vibrogene?"

"He was when his transmitter got fried."

"Damn! Better scramble the backup."

"Aye, aye, sir!" Jackson picked up a headphone and punched in the code for GSG-9, the German Special Antiterrorist Assault Unit.

Ten minutes later Admiral Gifford slumped white-faced into a chair. His knotted fist threatened to crush the headphones. "Christ almighty! I can't believe this!"

Jackson and Owen waited, puzzled.

"GSG-9 won't respond."

"What?"

"They say our authority has been pulled." Gifford looked stunned. "I also talked with the base commander. He cited specific orders not to intervene. No one will help. We only have clearance to leave. Somebody's sandbagged us, and it's coming from Washington."

Jackson whistled between his teeth.

The familiar burning of his electrocuted muscles wrenched Maddox out of the darkness into a blazing whiteness. He forced his eyes to crawl to this source that threatened to sear through his brain. That act caused pain even behind his eyes. Slowly a chalky ceiling studded with fluorescent lights materialized out of the haze. He was staring at the ceiling of the laboratory. He tried to move. More pain accompanied his effort. Heavy straps held him on a surgical table. Beside him Yael struggled with her bonds on the second table.

"Welcome back, Dr. Maddox." Erhardt Fuchs studied his specimens and then held up the shredded remains of Christopher's briefcase. Severed wires dangled impotently through the slashed fabric. "This obvious device will be of no use to you." The case dropped from his hand.

"Come on, Fuchs. They know all about you. You're finished." Maddox swiveled his head to watch the German.

The German shifted on his braces to free a hand from its metal shackle. He ran it through his thready hair.

"Release us and I'll try to help you." The physician tried to press his bluff. "Our backup will be here any minute."

"It doesn't matter, Dr. Maddox. My work is done. I have already distributed one purified vial of my virus—I call it my venom virus; poetic, don't you think?—to Khalid's men, and I have two vials here. While I was waiting for your pitiful charade to unfold I ran a computer analysis. My probability model predicted that one inoculation of venom virus will destroy the human race within eight months. The three together will take two months. Life on earth for our species will cease."

"Why are you doing this?"

"Why? I suppose I owe you an answer, Dr. Maddox. After all, it was your brilliant work that enabled me to splice the gene that produces the venom of *Pelamis* into the influenza virus. What a brilliant choice! I congratulate you, Doctor!"

"It wasn't meant for this!" Maddox cried. "For Christ's sake, it was an experiment!"

"Yes, yours. I simply applied your genius. If it weren't for Heisel—you may not remember him—"

"Heisel, the janitor?"

"The same. Unfortunately, his copy of your notes omitted the final steps in purification, a grave omission for which he paid with his life."

"You're mad."

"Am I? Perhaps. But I promised you an explanation. Do

you recall that glass and iron piece in my office? The one you called weird?"

"Yes." Keep him talking, Christopher figured. Any minute Gifford will be here. Just keep him talking.

"Good. I'll tell you a story connected with it. In 1944 I was a biological chemist involved in the war effort. My deformities kept me out of the army. I was not political—I know you've heard those pronouncements before, but it's true. I simply did my job. I helped make Zyklon-B."

"You're a murderer!" Yael shouted accusingly. "You made gas for the gas chambers!"

"I didn't care for the Führer," Fuchs continued. "I worked for my country. And for my family, my darling wife, Marie, and my daughter, Anna-Lise. The Jews meant nothing to me. I cared nothing for Hitler's weltanschauung. A *Judenfrei* Europe was not my concern. But that changed. You see, I lived in Dresden. I was called away to Birkenau, some problems with the shipping containers of the Zyklon.

"When I returned home, my world was gone. My house was gone. Dresden had been firebombed. My Anna-Lise, only two years old, and my wife . . . incinerated.

That piece in my office is all that remains of my house. My family, my life is melted into that shrine you call weird." The blue eyes darted about for something to strike and settled on Yael. "If I hadn't been checking on the Jews, I could have saved them." He dabbed at his wild eyes, and his metal crutches clanged against the floor.

"Look, this is crazy. You'll kill everyone."

"Exactly, Dr. Maddox. Afterwards, I was like a wild animal. I didn't eat or sleep as the Third Reich burned about me. I prayed to die, too. Then slowly I understood what the Führer meant by *Weltmacht* or *Niedergang*. We failed at world power; therefore, we must suffer not just defeat. *Niedergang* meant total destruction. World destruction."

The hairs bristled on Christopher's neck. Fuchs was wearing a protective jumpsuit of Tyvek.

The twisted man withdrew two black-capped vials from his pocket. He held the bottles up to the light. "When I release these two viruses the circle will be complete. The Führer's work and mine will be done. The world will be destroyed."

"But there's no antidote, no antiserum. You'll all die!" Yael protested.

Khalid Al Bakaar stopped at the doorway to the chamber to regard them with suspicion. He fingered a pistol in the sash of his robe.

"The Jewess lies, my friend. Do not listen." Fuchs placated the terrorist.

Khalid returned to his packing.

Fuchs bent close to Yael. "You're right," he hissed. "There is no antidote. I needed help, so I made an antiserum for him and his followers. And for some others. It's worthless because the virus mutates so easily, but only true scientists like ourselves know that. And these fools won't believe you. You'd be surprised at the greed of some, especially those in high places. They dream of power beyond comprehension: the world at their feet, the capacity to choose who will live and who will die. All dreams!" His laugh reverberated inside the chamber to terminate in a wheezing cough. "Don't be shocked, Dr. Maddox. I said I knew you were coming. I knew your every move. Yes, and I was the 'Sparrow' you sought in the desert. I needed your help, so I set that trap. But Khalid's fools botched the job. You see, I planned to obtain the final purification process from you."

"How did you know?"

"Very simple. Schmittler, the American congressman from New Jersey. He has access to your Admiral Gifford's transmissions. He also dreams of ruling the United States. He has the 'antiserum,' so he believes he and his cronies are safe. But he will die with the rest. That's my revenge for the American bombing of Dresden. Now, Doctor, would you help me if I let your charming friend go free?"

"No! God forgive me for what I've already done." Maddox turned toward Yael. His heart was breaking. "I . . . I can't tell him. I'm sorry."

She smiled at him.

"I thought not. No matter. Both of you will help me."

"What do you mean?"

"My dear young lady. As you and Dr. Maddox know, the gene splicing process sometimes yields strands of recombinant DNA that are capable of producing the sea snake venom outside of human cells . . . in the culture media. This has the untoward effect of creating a mix of venom virus with the capability of infecting a person plus actual sea snake neurotoxin. Unfortunately, this mix kills whomever it contacts. The subject dies from the neurotoxin contaminant before he has a chance to develop the viral infection and spread it to others. Dr. Maddox knows how to separate those two components so a person can be infected only by the venom virus. That way the virus is spread to others who develop influenza and within forty-eight hours die from neurotoxin that their own bodies produce. Without his final purification process I've had to rely on human test subjects. Crude but effective."

"You're nuts!" Maddox snarled.

"You two will be my final purification process. I'll test the two last batches on you. If it's pure, you will live for perhaps forty-eight hours. But if the serum is contaminated with neurotoxin, you'll die instantly from seizures and cardiorespiratory collapse. Quite simple, don't you agree? Two vials left. Two human volunteers."

Maddox writhed against his straps, but the heavy leather held firm. Something rolled from his pocket and fell to the floor. It bounced on the concrete and shattered.

"But what's this?" Erhardt bent over and picked up a black cap fastened tightly to the broken neck of a small vial. A small puddle of liquid glistened at his feet. The German scientist turned the remnant over in his hand. It looked identical to the intact vials in his other hand. His gaze returned to Maddox.

"Guess."

"Not an antiserum, Dr. Maddox? I thought better of you."

"Fuck you, you crazy Nazi!"

"Yes, well, enough of this. Would you like to select which vial to test on you and which for her?"

Maddox twisted his hand in the straps enough to allow his middle finger to point at the scientist in that well-known gesture.

Erhardt Fuchs smirked. "Ladies first. I mustn't forget my manners." He selected one vial. He nodded to his assistant, and both men donned their protective hoods. The aide clamped Yael's head against the table as Fuchs deliberately dripped four drops from the bottle into her nose. She sputtered as the material ran down the back of her throat, yet all the while her eyes blazed pure hatred and defiance at them.

"I'll kill you! You bastard!" Maddox broke the strap holding his right leg.

The men released their grip on Yael and stood back to observe the results. Maddox continued his stream of obscenities.

She turned her head to Maddox. "I love you, Christopher."

He nodded, too choked by emotion to reply.

Two minutes passed.

"Excellent," Fuchs chortled. "That batch is not contaminated. No neurotoxin impurities. Now for the good doctor."

Avoiding his flailing right leg, the assistant pinned Christopher's head down as Fuchs administered a dose from the last container.

"Aaah! It burns!" Maddox roared as the deadly drops entered his nostrils. His head twisted in anguish. Then his breathing rate jumped as he gasped for air.

Yael cried aloud.

Suddenly Christopher's whole body shuddered in a grand mal seizure. His fingers hooked into talons, his back arched against the restraints, and his neck bent into hyperextension. Blood filled his mouth to outline his teeth and seep from his lips. A deep purple suffused his face, and his breathing ceased. Agonizing seconds later his body collapsed beneath his bonds.

"A pity. That sample contains neurotoxin."

Silence filled the chamber save for Yael's quiet sobbing.

CHAPTER

—— 11 ——

Frankfurt International Airport, Germany

"Don't worry so about me, darling." Sally wrapped her arms around Hadi's neck to press her body against him. She kissed him, enjoying the stares of the other people in the terminal. Others could gawk with envy; now it was her turn to be happy. "I'll be just fine. Oh, two weeks! I don't know if I can wait that long. Two long weeks before we'll be together again. Today has been the happiest day of my life. Sounds corny, doesn't it? But it's true."

Truly, love had transformed the substitute teacher from Chicago into a ravishing woman. Her clothes were now in the latest style, her makeup subtly applied, and her hair fashionably permed.

"Will you write?" She glanced mischievously at him as her hand slid over the front of his trousers.

"I'll call you," he said, laughing.

"Oh, I don't want to go," she said with a pout. "I can still change my ticket," she added hopefully.

Hashim shook his head. "We've already had this talk."

"You're right. Damned Super Savers. Cost an arm and a leg to change."

"Two weeks will pass quickly, my love. Do you have all your luggage?" He counted the pieces. "One is missing."

"It's behind you, silly."

"So it is. Forgive my nervousness. I don't want anything to happen to you. I worry about flying."

"Don't."

They walked together down the terminal to the security barricade after checking her luggage. Sally fed her purse into the X-ray machine, then skipped through the metal detector. A dour security guard frowned disapprovingly. These American tourists had no respect for authority, he told himself. He looked suspiciously at Hashim as he entered the metal detector. And obviously screwing that Arab!

The alarm screamed.

Hashim looked shaken as the guard sprang from his chair. "I've done nothing," he protested.

"Remove your watch," the security officer ordered. He accepted the heavy imitation Rolex. "Now go through again."

Hashim passed through without tripping the alarm.

Sally grasped his arm and led him to a seat by the embarkation door. TransOceanic Flight 805 was already boarding. "Frankfurt to Los Angeles." She pointed to the monitor.

Hadi became serious as he held her hand. He withdrew a handful of objects from his pocket. Solemnly he handed each item to her. "Life Savers, to keep your mouth fresh. Antacids. Lomotil, in case you get traveler's diarrhea. And this I bought today." He held up a plastic traveling pillow. "So you can sleep without hurting your neck."

"You're so good to me."

He held her at arm's length. "Now, this is most important. Promise me you will do it."

"I promise."

He held up a plastic bottle of nasal spray. "Promise me you'll use this on the plane. Airplanes have less than four percent moisture in the circulating air. That's very bad for your sinuses. You must use this spray on the plane. Promise."

"Yes, silly. After all, you're the pharmacist. I promise." She hugged him, burrowing her head against his tweed jacket. "Besides, I've already used it. . . ."

"What? Already?"

"Yes, just after you moved into my hotel room. I got stuffy, and I found this in the medicine cabinet. I saw it with your cologne, and since we're sharing everything, I used it."

Hadi Hashim appeared shaken. "Already." The word choked in his throat.

"Is something wrong?"

"No, no. You must board now."

"Okay, love you." Sally tried to kiss him, but he retreated into the crowd. Their momentum carried her through the departure exit.

As she looked back she saw him hurry away.

Vibrogene, GmbH

"God will curse you for what you've done!" Yael fought back her tears.

"God died when my family died," Fuchs replied flatly while removing his hood. He looked at the two vials of venom virus in his hand. Carefully he placed them in his pocket. "Now we must go. Hurry, Khalid. My dear, since you've been helpful, I'll offer you your choice. A painful death from internal venom production or a quick end from a bullet. Quickly, what is it to be?"

"I have no wish to live without Christopher."

"Very good. Khalid will do the honors. It's cleaner this way. You might provide some information to Gifford, some detail I've overlooked." Fuchs signaled to the Arab.

Al Bakaar withdrew his automatic pistol and placed it against her temple. His thumb flipped the safety off while his index finger took up the slack in the trigger.

A grating noise caught his attention. Both men stared at the outside wall, the source of the sound.

Instantaneously the wall bulged inward for a split second before it dissolved in a cloud of glass shards, flying bricks, and two blazing lights.

The heavy chrome bumper and headlights of a truck bearing the sign "Papa's Pizza" crashed through the surface. Its wheels overran the table, crushing the structure and scattering the glassware. The truck halted in midair with front wheels spinning furiously. The headlights stared wildly into the room. Out tumbled a dazed Curtis Owen, followed by Gifford, Jackson, and Asher. All four carried H&K MP-5 submachine guns.

Simultaneously the entire wall of aquariums shattered under the truck's bumper, spilling water and writhing sea snakes into the chamber.

Owen slipped on the debris and fell facedown while the other three directed a withering fire at the inner door just as Fuchs's henchmen appeared. Bullets drove them back. Advancing under fire, Gifford and Jackson crouched amid the rubble while firing short, well-aimed bursts. The poorly trained Owen emptied his clip in a wild fusillade.

Jackson killed the assistant beside Fuchs, and a burst from Asher caught Khalid in the chest. The would-be prophet's chest erupted in a fountain of blood as the 9mm slugs tore through him. He spun away, and his bullet missed Yael's head to lodge in the operating table. The shot deafened her.

Now Fuchs's men returned the fire. Owen grunted as he fought to regain his feet. The admiral and Jackson continued to advance, coolly firing at the pockets of resistance. Smoke spiraled around the headlights, but miraculously, no rounds hit them.

Erhardt Fuchs sprang back from his dying assistant. Taking advantage of the confusion, he sought refuge behind the second operating table.

Yael screamed as she saw Maddox rise from the dead.

The unstrapped right leg of Christopher Maddox rose to kick at Fuchs as the German darted past. The well-aimed blow drove the madman headlong into an entangled mound of sea snakes.

Screaming, Fuchs clawed upright with a dozen serpents embedded in his face and neck. His flailing fingers raked at the reptiles. The man lurched forward, smashing a bottle of ether and pulling over an exam light. The globe ignited the vapors.

Erhardt Fuchs died from the venom before he crumpled into a blazing heap. The circle of *Niedergang*—the unfinished completion of the Third Reich, all the madness of a single man—ended in that corner as Fuchs burned like a nightmarish Medusa amid the writhing snakes.

Yael's mind toppled along the edge of insanity as she stared in horror at the fiery corpse. Bullets snapped past, but she was beyond noticing. The girl froze with wide eyes locked on that flaming specter. She never noticed Asher cut the straps, nor that Christopher gathered her in his arms to carry her to the safety of the truck.

"Let's go. Blow this place!" Gifford shouted to Jackson over the increasing return fire from outside the lab. "Use the satchel charges."

The Marine jerked his thumb up. Crouching, he set the detonators. He grasped Owen by his collar. "Let's go! Show time!"

Swiftly Jackson moved down the hallway, laying down fire with his MP-5 while tossing satchel charges into connecting laboratories. Owen followed, still trying to master his automatic weapon. They rounded a corner. Owen bumped into a man wearing a tweed coat.

"Wait! Don't shoot!" The man held both hands up. "Don't shoot!"

"Watch him," Jackson warned as he flung another explosive charge down the hall.

Curtis turned to follow the arc of the canvas bag. With lightning speed the captive drew a pistol and fired. Owen grunted with the impact of the bullet. Jackson whirled in the close quarters, dropping his submachine gun to grasp the terrorist's gun hand. The two struggled, hands and eyes locked, for endless seconds. The pistol waved above their heads.

Panic grew in Hadi Hashim's face as the strength of the Marine gradually overcame him. He peered into Jackson's hardened eyes and saw only death. The American grew stronger as they battled. Hysterically, Hashim played his last card. "Stop! Don't kill me! I'm a member of the Front for Liberation! I'm a political prisoner! I demand to be treated according to the Geneva Convention!"

"Fuck 'em." Jackson's lips curled in a feral snarl.

"Wait! I have important information about Flight 805!"

"That don't mean Jack shit to me, Ace." Jackson's left hand broke free and, in one fluid movement, drew a knife from his boot.

Hadi watched helplessly as the enraged Marine buried the KaBar up to its hilt above his Adam's apple. The terrorist lost all feeling below his neck, blood filled his mouth, and he died still gazing at the Marine. Jackson let the corpse drop. He crouched at his friend's side.

"Jeeesus Christ, little buddy." Jackson struggled to staunch the flow of blood from Owen's side. "I shoulda never let you come. Air force guys don't know how to fight."

"Yeah . . ." Curtis mumbled. His face turned ashen with his continued blood loss.

Jackson slapped his face. "Don't go out on me! Keep breathing! I'm not writing any fucking letters to your family!" he cursed. But the computer specialist was already unconscious.

Swearing, Jackson set the fuses on the last three satchel

charges and hurled them down the corridor. Then he slung Owen over his shoulder and raced back up the hall.

Asher helped load the wounded man into the truck. Jackson whirled his hand over his head to signal Gifford. The admiral jammed the gears into reverse and smashed the gas pedal to the floor. The heavy truck roared like an angry bear as it backed out of its hole. For an instant its sides caught on the building, then wrenched free, scattering bricks and powdered glass into the night air. The truck leapt backward over the manicured lawn, cutting deep gouges in the grass. Gifford spun the vehicle, and the truck careened into the darkness.

Behind, flashes of light pulsed from the ruptured wall of the Vibrogene building. Explosions rocked the evening. Windows shattered. Tongues of flame spurted from the portals, rapidly consuming the building.

CHAPTER

12

TransOceanic Airlines Flight 805

Sally awoke with a start. She swiped her hair away from her face. Several strands stuck to the corner of her mouth. The beige interior of the airliner's cabin materialized. She sneezed. Damn, she thought, I'm catching a cold. Combing through her handbag for a Kleenex, she felt miserable and lonely. She missed Hadi, and now her nose was runny. Her watch said four o'clock, but the faintest tinges of dawn colored gaps in the clouds. What time was it in L.A.? Sally sighed and refitted her head into her plastic travel pillow. Traces of his cologne sent twinges through her.

She sneezed again, then rifled through the bag until she found her nasal spray.

"I wouldn't recommend using that. . . ."

"What?" Sally squinted to focus on the face next to her. She wished she'd left her contacts in.

"They only last for a short time, and then you get a whopping rebound. Systemic decongestants work better, especially the long-acting kind." The voice belonged to kindly eyes with bifocals and a face straight out of a vintage Norman Rockwell painting.

"Well, my fiancé is a pharmacist, and he gave this to me," Sally retorted testily. Great. She was in no mood for a nosy neighbor.

"Oh, well. Perhaps I'm wrong."

"Are you a doctor?" She dabbed at her flowing nose.

"Retired. Ob-gyn. So I may not be up to date on nasal sprays. My specialty is—was—the other end."

"Is . . . was?"

He smiled. "Yeah, I just closed down my practice—after thirty years. It's hard to change. Say, I'm sorry if I butted in. Like I say, I'm having a hard time thinking of myself as retired."

Sally warmed to his openness. "I'm Sally Ericson from Chicago."

"Ames Cotter, San Diego." He shook her hand. "Looks like you've caught a nasty cold. If it gets worse, I've got some decongestants in my medical bag."

"You're retired, yet you still carry your medical bag?"

"Yeah, I feel naked without it." Cotter shrugged. "I know it's silly. . . ." His voice trailed off.

"Why did you retire? You don't seem like you were ready for it."

Dr. Cotter's face flushed. "Damned cost of malpractice insurance drove me out. I was paying over a hundred thousand a year. I couldn't stand it. That and . . ."

"What?"

"Oh, I got hit with a lawsuit last year. That finished me off. I got called by the E.R. to deliver this baby."

"E.R.?"

"Emergency room. Say, maybe you don't want to hear about this. Funny, I keep spouting to anyone who'll listen. Sort of psychotherapy, I guess."

"Go on. After all, we've got about ten more hours to kill."

"Well, I get this call in the middle of the night. Woman in labor. No prenatal care. Nothing. And to top it off, she's a known drug user."

"Oh, my."

"You guessed it. She was a crack user, and the baby was born with severe mental retardation. I got stuck with a contaminated needle and had to sweat it out until her HIV came back."

"HIV?"

"AIDS test."

Sally edged away.

"Don't worry. It was negative. But I was a nervous wreck, I'll tell you. And no sooner did the mother leave the hospital than she hit me with a malpractice suit."

"Oh, no."

"I won the case, but it finished me. Her lawyer ripped me apart on the stand. Made me feel like dirt. It was awful. So here I am: John Q. Retired. But it hurts to leave thirty years of work with a bad taste in your mouth."

Sally erupted into a series of sneezes. "I'm sorry," she snuffled behind a protective wad of tissues. "I hope you don't catch this."

"Probably will," Cotter warned philosophically. "The air is recirculated in these planes. We're all exposed."

Taongi Atoll, Marshall Islands

"The *itang* is the only hope of our people." Tangaroa pressed his message even though the two had been sailing all night. His time was short, and he would use every minute. "It is the talk of wisdom, the words of light, the winds that sail our culture through dangerous shoals that surround us. Without its knowledge our people will not know their safe course. They will be wrecked."

"But why must new ideas be dangerous to us?" Mau asked.

Tangaroa grunted, satisfied that the boy was listening and

not asleep. These recent days had been more than he had hoped. The boy's mind sought his teaching like a thirsty sponge.

"We use plastic Coke bottles to mark our fish traps. They float better than coconuts." Mau pressed his argument. "And tin cans work well for catching octopus."

"I'm not smart enough to answer you, Mau. I didn't go to the white man's school, and I can just write my name, but I navigate by ancient traditions. Thousands of years of knowledge can't be ignored without danger."

Mau yawned.

The old man ruffled the boy's hair. "As for your plastic bottles, I don't think the sea likes them. It never takes them in. Always it spits them onto the shore. Even the land doesn't know what to do with them. They're growing all over the place. They never die or go underground." He wagged his finger at the boy. "Your bottles will push us off our islands."

The moon broke through the scattered clouds to cast a pallid wash across the flat water. The wind had died hours ago, and this added light touched a glassy surface.

"The wind has gone home to the wind houses." The old navigator pointed to the cumulus clouds bordering the horizon. "It sleeps until the morning, then the wind will come back from its house." The old man knew dawn would bring freshening winds from the direction of the clouds. He prodded the dozing boy.

"I sit on Satawal. . . ." Mau mumbled a *wofanu*.

"Let's do the *paafu*, the numbering of the stars, one more time," Tangaroa coaxed. "Then you can sleep until the winds return.

The child nodded.

On a mat on the floor of the canoe he set an image of the canoe. He surrounded the boat with eight coconut fronds to represent the eight wave patterns that the *palu* could use to steer his craft. Then he arranged thirty-two stones about this circle, naming each stone as he placed it. North on this compass rose he placed Polaris, the North star. South, the Southern Cross. East and west were marked by Altair, rising in the east and setting in the west. Northeast and southwest were marked by the passage of Vega, and the arcing passage of Antares set the location for southeast to northwest. Finally he filled in the gaps of the rose with Cassiopeia, the Pleiades, and the Dippers.

"Good." The navigator praised him. "Remember the stars fight just like people. As they swim up to the top of the water they fight for air. They fight with everything, and that makes storms if the fight is hard. Everything fights," Tangaroa's jaw clenched as his old enemy, that recurrent chest pain, rattled inside his body.

Yes, the *palu* thought, strife is ever present. You, evil spirit inside my body, worm inside the tree trunk, you fight for my heart. Soon you can have it, but not yet, not just yet. You can't have it until I've finished with my work.

Weariness draped over his shoulders like a rain cloak. To strengthen himself he closed his eyes, and his mind returned to his dream. For the last two days it had been the same: a silver bird held in the mouth of a yellow and blue sea snake.

Giessen Army Base near Köln, Germany

"Abort takeoff, *Aesop*. I repeat: Abort takeoff! You do not have flight clearance. Shut down and taxi to runway zero-four-niner." The voice of the flight controller filled the darkened cockpit of the 707, adding to the combustible feelings of its occupants. Fluorescent images from the instrument panel painted the tense faces of the flight crew. The pilot glanced over his shoulder at Admiral Gifford.

"Power up, son." The level voice of his commander

reassured the pilot, a naval aviator especially picked by Gifford along with the rest of the crew.

"Aye, aye, sir."

Gifford thumbed the mike. "Clear the decks, boy. We're leaving."

"But you haven't filed a flight plan!" the flight controller protested.

"Need to know, boy," the admiral drawled in his best southern accent. "You don't need, so you don't know."

Edging the throttle handles forward, the flight crew drove the plane into the darkened sky over the objections of the ground controller. Gifford withdrew a map from his pocket and pointed to a location. The pilot and navigator exchanged glances. The grim set of the admiral's jaw did not allow for questioning. So the navigator punched the coordinates into his flight computer and fed the data to the autopilot. Gifford left the flight deck.

Back in the bowels of the plane Henry Clay confronted a grim landscape. The research quarter resembled a battle zone, or more precisely a field hospital.

Christopher Maddox bent over a pallid Curtis Owen while Jackson directed a flashlight at the source of continuing hemorrhage. Yael lay propped against the bulkhead sipping a mug of hot tea that Asher Lod helped her hold in trembling hands. Gifford moved closer.

Christopher's hand darted into the mass of clotted blood. "Got it!" The bloodied hand danced back, leaving a hemostat protruding from the mess. The gouts of blood stopped. "Subscapular artery," the physician added with finality. "He's lucky. The bullet grazed his ribs and tracked up into his armpit. But it missed the major nerves and his axillary artery. Otherwise he'd be dead." Deftly the doctor slipped a ligature around the clamp and secured the tie. Then he placed a clean dressing over the wound.

Gifford's shadow fell over the scene.

Maddox looked up. "Owen needs to get to a hospital. He needs a blood transfusion."

"No can do, Doctor. If what you told me during our truck ride back is true, we're all contaminated now. All but you. How did you do that?"

"Later. We've got to do something about Owen!"

"I know that, but landing is out. Can't you fix something up?"

"We need a blood bank. I don't even know his blood type!"

"A-positive, same as mine," Jackson interrupted. "Give him some of mine, Doc."

"I can't do that. The blood needs to be cross-matched. He might die from incompatible blood."

"Look," the Marine persisted, "he's going to die if he doesn't get blood—so what's the difference? We all know this air bus isn't the fucking National Institutes of Health. So give it your best shot. We got to try."

Gifford raised his eyebrows at Maddox's plea for backing. "The sergeant has an eloquent way with words, and I find no flaw in his logic. Besides, all this may be academic if we're infected by the virus."

Maddox nodded. He threaded a plastic cannula into a vein in Owen's arm and punctured a bulging vessel in the muscled forearm of the Marine with a similar needle. He connected these IV sites with a length of tubing. At the junction of the IV tubing and Jackson's indwelling catheter he interposed a three-way stopcock and a 50cc syringe.

"Well, here goes nothing. You'd better get comfortable, Jackson. It wouldn't be seemly for a jarhead to pass out."

"Never happen, Doc. Pump away."

Maddox withdrew a syringe full of blood from Jackson, twisted the stopcock, and pumped it into the prostrate computer specialist. Syringe after syringe, the life-sustaining plasma flowed across the yard of narrow tubing

Miraculously, life returned to Owen with each pump. The life-giving fluid carried oxygen to his tissues and removed impurities to the organs designed for their elimination.

Owen stirred. Maddox pumped harder, and soon the little man's blood pressure was back up to normal. He grinned crookedly at them.

"You're Marine, buddy!" Jackson punched him gently on his good shoulder. "Now you got my special antibodies to cheap whiskey and penicillin-resistant clap."

"Semper Fi," Curtis whispered.

Gifford glanced at his watch. "Okay, I figure Giessen is burning up the phone lines to Washington. In about one hour Washington will query us. Then all hell will break loose. Let's use this time for debriefing. Owen, are you up to this?"

"Yes, sir."

"How about you, Dr. Ivanov?"

Yael nodded. Maddox tucked the corner of her blanket under her chin.

Forty-five minutes later Henry Clay rechecked his notes. "Go over that again, Maddox. I still don't see how you got all the symptoms of sea snake neurotoxin, yet still survived."

"But I didn't, you see. The batch that Fuchs tested on me was pure. Fortunately it didn't have any neurotoxin contamination—just pure virus, same as Yael's."

"But your seizures," Yael protested. "I saw you have seizures . . . and the blood. I thought you were dead."

"I faked it. In the plane crash that killed my wife . . ." Maddox paused. Emotions rippled over his face. He could talk about it. Now it seemed in the distant past, like a bad dream. "I suffered a head injury. Ever since then, if I hyperventilate, I develop grand mal seizures. I've got an irritable focus on the cortex of my brain. All I've got to do is start breathing fast, blow off my carbon dioxide, and it happens."

"Like when you were frightened on the Vigilante!" Asher shouted.

"Right."

"But the bleeding—just like the anticlotting effects of sea snake venom." Yael trembled. Her fate was still undecided.

"I bit the inside of my cheek. Hurt like hell, but it bled enough to be convincing. I figured Fuchs wouldn't look too closely in my mouth."

"Jesus, Doc." Jackson whistled. "That's pretty smart."

"But why aren't you infected with the venom-producing virus now like she is?" Gifford persisted.

"I dosed myself with an antiserum I made from Asher back in Hawaii. We know his flu blocked the venom virus. To be on the safe side, I added some complement. I injected that mix before we went to Vibrogene and swabbed it in my nose and throat. It was a long shot, but it must have worked. I'm going to run a few tests on myself to be sure."

"Well, why don't you give some of that antiserum to all of us?"

"I can't, Admiral. The bottle broke in the Vibrogene lab. I can't make more from Asher because he's over his cold now." He looked at Yael. "I wish I could. God, if only I had more."

They all turned to see Owen chuckling as he struggled to sit upright. The little computer programmer pointed to the bank of screens above his head.

"Look. Dr. Maddox's tracer is working again. I told you they're well built."

"My tracer?" Chris squinted at the series of sine waves on the monitor.

Gifford nodded. "A homing device. Injected in your arm so we could track you."

"You bastard! You told me it was yellow fever shots. No wonder my arm hurt like—"

"Quit your griping," Gifford interrupted. "It saved your life. Besides, we could've injected it in your fanny."

Abruptly Maddox laughed.

"What's so funny?"

"Being rescued by a pizza truck just struck me as being totally absurd."

"That's right. Jackson, where did you get our wall buster, anyway?"

"Midnight requisition, Admiral. In the best tradition of the Corps, I borrowed it from the army. I guess the base has frequent pizza deliveries. You told me to find a vehicle, sir. When this truck drove through the gate I said to myself, now this looks like a vehicle. So I requisitioned it. Turned out to be built on a surplus deuce and a half—just what the admiral ordered."

"You didn't kill anybody to get it, did you?"

"No, sir. But there's two MPs and a German pizza deliveryman tied up in the bushes back in Giessen. Bet they'll have more respect for Force Recon now."

Gifford nodded.

"Goddamn, sir. I forgot something."

"What?"

"The raghead back at Vibrogene, the one who snaked Owen, said something about a flight. Was it 809? No, 805. That's what it was—Flight 805. He said he had important information about Flight 805."

"What else did he say?" Gifford was instantly alert.

Jackson looked embarrassed. "Ah, those were his last words. . . ."

"Admiral." Maddox spoke first. "Fuchs mentioned three vials, one of which he'd already given to one of Khalid's men. Do you think it's on Flight 805 with a terrorist?"

Gifford chewed his lip. "We need to check it out. Owen, do you feel up to talking to your computer?"

"If Jackson can help me to the console, I can do it, Admiral."

Twelve minutes later Curtis handed his printout to Gifford. "TransOceanic Airlines has a Flight 805. Frankfurt to Los Angeles. It left two hours before we took off. But a cross-check of names and passports doesn't help. No Arabic names. Mostly American passports with a few German, Swiss, and Dutch."

"Keep working on it, Curtis." Hardly had Henry Clay

finished his sentence when the plane's navigator announced an incoming message, flash priority—from the president. "Pipe it through," Gifford grunted. He glanced at his watch. Right on time.

"Henry?"

"Here, Mr. President."

"Henry, what the hell is going on? First you scare the shit out of the National Security Council with this wild story of poison flu germs, and now I get pulled out of a meeting with the Polish trade delegation because you're blowing up half of Germany. You'd better have a good explanation. The German ambassador's about to have a stroke."

"Vibrogene was the center of the venom virus production, Mr. President," Gifford responded evenly. His measured tones belied his true feelings. "Erhardt Fuchs, an ex-Nazi, was the mastermind—"

"Oh, God!" The president cut him off. "Not this virus stuff again! And no Nazis! No one wants to hear about Nazis. They're a dead horse, do you understand? The Wall is down, Gifford. Germany is reunited. Even the Russians are buying it now. So please don't dig up any crazy Nazis."

"The prez sounds pissed," Jackson whispered to Owen.

"Please, Mr. President . . ."

"No. No. No. I don't want to hear anything about this! Where are you now, Henry?" The president adopted a conciliatory tone, the kind he liked to use when he was feeling magnanimous.

Gifford slowly drew in his breath. He knew what was coming next. "Airborne, sir. We've plotted a course for Diego Garcia, in the Indian Ocean."

"Henry, you've been working very hard recently. And we're all grateful for your dedication. But . . . well . . . I think you need a rest. You know, take some time off, play a little golf, do some sailing. You've done a fine job."

"Please, sir! It's not finished."

It hurt Jackson to see his skipper on the verge of begging.

He wanted to scream: Listen to the admiral, you lump of political shit! But he held his peace.

The president wasn't listening. "Henry, you fly to Garcia and wait for further orders."

"Am I relieved of duty, sir?"

"Damnit, Henry, don't put words in my mouth. Let's say you're on R&R. Look, I've got to run. The delegation is waiting. I'm glad we had this talk. Oh, you know it's an election year, and I'm busier than usual. So Jim Schmittler will be taking over your . . . ah . . . direction. He's got the seniority on the committee. You'll report directly to him."

"Representative Schmittler." Gifford marveled at the irony. Truly, the demons that dogged human effort, snagging their every footstep, had a marvelous sense of humor.

"Schmittler?" Yael and Maddox looked at each other. Her eyes widened.

But the president was gone. Another voice emanated from the overhead speaker. This one was thready, more irritating in pitch and wheedling in nature. "Admiral Gifford, I'm in charge now."

Maddox recognized the nasal accent that he had encountered from pretentious middlemen. The vaunted phrases dripped from the amplifier.

"Sir, we'll continue on to Diego Garcia as agreed upon by the president, but we'll need to refuel. May we have permission for a midair refueling?"

"Of course, Gifford." Schmittler's gloating saturated the room. "Bye." The microphone sputtered into silence.

Maddox noted a slight smile flicker across the old man's face.

"But this Schmittler's one of them!" Yael protested to Gifford.

"What do you mean?"

"She's right, Admiral," said Maddox, remembering now. "Fuchs said this guy Schmittler was working with him."

"Are you sure?"

Yael's head bobbed. "Fuchs fooled him into thinking he had the antidote. He was feeding all your information to Fuchs."

"God in Heaven!" Gifford sprang to his feet. "That means he'll want us to fail! I've got to tell the president."

"Admiral!" Distress filled Owen's outburst. "They just cut off our computer links!"

"Damn! What do we have left?"

Curtis Owen's fingers played over the keyboard, coaxing a reluctant reply. Quickly he ticked off their remaining resources. "The onboard computers are functioning, and they have the data banks I downloaded before they cut us loose, but we've no links to NASA, Langley, or Los Alamos. No Crays. No secured phone links, either. They've changed our access codes. We're blind."

"Can you break the access codes?"

Owen shook his head.

"Okay, do the best you can. One for them, one for us."

"One for us?" Maddox asked.

"Yeah, Schmittler's no good at playing poker. The in-air refueling he agreed to gives us enough fuel to reach Hawaii."

"We're not giving up, then?" Asher questioned.

"No way in hell. From what you all told me, I have to assume there's a terrorist on TOA Flight 805 with the last vial of virus. As I see it, there are two threats to the world from this venom-producing virus. Flight 805 and us." He looked directly at Yael. She nodded.

"So?" Maddox bristled. "What does that mean?"

"With refueling we can catch them before they land in Honolulu."

"And then what?" Maddox didn't really want to know.

"Pray you and Dr. Ivanov—and Owen with his crippled computer—come up with a solution by then."

"But what if we don't?" Christopher protested. He watched the others look away.

"Operation Blazo," Jackson answered.

"What the hell is Blazo?"

"Our contingency plan, if all else fails."

Maddox fought against comprehension. He refused to believe.

Jackson shrugged. "Simple, Doc. We kamikaze them."

CHAPTER
—— 13 ——

TransOceanic Airlines Flight 805

Ames Cotter clutched the armrests of his seat as the Boeing 747 jostled about in the clear-air turbulence. He pressed his face against the window, clinging to the mistaken belief that he could spot any trouble. Not that I could do anything about it, he reminded himself. He wasn't in charge. He didn't even know how to fly. Like most doctors, he had the need to be in control, and situations like flying were doubly stressful for this reason. He looked carefully and saw nothing.

Outside the azure sky filled his window, while far below tiny waves flickered like crystal corrugations across the Indian Ocean. It was a beautiful day—too bad he wasn't enjoying it. He lamented his fear of flying. It wasn't rational, and he hated it. Chewing on his lip, he turned for the hundredth time to the inane crossword puzzle at the back of the flight magazine. He hated crossword puzzles as much as flying. A yawn slipped out. He wished he'd bought a handful of magazines back in Frankfurt. But he was trying to be frugal. Part of being retired, he told himself.

A spray of saliva rained across his face.

"Oh, God. I'm sorry," Sally Ericson sputtered between paroxysms of sneezing and coughing. She offered him a tissue.

"No, thank you." Cotter wiped his face with his handkerchief. "Christ," he fumed. "Cover your mouth when you cough."

Sally started to cry. "I'm really sorry. That caught me by surprise. I'm so ashamed. Now you'll catch this."

"Really, it's all right." A change of seating flashed through his mind. Only the smoking section had empties. Was the risk of cancer better than this? he asked himself. This girl had it bad. Well, she insisted on using her nose spray . . . so to hell with her. He'd done his part for humanity. He glanced at her.

It was then he noticed the muscle tic in her right cheek. I'm slipping, he thought. I don't remember her having that before. . . .

Aesop, *Indian Ocean*

Christopher Maddox pressed his fingertips against the quartz viewing port of the isolation chamber. Inside the sealed chamber that Jackson grimly referred to as the oven Yael's fingers sought his. Two inches separated them. She smiled bravely, her lips moving to blow a soft kiss to him.

"God, Yael, this isn't necessary." His voice cracked.

"Yes it is, my love." Her warmth passed even through the intercom. "We have a responsibility beyond ourselves. We're scientists, and we should act like scientists. We both know that the virus seems to be contagious during the initiation of upper respiratory symptoms. That may be the

only time it's infective. I don't have any symptoms . . . yet."
She paused to shudder. Then her composure returned. "It
makes good sense to isolate me before any signs develop."

"Yes." He didn't care about anything but her. His work
had put her there. His folly, or was it his vanity? He'd had to
do what others couldn't, or wouldn't, and look what his
success had caused—the impending death of the woman he
loved—again. It was too much to bear.

Now this translucent barrier held him once more. Flash-
backs of his wife trapped behind the airplane's Plexiglas
seared his perception. That remembrance awakened old
wounds like raw nerve endings touched by a flaming match.
He was losing control. The portal flickered back and forth in
his mind. The stroboscopic effect grew.

Horrified, Maddox watched his mind blend his nightmares. Yael burst into flames. His dead wife seized from the
venom. Faster and faster the separate occurrences played
out before him, merging and mixing until they became a
single event. He reeled beneath these mental blows.

"Don't give up." A soothing voice anointed his wounds,
applying a salve to his suffering. The madness receded.

Maddox opened his clenched eyes to gaze into the violet
aura of the woman he loved. She was still smiling. "I . . . I
won't, Yael. I'll find a way. There's got to be a way."

"I know you will."

TransOceanic Airlines Flight 805

One hour later, three hundred nautical miles ahead of
Aesop, Sally Ericson's nose started to bleed.

Aesop, *Indian Ocean*

Curtis Owen's vision blurred as a cold sweat rolled over him. His hands trembled, fingers missing the keys, yet his will held him in his seat while he dug for clues in the remaining data banks of the onboard computers. Driving him was a vision of his daughter. He desperately wanted her to see another birthday. His head swayed.

"Doc!" The Marine caught Owen as he slid from the console.

Beside him, Maddox broke his concentration and tore his gaze from his screen. Since Yael's imprisonment in the isolation chamber Maddox had been like a madman, refusing sleep, eating little, and never pausing for more than moments at a time in his relentless effort to save the girl. "Lay him down," he commanded as he returned to his CRT. "He's still a little short on blood volume. Keep him warm. Give him warm fluids."

Admiral Gifford looked up from the map he was studying. Good, he thought. I guessed right on Maddox. He couldn't give a rat's ass about the world, but he loves that girl. She's the key. He'll tear this place apart trying to save her. And the viewing port is crucial, a nice touch. Something to do with the death of his wife. He congratulated himself for reading the psychological reports on Dr. Maddox.

Listen to yourself, another part of him said. What kind of person are you to dangle their love like a stinking piece of fish bait? Wouldn't your wife be proud of you? Thank God she's not alive to see this.

Yes, he admitted. Thank God she isn't here to see what I've become. And she'd never approve. But he'd still do it this way, he admitted. The stakes were too high, and he only had this single card to play. What a lousy hand he'd been dealt! Maddox, the joker. By God, he'd turn this joker into a king. Yes, he'd do it the same way.

Gifford turned back to the two parallel lines drawn on the map, one marking the course of TOA Flight 805, the other the path of *Aesop*. *Aesop* was catching up.

TransOceanic Airlines Flight 805

Sally Ericson rose unsteadily to her feet. She swayed backward, waking the sleeping Dr. Cotter. He stared at the blood-dappled handkerchief pressed to her face.

"Sorry," she mumbled in confusion. "I don't feel well. . . ." The words frayed away into nothingness as she staggered toward the aft lavatories.

A scream brought Cotter to his feet. Halfway down the aisle of the 747 a middle-aged woman was shrieking and pointing at a figure crumpled in the narrow corridor. Cotter recognized the tan sweater of his neighbor.

Sprinting aft, Cotter was at her side before the startled stewardess. Sally Ericson jerked about the floor in full-blown seizures. Bloody froth spewed from her mouth while the whites of her upturned eyes stared unseeingly. Her seizing limbs thrashed against the seating.

The standing woman screamed as she tried to claw through the bulkhead, unaware that outside lay nothing but thirty-five thousand feet of empty air.

"Shut up!" Cotter commanded. Just then the seizures stopped, along with Sally's breathing. Her face darkened to a violaceous hue. "Christ!" the physician cursed. He dropped to his knees, wiped the froth from the victim's mouth, and began mouth-to-mouth resuscitation.

Behind him the flight attendant stood clutching a blanket.

Cotter gave four sharp breaths, satisfying himself that her chest moved with each puff. He felt for a pulse. A thready beat met his search. Good, no cardiac arrest.

"Get my bag! Black bag! Overhead, row fourteen!" he sputtered between breaths. His arm waved at the attendant. She comprehended and raced away to return with his worn medical kit. Cotter gave another series of artificial respirations while he dug in the kit.

Crouching awkwardly in the aisle, he inserted the narrow blade of the laryngoscope into her throat. Blood, mucus, and food particles obscured the passage, but he succeeded in blindly passing the endotrachial tube into her windpipe on the first try. He taped the plastic tube to her face and connected it to an Ambu bag. A quick squeeze of the black balloon moved Sally's chest. He pumped a syringeful of air into the tiny inflatable cuff at the end of the endotrachial tube to seal any air leaking around the cannula. Cotter looked up.

The stewardess had vanished. "Nurse"—he grabbed the screaming lady—"squeeze the Ambu twenty times a minute. Start the count!"

"I'm not a nurse!" protested the woman.

"By the power invested in me, I make you a temporary nurse!" Cotter applied his benediction. The woman nodded solemnly and began to ventilate the unconscious girl.

Cotter rocked back on his heels to assess the situation. Sally remained unconscious. Intermittent seizures racked her body, but the cuffed tube ventilated her and kept her from choking on her bloody saliva. Her pulse was thin and irregular. Rummaging in his bag, he found what he needed and started an IV infusion of saline. What the devil was this, he pondered while he gave an encouraging smile to his new nurse. Really, she was doing a fine job. He wished for a suction apparatus. Sally's lungs kept filling up with bloody froth, and it became hard to ventilate her. So periodically he'd turn her on her side to let the bloody bubbles drain out the tube before resuming respiration.

The flight attendant returned with the copilot. The officer knelt behind Cotter.

"You the captain?" the physician asked after rechecking his patient's vital signs.

"First officer. John Simmons. Greg Whitley is the captain of this flight. How is she, Doc?"

"Not good, Mr. Simmons. Major seizure and some kind of bleeding disorder. She's critical. We've got to get her to a hospital fast."

"That's impossible. We're over water." Simmons ran his fingers through his hair. "Perfect timing," he lamented. "We're right in the middle of nowhere. Right now we're 1600 miles north and east of Manila. Guam's about 560 nautical miles astern. The closest island with a strip long enough for this baby is Wake Island, but that's another 800 miles ahead. Wake's restricted—a naval base without any medical facilities."

"Well, turn back to Manila. Look, I don't know how long she'll last."

"Easy, Doc. Normally we could, but we're riding a jet stream—150-knot tail wind. If we turned back to Manila, we'd be bucking that. It'd take us as long as it would to fly on to Honolulu."

Cotter thought for a moment. "Can you radio her symptoms to a hospital? That might help. For Christ's sake, I'm a gynecologist. All I can say for sure is that she's definitely not in labor. Maybe there's an internist on board."

"Come forward with me. Let's talk to the captain. Will she be okay for a couple moments?"

Cotter shrugged. "I hope so. My nurse is taking good care of her." He patted the woman on her shoulder, eliciting a smile. "When you get tired, show the flight attendant how to ventilate her. I'll be right back."

Startled passengers watched Dr. Cotter follow the copilot up the spiral stairway, through the upper lounge, and onto the flight deck. Several noted the spatters of blood on his jacket and sports shirt.

The head flight attendant paged vainly for other physicians on board. She got no response except for three nurses who immediately began a rotation with the Ambu bag. A makeshift suction was constructed from an ear syringe. Cotter's substitute reluctantly returned to her seat.

Captain Greg Whitley listened to Cotter while he kept a continuous scan out the cockpit windows. A retired navy pilot, he loved flying, even these big 747s. True, the Boeing was sluggish and ponderous compared to military planes, but Whitley appreciated their rugged engineering. Besides, this flying was better than no flying. He realized the commercial need for ex–Intruder pilots was nonexistent.

He'd jumped at the offer to join TransOceanic on their cross-Pacific route. Momentarily his gaze was diverted to the panels of gauges and switches that carpeted the walls and ceiling and flowed about his seat. He tapped at a bank of dials.

"Better check the fuel gauges," he called over his shoulder to the flight engineer. "They're showing a thousand pounds less than I'd expect."

The engineer bent to this task.

"Okay, Dr. Cotter." Whitley turned at last to face the physician, but not until Simmons returned to his seat and picked up the vigil. "Is this lady dying?"

"She will die unless she gets the proper treatment. Captain, I haven't got a clue as to what the problem is!" Cotter waved his arms, unaware that the captain was staring at him. His right hand held Sally Ericson's purse.

"Is that yours?"

"What? No! For God's sake, it's the patient's. The stewardess got it for me. Nothing in it in the way of medication except birth control pills and some generic nasal spray— without a label."

"How do you know it's nose drops? Could be drugs."

"She told me before she had these seizures. Besides, she was using them for nasal congestion."

"All right. Look, we're over the mid-Pacific. No place for

an emergency landing. With this tail wind our best bet is to plow on to Honolulu. They've got the best medical facilities there anyway."

"How long will that take?"

"Three hours and forty-five minutes. I'll radio ahead and request priority clearance. That should shave twenty minutes off our time."

"Could you ask to talk to some medical specialists? This is way out of my field." Cotter felt like adding that he was retired. "Maybe this is some sort of tropical disease."

"From Frankfurt?" the copilot remarked.

Twenty minutes later Cotter tallied the results of his conversations with personnel at Queen's Hospital in Honolulu. All agreed with his supportive treatment in view of the limited facilities available. One physician reminded him that he was probably protected from lawsuit under the State of Hawaii's Good Samaritan laws. Just what I wanted to hear, Cotter mused. The consensus held to cerebral hemorrhage, possibly rupture of a congenital cerebral aneurysm. No other treatment was suggested. He'd have to wait until they landed. Cotter rose to leave, dejected because he knew this girl wouldn't last that long.

"Ahoy, Flight 805." The radio crackled into life. "Flight 805, this is Majuro Station. Come in, 805." The heavy Australian accent was evident, even electronically.

"We read you, Majuro. Go ahead."

"Been monitoring your transmissions, mate. The name's Thomas—from Australia. I'm doing oceanic research here in the Marshall Islands. Crown of thorns work. You know those bugger starfish are chewing up our barrier reef."

"Go on."

"Well, I'm no doctor, you understand. But this sounds like a sea snake bite. . . ."

"Sea snake?" Whitley looked at Cotter.

"Yeah, mate. It's a neurotoxin. Buggers up the central nervous system something fierce. It also contains a hemolytic factor that causes bleeding like you described."

"Sea snakes in Germany? There sure isn't one on my aircraft." Whitley retorted.

"Just the same, mate, you might try atropine to reduce the secretions—that is, if you've got it. Keeps the lungs clear."

Captain Whitley turned in time to see the back of Ames Cotter as the physician sprinted back to his patient.

CHAPTER

—— 14 ——

Aesop, *Mid-Pacific*

"Ah, shit! Another stone wall!" Christopher Maddox raised his coffee mug in front of his CRT screen, desperately wanting to smash the heavy ceramic cup into the fractious screen. Beside him Curtis Owen grimaced at the chance of injury to an extension of his body. The mug darted inches from the terminal before Maddox thumped it down. Coffee slopped over his hands. He glanced into the viewing port. Yael was sleeping.

"Same here, Doc." Curtis Owen had regained strength with his last rest; now he crawled back to his post. "We've cross-checked every reference to virus in the data banks. This makes the eighth time. Do you see any lead we've overlooked?"

"No. There's no way to produce an effective vaccine against this influenza virus. Its DNA daisy-chains itself into new antigenic profiles too easily. We need a fresh approach. Let's look at the problem from sea snakes."

The computer responded in seconds.

"What does that mean?" The coffee cup menaced the computer. "I'd like to . . ."

"Easy, there's no data bank on sea snakes. We were cut off before I downloaded that." Owen pushed back from his console. "That's all we've got." Weariness tormented him. He rubbed his balding head. Suddenly he felt old, helpless. His wife and daughter occupied his thoughts. He'd never see them again. He'd never see Annie have her birthday. "I'm glad I ordered Annie that phone," Owen lamented to his computer.

"The phone!" Maddox and Owen responded simultaneously. "The phone!" They danced about, laughing, crying, and slapping each other on the back.

"That's it, Skipper. They've snapped," Jackson scoffed, looking up from cleaning his Colt .45 automatic. Like all good Marines, he cleaned his weapons when faced with nothing else to do.

"What do you mean, phone?" Gifford peered over his half-glasses at the saucer-eyed pair.

"Owen's two-million-dollar modem! The one he built from computer parts. We can access commercial databases with that, using the phone lines. Now we can get more information."

Owen's head bobbed enthusiastically.

"By God, you're right. Get on it!"

Within an hour the two men had logged onto Compu-Serve, the giant computer network that linked thousands of personal computer subscribers and afforded access rights to giant databases such as Dialog. All references to sea snakes were searched. Reams of paper printouts littered the deck.

"This is good stuff." Owen breast-stroked over the paper sea to feed another box of computer paper into the printer. "But I wish we'd used a phone number other than mine to charge all this to." Mentally he calculated that his phone and CompuServe charges had reached the six-figure mark. What the hell, he decided. He enjoyed being a big spender. Life in the fast lane had its risks.

"Damn, all this material on polyvalent sea snake venom isn't relevant." Maddox set aside his stack. "What's to keep the body from producing more venom? You'd have to continuously infuse antiserum."

Yael tapped on the window. "Unless you could give a large dose of antibodies before the virus got a foothold."

Maddox shook his head. "Timing is too critical."

"What about a gene for the snake venom antibody? From repetitive exposures," Yael persisted. "Maybe someone who survived more than one sea snake bite?"

"You mean Superman? Honey, I don't know of anyone who's survived multiple bites. Especially *Pelamis*. Its bite is uniformly fatal."

"How about divers? Skin divers?" She wrinkled her nose at him as if to say: gotcha.

He wanted to rejoice because she loved him and cry because he couldn't help her. The conflicting feelings churned inside, but she wouldn't let him halt. Her optimism smothered his dark side. "Come on, scuba divers?"

"Try it!"

Maddox laughed, but he punched GO SCUBA into the computer. Directly the screen welcomed him to the Scuba Divers Forum on CompuServe.

"Has anyone been bitten by a sea snake, specifically *Pelamis?*" he asked out loud as he typed his inquiry.

Seconds later eight replies covered his screen. They ranged from serious to irreverent—none were helpful. Christopher felt the cold hand of despair clutching again. He squeezed his eyes tightly to hold back the tears.

He typed: In God's name, this is serious. Can't anyone help?

The screen stared blankly.

The same prayer he had whispered a thousand times since Germany spilled silently from his lips. He pleaded for strength, for knowledge to save this person who brought light into his life.

His monitor flashed. Emerald characters marched across the CRT. Owen and Maddox watched, spellbound by the characters. Even Jackson stopped his relentless cleaning to stand beside Admiral Gifford as the four regarded the message:

From Rev. Samuel Castle, Methodist Schools, Taongi Atoll, Marshall Islands: You should not take the Lord's name in vain. If you are serious, there is a man on this island who has survived sea snake bites.

Maddox held his breath as he responded.

From Aesop: We're deadly serious, Reverend. Are you sure?

From Castle: Yes, I have not seen it, but all the islanders swear to it. His name is Tangaroa.

From Aesop: More than one bite?

From Castle: Many. Over many years.

From Aesop: Is he in good health?

From Castle: As far as I know, although he is elderly. He is the palu for this island and is held in high esteem by the islanders. But he refuses to come to church.

From Aesop: Palu?

From Castle: The palu is the navigator of the outrigger canoes.

From Aesop: Where is Taongi, Reverend?

From Castle: Northernmost atoll in Marshall Islands. North and west of Bikini Atoll. North of Majuro by about 600 miles.

"I got it." Gifford punched his finger into the map he'd draped over Jackson's shoulder. "Four hundred nautical miles southwest of Wake Island. Sweet Jesus! We're within range!"

"Don't let the good reverend hear you, Skipper," the Marine cautioned. His response drew curious stares from Gifford.

From Aesop: Does Taongi have an airstrip? One where jets can land?

From Castle: No airstrip. Only contact is by boat.

The four men stared at the last line. Its disinterested characters proclaimed a death sentence for them and the world as certain as loss of the sun.

"If only we had access to Wake." Gifford turned away, not

wanting to see the look on Maddox's face. "And a helicopter . . ."

But they didn't. He was locked out of his own government, the one he'd served for almost thirty years. Easy, don't give in to those feelings, he counseled himself. Keep your head straight. Keep thinking. Find a way.

"Admiral!" The copilot of *Aesop* appeared in the crawlway. He waved a transcript urgently at Gifford. "I've picked up transmissions from TOA 805. They're requesting emergency medical clearance for landing."

Gifford pored over the printout. His face clouded. "We were wrong. Flight 805 doesn't have a terrorist on board. It's got the terror itself."

Owen read the critical phrases. "Woman passenger. Bloody seizures. Does that mean the whole plane is infected, Admiral?"

"I think so, son. Two hundred and seventy passengers. Looks like it's on board. I would have thought it was a little premature to board an infected carrier, but who knows? We were dealing with a demented mind in Fuchs."

"Maybe they had a slipup like before, Admiral Gifford." Asher had returned from the cockpit with the copilot.

"Possible. How far are they from Honolulu?"

"Three hours."

"We can't let them land. Can we contact Washington, maybe Honolulu? We've got to notify them. Got to try again to make them listen."

The copilot ran his hand over the wall of communications devices. The transmitter lights, LEDs, and gauges stared blindly back. All were turned off. This darkened bank of electronic equipment stood out from the nearby flashing devices like a string of dead Christmas tree lights. "Negative. We only have short-range communications—line of sight. Long range is through AWACS. They locked us out of that."

"Can we overtake them?"

The copilot was prepared for that question. "Since our refueling, we've steadily gained on them. With full burners we'll be in position in thirty minutes."

"Blazo." Jackson sucked in a mouthful of stale air.

"Wait! Goddamnit, wait!" Maddox was on his feet. "We don't have to do it this way! We can save them . . . and us! This *palu* guy may have the key!"

"I know that, Doctor. But we have no way of landing on Taongi in this jet. To try would mean our ending in a fireball on that coral atoll. And the infected TOA flight would reach Honolulu. You know what that'd mean. We'd die for nothing."

"Oh! A meaningful death, is that what you want?"

Jackson stepped in front of his skipper, shielding him from Maddox. "Easy, Doc."

"No, Dr. Maddox. I want a meaningful life, but it may not happen." Gifford turned to the copilot. "Commence Blazo."

Taongi Atoll, Marshall Islands

"There is a freshwater pool on the island Puluwat where dolphins come to bathe. In the dark of the night they slip out of their skins and become women." Tangaroa watched the moonlight reflected in the widened eyes of his pupil.

"Really?"

"It's the truth." The old man bobbed his head. "I've seen it. In the morning they put their skins back on and return to the sea."

"Reverend Castle says such things aren't possible."

"Screw Castle," Tangaroa belched. He spread his arms wide and turned his face to the sky. "And screw his automobile. It cuts tracks all over my island. See! No lightning strikes me dead. And I'll say it again. Screw Castle!"

"He doesn't do that."

"It might be good for him," the *palu* continued.

Mau nodded in agreement. Reverend Castle's celibacy didn't seem natural.

"Look! Over there! See that?" Tangaroa pointed off the bow. A barely perceptible mass floated on the water. Only its roughened texture, highlighted by the moonbeams, separated it from the enormous expanse of the Pacific.

The boy and the man directed their vessel to the tangled mat of vegetation. Tangaroa scrambled across the outrigger platform to scrutinize the debris. His eyes lighted.

"Sagur! Sagur!" The *palu* thrust his hand into the pile and withdrew a length of bamboo. "Sagur, the demigod, lives in bamboo. We must *Atirro* him." He placed the bamboo beside him on the platform and bowed solemnly to the stick. "To ignore Sagur would be very bad. When a navigator is lost at sea, Sagur will tell his future."

Tangaroa began an ancient chant to the fragment of bamboo. He lifted the wood high in his hand and dived into the dark water.

Startled, Mau rushed to the side of the canoe. Only bubbles rose to the surface. Then the bamboo shot to the surface to bob at a tangent to the hull of the boat.

Moments later the *palu*'s head broke water. "Good! Good! Sagur was pleased with my song. See, he acts like a skid for rolling the canoe ashore. We will see land today."

"Tangaroa!" the boy screamed in terror as the old man pulled himself onto the outrigger platform.

Tangaroa followed Mau's quivering finger. It pointed to his right side.

A wriggling yellow and blue ribbon hung from his hip.

Eyeing him maliciously, the sea snake clamped its jaws tighter as its cheek muscles pumped deadly venom through hypodermic-needlelike fangs. The jaws chewed repeatedly, and the cheeks twitched again.

"Ah, my little friend." Tangaroa unhooked the snake from his flesh. "Did I disturb you? Were you waiting in the seaweed for an unwary fish?" He turned the rounded head from side to side.

The snake's unblinking eyes followed him. You're a dead man, they seemed to say.

"You'll die!" Mau wailed. Every islander knew of this horrible death.

"No," the navigator replied fiercely. He tapped his snake tattoo. "I won't die from the bite of my brother. He and his brothers have bitten me often since that first bite when I was younger. Your first bite almost did kill me." He waved the reptile in the air.

Its eyes never left him.

"But while I fought your poison I had my dream. The old gods came to tell me I would save the world." Tangaroa laughed. "Thank you for that, little brother." He dropped the serpent into the water. It disappeared as a gust of wind swept across the sea.

TransOceanic Airlines Flight 805

"Quick, get the adrenaline ready!" Ames Cotter raised his head from the chest of Sally Ericson. The background noise of the jet engines made his stethoscope useless, so he placed his ear to her chest to monitor her heart rate. The atropine held her lungs to a manageable state of dryness, but it also pushed her heart rate beyond safe limits. Internal bleeding from the anticoagulant effects of the venom continued to drain her blood volume. Cotter was forced to add pressor agents that clamped down on the size of his patient's blood vessels. Less circulating volume and a frantically beating heart spelled trouble. Any second her heart might fibrillate.

A flight attendant whispered in his ear. He looked up. A respectful column of onlookers manned the seats surrounding his makeshift clinic. The curious and the fearful watched.

"I've got to go forward. Keep an eye on her," Cotter said to his real nurse, thankful that she had turned out to be an intensive care nurse. She knew more about this stuff than he did.

"How's she doing, Doctor?" Whitley asked. Besides the sick passenger, the fuel gauges were acting up. The flight engineer had pulled the panel and checked the fuses, but the entire bank was acting strangely, fluctuating between readings that ran over a thousand pounds high and then low. They'd isolated the problem to a flaky rheostat. But exact measurement of the remaining fuel was impossible. No problem, Whitley reassured himself. They had plenty of fuel to reach Hawaii. Only circling in a lengthy holding pattern could be a problem. Fortunately, the medical emergency assured them immediate landing rights.

"Not well, Captain. She's barely holding on."

"Three more hours. Think she'll make it?"

"Don't know."

The flight engineer tapped his radar screen. "Captain, bogey on our six, closing fast." Like Whitley he was an ex-Navy man and used the military jargon for the six o'clock position—the tail location—that represented the cone of vulnerability of an aircraft. Successful attacks came from six o'clock.

"What the hell? This is our lane." Whitley studied his scope. "Another commercial?" Some international lines, notably the Koreans, flew all over the place.

"Negative. Electronic signature looks military."

Whitley relaxed. "Fun and games. Probably some jet jockey out of Hickam playing games." They loved to play cat and mouse on the way back to base, dropping out of the sun on hapless airliners. But all broke off outside the reserved space surrounding their prey. "Is he going to overfly us?"

"Negative. He's at the same altitude we are. Coming on fast. He's four miles within our airspace now."

"Get him on the radio. His ass is grass. I'll have him standing tall before his C.O. for breaking international regs."

"No good, sir. I've tried to raise him, but he doesn't answer."

"What? Come right five degrees." Whitley ordered his copilot.

"Right five degrees."

"He's changed right five degrees, sir. Right on our tail."

"Shit! What's wrong with him?"

"Left ten degrees."

"Left ten degrees."

"Still with us!" The copilot's voice cracked. "One mile! He's going to hit us!"

Aesop, *Mid-Pacific*

"Aesop! Aesop! Do you read? This is a flash priority!" The speakers lining the walls of the science bay barked into life.

Gifford hit the communicator button. "This is *Aesop.*" His voice was calm. No hint of the tension that filled the plane to the point of combustion leaked into his response.

"Henry? Is that you, Henry?"

"I'm here, Mr. President."

"Thank God, Henry!" The chief executive's voice bordered on hysteria. "You've got to help me, Henry!"

"Sir?"

"Something terrible's happened. Schmittler's dead! He got a transmission about some airliner with a sick passenger. He said it was loaded with this crazy virus—the one you warned me about! I should have listened to you, Henry!"

"Go on, sir. What happened to Schmittler?"

"Yes. Yes. I've got to get control of myself. Schmittler told his aides that this plane carried this deadly plague . . . and that only he . . . only he had the antidote. He was laughing. My God, Henry, the Capitol is in a panic!" The president was gulping air. "But he took the antidote, and . . . my God, you should have seen his face! It was ghastly. He died of these terrible seizures—right here in the White House!"

"Score one for Fuchs." Jackson grunted. "He fucked the rep."

"Sloppy chemistry," Maddox added. "Contaminated with the venom."

"I'm putting you back in charge. Immediately, Henry! Do you hear? Everything! Anything you need! Please fix it, Henry!"

"Aye, aye, sir!"

Jackson and Owen broke into huge smiles. The cheering lasted only a moment before the terrible realization dawned on them.

"Blazo!"

"Abort! Abort!" Jackson sprinted forward, hurdling the door partitions and screaming at the top of his voice. Twisting past the last metal barrier, the Marine dived headfirst into the cockpit.

The forty-five-foot-high tail section of the TransOceanic Boeing 747SP filled the windows of *Aesop,* gleaming in the tropical sun in stunning colors of orange and silver. To Jackson the huge rudder beckoned, a door to hell. Rivets, bolts, metal plates, and paint markings zoomed larger.

TransOceanic Airlines Flight 805

Captain Whitley pulled hard on his yoke in a desperate attempt to avoid collision. Seat belts held the flight crew, but the physician still stood behind them. Ames Cotter soared over the back of Simmons, driving his head into the overhead instruments and shoving the four throttles into the idle position. The ponderous 747 decelerated sharply.

Aesop, *Mid-Pacific*

Jackson bellowed, "Cancel Blazo!"

The flight crew's heads snapped as one to the Marine. Instantaneously the pilot jerked hard on the yoke, pushing *Aesop* into a steep banking climb to the left. G-forces skidded the sergeant backward, slamming him into a bulkhead.

Playing before their eyes like a slow-motion movie, *Aesop* struggled against the momentum that swept it to death. The 747's tail planes tilted in a frenzied sweep, a sail capsizing in an invisible sea. Ponderously, reluctantly, *Aesop* clawed toward safety.

The orange and silver sail side-slipped. Cheering erupted inside the cockpit as the 747's tail dropped away.

Terribly, at the moment of salvation, fate smirked. The 747's massive Pratt and Whitney engines dropped into idle. The giant tail appeared to jump backward into *Aesop*. Turbulence from the uneven jet stream caught the undersurface of *Aesop,* striking the leading edge of the port wing and thrusting it back. *Aesop* shuddered and yawed to port. The opposite wingtip swung around. The wingtip satellite antenna, jutting forward of the wing's edge like a scythe, sliced through the tail section of the Boeing 747.

Silver shards fluttered past the stricken aircraft as the reinforced tip of *Aesop*'s wing sheared away the 747's tail before snapping off itself.

"Shit!" the pilot swore as metal fragments rained over his windows. "We hit them!"

The wounded *Aesop* lurched away under the struggling control of the flight crew. Jackson caught a glimpse of the afflicted Boeing's tail section as it passed. Ragged edges exposed a massive open wound that reminded him of a severed limb. The image of a giant shark bite flared in the Marine's mind. Like blood staining the water from such a shark bite, additional sections broke off to float past. Severed hydraulic lines and electric cables, the vessels and nerves of this metallic giant, trailed from the laceration.

TransOceanic Airlines Flight 805

A cloud of silver and charcoal powder, dust and metal particles from beneath the instrument panels and every corner of the cockpit, exploded into Whitley's face. Concurrently, the rudder pedals jumped forward under his feet, smashing his knees into his chest. Headsets flew backward off the heads of the flight crew. The cabin door blew open, and clipboards, hats, and papers spiraled into the first class compartment with the tornado of dust.

Stunned, Dr. Cotter felt himself lift off the floor, weightless as the plane slowed, then nosed down into a dive. Blood poured into his face from the laceration of his scalp.

"Shit! That motherfucker rammed us!" Captain Whitley forgot airlines protocol in his fury. What madness was this? They'd been struck aft of the midsection. The yoke grew sluggish in his hands as the plane nosed downward toward the blue expanse of the Pacific. The floor pedals remained jammed.

Instantly the pilot recognized that his ship was heading into a nose-down dive from which no recovery would be possible. Whitley shoved the throttles into full power. Four Pratt and Whitney JT9D-7 jet engines surged, each producing 50,000 pounds of thrust. The 747 leapt forward and pitched its nose upward into level flight.

"Losing hydraulic pressure!" the flight engineer noted. "Big leak!" Red warning lights covered his control board. The engineer worked feverishly to staunch this hemorrhage.

"Switch to backup pumps!" Whitley barked.

Already the in-line safety sensors on the four separate hydraulic lines to the tail had blown their fuses, and shutoff valves worked to stop the leak of vital hydraulic fluid.

The bleeding stopped. The yoke relaxed. Hydraulic pressure returned. Whitley silently blessed the Boeing engineers for building backup pressure lines and safety cutoff valves into the tail control system. The Boeing 747 had four separate hydraulic systems, and a single intact system could control the ship. All lines ran along the undersurface of the passenger floor and could be destroyed by a collapse of that structure in the event of massive depressurization. But Boeing engineers had widely separated the out-and-return tubes, two on the port side and two on the starboard side, to protect them. Additionally, the control cables to the rudder, stabilizers, and elevators course along the inner surface of the plane's ceiling to the tail. Again, Whitley blessed the thoughtfulness of the designers.

The plane leveled off at 20,000 feet.

"Get aft and give me a visual, Simmons." The copilot scampered away at Whitley's order, stepping over the bleeding doctor. The captain checked his controls. Gingerly he tested the yoke. Gently he banked first to the right, then left. The wingtips dipped obediently. "Okay. Wing surfaces appear intact. So far so good. Ailerons a little touchy. Need light touch," Whitley remarked to the engineer. "Now yaw..." His white-faced companion nodded. Whitley worked the foot pedals to the tail rudder. Nothing happened. Try as he might, all his force failed to move the pedals.

"No yaw," the flight engineer observed. He matched his warning lights. "Tail rudder is out."

"Pitch." Whitley tried the elevators, the flaps on the trailing edge of the horizontal portion of the tail that controlled the nose-up-nose-down attitude of the airplane. Nothing.

"Shit."

"Okay, okay. Stabilizers." The captain pulled the manual lever to operate those flaps on the front of the horizontal tail that trim the ship into correct flying position. The suitcase-shaped handle flopped impotently. "No stabilizers."

Simmons returned. Quickly he listed his findings. "Hull's intact. Pressure okay. No smoke. No fire. A couple of the interior hatches were jarred loose, but that's all I can find. Personal effects all over the aisles." He shrugged. "Looks good."

"Passengers?"

"Scared as hell, but the attendants have everything under control. Everybody's got on a life jacket. Thank God we had the fasten seatbelt sign on. That sick girl is still down."

"Okay." Whitley listened with one ear as he completed his diagnosis. "Looks like our tail rudder is out. Stabilizers and elevators, too."

"Jesus Christ!" Simmons blurted out. "Remember that JAL flight? August, 1985. It lost its rudder, too. Flew around until it crashed into a mountain!"

"They lost their hydraulics when an aft hatch blew out," the flight engineer added.

"Yeah," Whitley agreed. "The hydraulics got crimped

where they went through a hole in the aft pressure bulkhead. But Boeing changed that. And we've got our hydraulics."

"But it looks like we don't have our tail!"

"Easy." Whitley's mind was racing over his options. "We do like McCormick did."

"McCormick?"

"Yeah, Bryce McCormick. American Airlines, 1972. McCormick was flying a DC-10 when one of the cargo doors blew out. Lost his rudder."

"Yeah! I remember!" The navigator's face brightened. "He landed safely using his engines to control the plane."

"But the DC-10 is easier to control because all three engines are mounted on the tail!" Simmons reminded them.

"We can do it," Whitley resolved. "I've spent a lot of hours in the flight simulator practicing throttle flying just in case I ever lost my hydraulics. I could fly the simulator from climb-out around to approach with just the throttles. By varying the engine thrust you can do it."

"Procedure for a midair collision calls for a controlled emergency descent," the flight engineer recited half-heartedly as he worried over the red lights that now dominated his panels.

"In the Pacific?" Simmons looked out at the blue expanse beneath them.

"Right. Let's do it." Whitley checked his headings. "Get a fix on the nearest airfield."

"We're off course. Honolulu's twelve hundred nautical miles ahead, but we're twenty-five degrees south of our flight plan. Wake Island is 428 nautical miles south of us. Wake's got a naval airfield long enough to handle us."

"Wake it is. Do you agree?"

"Yeah," the engineer said. "I don't know how long the aft pressure bulkheads will hold together. The sooner we set down, the better."

"All right." Whitley licked his lips, reached gingerly forward, and gently pulled back on the throttle handles for the two starboard engines. "Cutting back one and two."

All three men watched the power gauges register a decrease in thrust from those engines. The 747 side-slipped to starboard momentarily before righting itself.

"What happened, Greg? We're back on heading."

"I don't know. She started to move, then she slipped back."

"Try again!" Simmons coaxed.

Whitley nudged the throttles again. Again the plane shifted, only to return to its previous course.

"How about using the ailerons? Bank more."

"Can't, John. If I bank more than fifteen degrees, we'll go into a spin. I remember that from the simulator."

The navigator rechecked his screens. "We need ninety degrees to starboard to make Wake Island."

"Can't do it. We'll have to try for Honolulu." The pilot reduced thrust—this time to the port engines. "Cutting back on three and four."

Once more TOA Flight 805 moved reluctantly north a few degrees, only to revert to its old path. Something seemed to be nudging it back into line.

"It won't go. Something's pushing us along this course."

"It's no good, Captain. We're twenty-five degrees off course for Hawaii. We won't intercept the island. What's wrong?"

Greg Whitley thought for a moment as he experimented with engine power. The terrible revelation dawned on him. He looked out at the unseen force that controlled his plane. A feeling of desolation grew inside him.

"The jet stream."

"What?"

"We're caught in the jet stream. Without a rudder we can't steer out of the stream. That's what's pushing us back into line."

"Oh, my God."

"It's pushing us straight out into two thousand miles of empty ocean. . . ."

CHAPTER
—— 15 ——

Taongi Atoll, Marshall Islands

"I'm sorry I doubted you." Mau tagged behind the old man like a puppy. "You're the greatest. You can be my father. I . . . I'll work hard to be a *palu*. You'll see."

Tangaroa paused to lean against the stern of his canoe. Was it the pain in his chest that stopped him from beaching his craft, or was it anguish? He must tell the boy now. His feet ground deeper into the sand.

The boy babbled on.

"Stop," the *palu* commanded.

Mau fell silent.

"You cannot be my son. I can't . . ." Tangaroa started.

The words struck Mau like lightning. His face drained. "You can't adopt me?" he asked incredulously. Then a thought as twisted as his foot filled his mind. He looked down at his deformity. The boy's world shattered. "It's because I'm crippled, isn't it?" he cried.

"No," Tangaroa protested, but the weight on his chest strangled his words.

"Yes, it is!"

The navigator struggled for air.

"I hate you. I hate you." Mau ran crying in the direction of the church school.

Tangaroa dropped to his knees. His head came to rest against his canoe.

Aesop, *Mid-Pacific*

Bereft of the outer third of its starboard wing, the Boeing E6-A shuddered into a looping dive toward the ocean. Admiral Gifford felt the impact and guessed the next reaction of the wounded aircraft. Jamming himself beneath the computer consoles, he grabbed the wounded Owen and Maddox and pinned them into their chairs before the plane's plunge lifted them weightlessly into the air. Clipboards, pens, and coffee cups filled the air of the dropping plane, but Gifford held tighter.

In the cockpit the flight crew fought for control. The pilot blinked away tears as he adjusted trim and shifted fuel in the wing tanks to balance *Aesop*. The craft completed a giant loop before wobbling into level flight like a wing-shot albatross.

Owen dug his face out of his keyboard to witness the rebirth of arrays of lights erupting over the screens, CRTs, and panels of all the computers.

"Admiral, they're back!" Warmth and excitement in his voice left little doubt that the computer analyst viewed the return of his cherished computers with the same enthusiasm a preacher would have for the Second Coming. "We're back on line!" The little man retrieved his glasses from the back of his neck. His fingers danced over the keys.

"Sweet Jesus!" Gifford exclaimed, voicing his thanks as much for the stabilized craft as for the computers.

"We clipped 'em, Skipper!" Jackson's head popped through the hatch a split second later.

"Get me a damage report!"

"Sliced off their tail aft of the fuselage, but they're in level flight. We're missing the starboard wing outboard of the number one engine. Pilot says we're controllable." The Marine flatly ticked off the account. Years of training left no room for emotion.

Gifford digested the report as his mind raced ahead. New possibilities flashed across his thoughts. He released his hold on Maddox. "Doctor, do you think this guy on . . . what's the name of that island?"

"Taongi," Maddox and Owen responded as one. Asher crawled to their side. A dark bruise ballooned over his nose where he'd hit the ceiling.

"Right. Taongi Atoll. What's the chance of you being able to produce an antiserum from that fellow?"

"I'm sure of it, Admiral."

"Would it block the venom?"

"It should work like a smallpox vaccination. Once the body's immune system gets clued in to the protein arrangement of the sea snake venom, its T-cells and helper cells should be able to release antibodies as needed. I just need to get enough serum from this islander to make the antiserum. He's the key, Admiral. If he's survived multiple sea snake bites, he's a walking warehouse of antibodies to their venom. And if the antiserum is administered before symptoms develop . . ."

"Can you make enough for every passenger on that 747?" Gifford skewered Maddox with a piercing gaze.

Maddox averted his eyes only to see Yael watching him across the quartz glass barrier. He stuttered.

"Christopher," her voice warned him. "One man couldn't donate enough serum for several hundred people and survive. It would take all of his blood volume."

"Look, Admiral"—he chose to ignore her—"I . . . I can

get enough to protect all on board this plane." Shut up, he was screaming inside. Let me save you.

"But not enough for those on the 747."

"No." Maddox fought an involuntary tic dancing at the corner of his lip.

"Well, that's not good enough, is it, Doctor?"

"So what? A minute ago you were happy to blast them out of the sky. What's changed?"

"A minute ago I didn't have any alternative." Gifford's voice carried a cold, tempered edge. Jackson, his faithful Marine, recognized the tone and the deadly menace it projected. Like a honed weapon, it meant his boss was poised to strike. "Contrary to your opinion of me, Doctor, I don't enjoy killing. I like to think of myself as a surgeon, incising tumors as needed to save the whole patient."

"Great! You're lecturing me about medicine?"

"Whatever." Gifford let his anger ebb. He couldn't afford that luxury at this time. "If we could isolate this Trans-Oceanic flight, say on Wake Island, is it possible you could manufacture more antiserum from this islander's samples? Enough for all the exposed passengers?"

"It'd have to be within the forty-eight-hour limit . . . before their own cells produced enough venom to kill them," Maddox replied slowly. A light dawned. Here was his chance to save Yael. "I'd have to inoculate all of us first."

Gifford's eyebrows arched. "Blackmail, Doctor?"

"No, sir. It's just that we've been infected first. At least a good day before all of those passengers except the carrier. We're likely to drop in our tracks before a new batch of antiserum is finished." Maddox strained to sound upbeat. Inside he calculated the odds of his producing enough antiserum for over three hundred people within two days. It couldn't be done. He'd try with all his heart, but he knew he'd fail. Those people were doomed. Yet here was a chance to save Yael. A part of him sensed she was about to protest, to reveal the futility of all this. Silently his hand slipped behind him to switch off the intercom to the isolation chamber.

"It's a long shot, but worth a try." Gifford nodded. "Jackson, get me Wake on the horn. Tell them we'll be landing. I want a helicopter fueled and waiting on the pad. One with a range of six hundred nautical miles to take the good doctor to Taongi."

"Aye, aye, Skipper."

"Owen!"

"Yessir?"

"Get CINCPAC on a scrambled line. Flash them my presidential authorization in case they weren't notified. Tell them I want Wake Island isolated. No one in or out without my authority. Then get TOA Flight 805. I want to talk to them."

Curtis Owen fired off the coded message to the commander-in-chief of the navy's Pacific fleet and received an instantaneous confirmation. "CINCPAC's on top of this, sir." Then he contacted the crippled 747.

"TOA 805. This is *Aesop*. Do you read me?"

"Roger, *Aesop*. What the hell were you doing? You rammed our tail. Over."

"Flight 805, this is Admiral Gifford, director of counterterrorist activities."

"What's going on, Admiral?"

"Flight 805, you have a woman passenger on board who is infected with a deadly virus. Your whole plane is in-fected—"

"You mean the woman with the seizures?"

"Right. We have reason to believe she's part of an Arab terrorist plot to spread this virus."

"Jesus Christ!" Greg Whitley forgot FAA protocol. Events were proceeding too fast for him.

"Flight 805. Everyone, repeat, everyone on board is now infected. You cannot land in Honolulu. Change course to Wake Island. You will be isolated and treated there. Do you read me?"

"Jesus Christ," Whitley mumbled. The gravity of his situation shocked him back into reality with the stringency of an icy shower. "Negative on Wake."

"Flight 805. You must land on Wake. If you attempt to land at Honolulu, you will be shot down."

"No need to call in the Tomcats, Admiral. We can't land on Wake *or* on Honolulu." The irony seeped over the electronic links. "My controls are damaged. With this tailwind, I can only keep the plane level and headed on a course of 94.5 degrees magnetic. Admiral, we're headed for a blue hole in the Pacific. And there's nothing I can do to stop us!" Whitley's voice broke into shards of frustration and anger.

"What's your name, son?"

"Greg Whitley, sir. Used to be in the navy before I took this job."

"How much fuel do you have, Greg?"

"Enough for four more hours, Admiral. But the gauges are acting a bit funny, so it may be half an hour more or less. Not enough to reach any land in this direction."

Gifford's mind churned about, seeking solutions to a problem he had helped create. "What did you fly in the Canoe Club, Greg?"

"A-6s, sir. Intruders."

"Good planes. You probably saw your share of carriers."

"Yes, sir. I sure hated those night ops, though."

"They're no fun, Greg. I don't know anyone who likes night landings on a carrier."

Curtis Owen tapped Gifford's shoulder and pointed to twin radar screens behind the admiral. Now that Washington had reestablished their codes, the screens were picking up data from a distant AWACS. Just over the earth's horizon the high-flying advanced warning and command system fed extended radar information to *Aesop*, far-reaching patterns beyond the curvature of the earth that blocked conventional radar. The dual screens painted geometric symbols in vivid emerald hues above the center of the sweeping arm. Numbers accompanied the diamond shapes. Gifford rechecked the radar locations with NAV-SAT figures from the overhead navigation satellites.

"Hold on, Greg. You're heading in the direction of Carrier Air Wing 15."

"I don't see anything on my radar."

"They're over the horizon. About six hundred nautical miles."

"Who's with CVW-15, Admiral?"

"CVN 70."

"The *Carl Vinson!* That's my old ship! She's a nice one, sir." Whitley wished he was back on his old carrier. The *Vinson* had always been a refuge in this world of water.

"Seventy's got lots of support, Greg. HS-4s on board." Gifford recalled that the helicopter antisubmarine squadron attached to the carrier also functioned as rescue and recovery during flight ops. "And I'll get PatWingPac to send Patrol Wing 2 from Barber's Point. Their P-3 Orions should be on station from Oahu in two hours. How many do you have on board?"

"Almost a full house, Admiral. Two hundred and seventy-two, counting the crew. Are we thinking about ditching, sir?"

"Looks like the only option, son."

Gifford knew that Whitley was doing mental arithmetic, as he was. Both realized the figures would come up short. The SH-3 Sea Kings were designed for antisubmarine warfare, plane guard, and SAR. Unlike their half-brothers, the Coast Guard HH-3F Pelicans, especially built for rescue, the Sea Kings couldn't land in the water or carry the load of fifteen passengers that the Pelicans could. Dropping inflatable rafts would be chancy if the wind picked up and flipped the rafts over or blew them out of swimming range. Individual hoisting would take hours.

Even using whale boats, and the carrier escort ships with over-the-side cargo nets, many would be lost. The admiral's mind painted an image of screaming heads bobbing in a sea turning red as would-be rescue propellers churned into the mass of humanity, elderly and out-of-shape passengers clutching and twisting in the boarding nets. Some would reach the top as others slipped and fell back shrieking. Or those hopelessly tangled in the nets would be bashed to a pulp against the rolling sides of the ship.

Gifford's thoughts pressed on, giving him no relief. He saw more blood . . . and night arriving. And the sharks . . .

"It's going to be a cluster fuck, Skipper," Jackson reasoned.

Gifford wiped his hand wearily across his face and nodded.

CHAPTER

—— 16 ——

Taongi Atoll, Marshall Islands, Mid-Pacific

"There it is, Doc! Taongi!" the navy pilot shouted over the roar of twin General Electric T64-415 turboshafts as he banked the RH-53D Sea Stallion to give Maddox a view of the necklace of coral islands that glistened from their cobalt setting.

History held a bitter place for these verdant isles that rose from these azure waters of the Pacific. Nestled in an ocean called Pacific, not peace, but war and modern destruction surfeited the inhabitants of the Marshall Islands. Few pieces of remote paradise bore the burden of names like Kwajalein, with its bloody fighting in the Second World War, or Bikini Atoll and Eniwetok, sites of atom bomb testing.

Cancer of the thyroid rose in increasing numbers among those Marshallese islanders exposed to radiation fallout as children. Worse than the radiation, western civilization eroded the islanders' culture without replacing what it destroyed. Life-styles suited for Los Angeles had no merit in the Marshalls.

Taongi Atoll, farthest north of the islands, suffered less by virtue of its isolation. Civilization leaked to them only twice a week on the freighter from Ponape and Majuro.

So the throbbing sound in the air drew an excited crowd.

Maddox watched the largest island grow as the Sikorsky helicopter flew on. A coral reef ringed the white sand beaches, containing brilliant blue shallows and separating the deep cobalt sea. Palm trees reached from volcanic boulders to grasp at the aircraft as it overflew the island in search of a place to land. Scattered clusters of people spilled out of thatched houses as the plane passed. Many of the women were bare-breasted. All faces turned up to this wonder.

"A real paradise, eh, Doc? Complete with native girls."

Maddox thought of Yael. A beach for them to share, time for themselves—these things floated beyond his grasp.

"Uh-oh." The pilot grimaced as the Sea King crossed a tin-roofed board building with a steeple sprouting a whitewashed cross. "The missionaries beat us," he added ominously.

The Sea King circled the atoll until the pilot located a suitable landing zone. Pilot and copilot agreed on a powdery expanse of sand near the northern tip of the island. Neither of the two aviators voiced thoughts on this mission or why the crew had been stripped to just the two of them. It was classified, they'd been told. The heavy assault helicopter normally carried a crew of seven.

The pilot, a lieutenant, worried that he had received his orders directly from a vice-admiral. That was bad luck, he reasoned. Now this gold-armed admiral knew his name. Bad luck for sure. Best not to have admirals know you exist.

The RH-53D descended onto the beach like a wrathful god in a whirlwind of stinging sand, shredding branches from the coconut palms and blowing fishnets into the surf. Propwash beat the lagoon to a froth. Below, the islanders mouthed moans that the thundering rotors snatched from their throats.

The Sea King bounced to earth, crushing the outrigger of

a canoe beneath one tire. The fliers cut power, and the three blades spun to a halt.

"She's all yours, Doc. We've got orders to stay aboard and maintain radio contact." The copilot faked a sigh. "Looks like you've got all the wahines to yourself." He didn't mention his other orders—to shoot Dr. Maddox if he refused to return with the aircraft.

Christopher Maddox stepped onto the sand and looked about. The shore was empty. Frightened natives huddled behind trees and clustered at the forest edge.

"You must forgive their alarm. They've never seen a helicopter before."

Maddox turned to watch a short man hurrying from the direction of the frame building. Thinning gray hair failed to protect the man's head from the sun as he clutched a straw hat that had long ago forgotten its shape. A florid complexion blended with his reddened scalp. Clearly this man's skin had not been designed for the tropics. Solar radiation and wind had beaten it into submission.

"They don't know if this is an evil omen. To them it resembles a giant dragonfly." The man grasped the doctor's hand and pumped it warmly. "I'm John Castle. Reverend John Castle of the Methodist mission here."

"Christopher Maddox."

"Commander Maddox, am I right?" Castle eyed the shoulder patches on the jumpsuit. "I was in the navy myself. Now I'm a soldier of God."

Maddox watched this curious little man who fairly jumped with excitement, his bare feet shuffling in the sand as he continued his prolonged handshake. The sun had destroyed him so thoroughly, it was impossible to guess his age. Maddox figured anywhere from forty to sixty. Christopher had the impression that the man had come to bring civilization to these islands, and in the prolonged battle that had ensued, the island was winning, leisurely molding the reverend into one of its own.

"Tea, Commander? The mission is over there . . . ."

"Thank you, Reverend, but this is an emergency. No time."

The little man appeared crestfallen. "I'd hoped to show you to the faithful . . . to have you talk to them . . . to sort of reinforce my work. The people here are good people, but backward. Recently there has been a rebirth of old superstitions. Your helicopter, for example, may be taken as a sign of displeasure of the old gods instead of a shining example of Christianity. . . ."

"What?" Confused, Maddox looked at the Sikorsky.

"One man in particular . . ." The minister pressed his suit.

"I'm sorry, Reverend. The lives of thousands depend on us. Time is running out."

"Oh, dear! Yes, you're right. I'm being selfish."

"You mentioned a man who's survived many sea snake bites." Maddox bored onward. A mental clock with Yael's face ticked off the seconds inside his brain.

"Yes, Tangaroa. A stiff-necked and proud man. The very same who fosters these godless superstitions. If it wasn't for his status as navigator, I would have him cast out of this community." Castle smoothed his formless white jacket to emphasize his importance.

"Tangaroa? Where is he? I've got to see him immediately."

"Yes, yes. Immediately." Castle's face blanched. "I've not seen him around for several days. Not since we had a nasty argument. Oh, dear, I hope he's not out sailing. Sometimes he takes an outrigger out for days."

Maddox felt his heart drop.

"Wait. He usually takes a boy with him." Castle scanned the crowd that hung back, waiting for the silver dragonfly to devour the minister. His eyes settled on one who stood alone from the rest, one wearing a *thu* and a torn Hawaiian T-shirt. "Yes, there he is! Joseph, come here. Don't be afraid."

The boy walked to them.

"Joseph, this is Commander Maddox, a great warrior for God."

Maddox winced. The boy's fast eyes caught this.

"Joseph," Castle continued, "where is Tangaroa? Is he on the island?"

The boy nodded while keeping penetrating eyes on Maddox. Christopher sensed the boy had been expecting him. The thought was unnerving.

"Good. You must take Commander Maddox to see him at once. It's very, very important."

Joseph nodded. He turned and limped off in the direction of a rocky point that pierced the edge of the beach. Maddox noticed the child dragged a deformed foot. *Talipes equinovarus,* clubfoot, his medical mind noted. Castle hurried after them.

The child led them through thorn bushes and *kiawe* trees that appeared to part for him while snagging the minister. They followed into a sunlit clearing that faced the sea.

Wild cymbidium and pikake filled the air with their scents. Snowy kukui blossoms alternated with bougainvillea and torch ginger, decorating the forest walls in scarlet and white. A weathered hut of coconut palms and *kiawe* branches rested in the clearing. A trim outrigger canoe guarded the shallow lagoon facing the hut. Sanderlings and ruddy turnstones hopped about on guard duty while brown noddies and sooty terns flew air cover. The site seemed timeless.

The boy limped to the doorway and bowed to the tapa cloth that hung across the opening. *"Atirro,* Tangaroa. I bring the man." Then he drew the curtain aside and turned to look back at his followers.

Maddox noticed tears in the boy's eyes.

"Atirro, man of the west," a voice beckoned.

Maddox stooped to enter the thatched hut. His eyes adjusted to the darkness. Sunlight filtered through the wicker walls to cast stripes across the interior. The doctor searched the gloom until his eyes fastened on something glowing amid the patterns of light.

Shocked, Maddox was staring into the eyes of Tangaroa. The man lay inches away on a tapa cloth mat.

Clearly, the old man was dying.

U.S. Navy Nuclear Carrier Carl Vinson, CVN-70, CVW-15, Mid-Pacific

"Admiral, Vice-admiral Gifford on the line." The communications officer held the telephone receiver away from his body as if it were a scorpion.

Clement Turner, rear admiral and commander of Carrier Wing 15, stopped gnawing on his fingernail to look at the deadly phone. His Hawkeye AWACS had been monitoring *Aesop*'s coded transmissions as well as the shortwaves between them and TOA 805. He didn't want this, and he didn't need this. But Truck Turner knew this rasher of shit had his name on it. He sighed as he accepted the scorpion.

"Hello, Clay," Turner greeted his old Annapolis classmate.

"Truck. How's the family?"

"They're fine, Clay."

"I'm glad to hear that."

"Are we finished with the amenities, sir?" Turner had worked his way up the ladder through naval aviation with a distinguished combat record in Vietnam. He was a full-blooded brown shoe who should have had his third admiral's stripe, except that his bluntness and incessant concern for his pilots had ruffled a few feathers. Turner remembered the steel that hid behind Henry Clay's southern gentility.

"Yes." That steel glinted.

"Good. Admiral, I wish to go on record as protesting the use of my air wing for—"

"So noted." Gifford cut him short.

"Thank you, sir. Now what do you need me to do?"

"I knew I could count on you, Truck. You've been monitoring this . . . this situation?"

"Yes, sir."

"POTUS"—Gifford used the acronym for president of the United States that the White House staff fostered—"has got his ass in a wringer. His boys dropped the ball with this terrorist virus. Well, we've snuffed out the source, but a carrier got on this TransOceanic flight. The whole damned plane is infected."

"I heard that, Clay."

"You also know it's an election year, Truck."

"Yup. I guessed all those passengers have voting relatives."

"You called it right. We can't let them land anywhere they please—"

"You saw to that, Clay."

"Yeah, well, I take full responsibility for that." Gifford accepted his role. He had a lot to account for when he stood before his Maker. A fleeting doubt crossed his mind: If there was a Heaven, he knew his wife would be there. Would he be allowed in? It was a cruel thought, to be denied her company in death as well as in life. "But it also looks like we may be able to inoculate the passengers. So the bottom line is we need a maximum effort to save them."

Turner had been working on the logistics since he'd become aware of the problem. "Henry Clay, I can't let you infect the entire air wing."

"No, that would exponentially increase the risk of this virus getting away from us."

"Right. I propose dispersing the escort ships, detaching the air wing squadrons to Wheeler, Barber's Point, and Kaneoe. Leave just HS-4 to help in the rescue. The *Vinson* will go to general quarters and nuclear contamination status. That'll seal off the majority of the spaces and protect the crew. We'll issue rubberized biological warfare outfits to the Marines and bosuns manning the lifeboats. Anyone in direct contact with the passengers will wear them—medical personnel, helo crews. And they'll all go to sick bay, where they'll be isolated until your wonder boy cures them or they die."

"Without the escorts you'll triple the time it takes to get them out of the water."

"I know. But it's the only way."

"I thought as much. What do you think the casualty rate will run?" Gifford had a hard time thinking of the civilians on board TOA 805 in military terms, as casualties. Perhaps he was getting too old.

"Not counting killed or trapped in the plane from a hard landing in the water?"

"Yes."

"Sixty to eighty percent."

Taongi Atoll, Marshall Islands, Mid-Pacific

"I've waited for you." Tangaroa raised his head to watch Maddox enter his hut. The sunlight poured through the door behind the doctor as he knelt on the earthen floor. The halo that backlit his visitor confirmed the old man's belief that his visitor came from the gods . . . the old gods. The navigator struggled to rise but failed, falling back, ashamed of his weakness. "Forgive my weakness. I have nothing to offer you to drink."

"You were expecting me?" Maddox rasped as he tried to clear his throat. This old man, the hut—all this unnerved him.

Tangaroa nodded. He pointed to a palm leaf covered with an elaborate design of knots. "The *pwe* told me of your coming."

"*Pwe?*"

"The natives believe they can tell the future by tying knots in palm fronds," Reverend Castle answered as he followed Maddox into the hut. "That palm over there must be his *pwe.*"

Fire blazed in Tangaroa's eyes, and his lips twisted into a snarl. "What are you doing here?"

"Oh, I'm not mentioned in your *pwe?*" Castle returned the enmity. Then he collected himself and solemnly added, "I'm here on God's work. To save your soul."

"You cannot have it!" the navigator barked, but the effort caused a spasm of dry coughing. "My spirit does not walk with you." The weathered hand rested on Maddox's shoulder. "You are a master of medicine, a *sausafay?*"

Christopher nodded.

"Send him away, *sausafay*. Protect my spirit from his robbing hands. I'm too tired to sing the chants to protect myself. There is much to be done and little time."

"I . . . I don't know your language, navigator," the physician stuttered.

"The boy, Mau, has a clever tongue. He can translate."

"Mau?" Maddox was confused.

"Joseph! His Christian name is Joseph," Castle insisted.

"He is Mau, the hawksbill turtle."

Maddox watched the two men fight, the prideful minister and the old man, stubborn even as he lay dying. Yael's face materialized in the patterns of light. His way was clear. Nothing mattered but her. "Stop!" he commanded. "Get out!" He pushed the sputtering Castle through the doorway and headlong into the sand.

Mau's jaw dropped, and his eyes grew wide with wonder. This stranger had the power to command the servant of God. No lightning struck him down.

"Good." Tangaroa smiled. "You are as I expected. You

have the power. Together we will chart the *yalap,* the great path, between our hearts."

Maddox settled back on his heels. "Is it true the sea snake can't harm you?"

Tangaroa nodded.

"What did these snakes that bit you look like?"

Tangaroa mumbled a name that meant nothing to Maddox. He looked to the boy.

"The yellow and blue ones—with the flat, spotted tail—like a fish."

"Pelamis!" Maddox sang. It was true. He couldn't believe it. "Look, you have—inside you—the power to fight the poison of the yellow and blue sea snake. Many people are sick with the poison of that snake. And you have the answer to saving their lives. I need to take you back with me so we can . . ." The doctor stopped. He gazed at the withered husk that lay before him. Once this person had been robust, strong, and brimming with force. But life had drained all that. Only the shriveled pith, the glowing embers remained. The man couldn't be moved. Only a few minutes of life were left in him.

"You know I'm dying." The navigator read his thoughts.

"It's useless. Finished. They're all finished." Maddox buried his head in his hands.

"You worry about your woman and all those on the great metal bird." The hand returned to his shoulder.

Maddox stammered. "How did you know?"

The hand swept toward the palm leaf. "The *pwe.* It tells me the future."

"How many are in the sky?" Maddox questioned.

Tangaroa's hands flashed an accounting. Christopher looked at Mau.

"About three hundred," was the boy's reply.

The hairs on the back of the physician's neck prickled.

"Don't be surprised, *sausafay.* Alulap, the great spirit, sees far beyond this island. When I lay sick from the first sea snake bite, Alulap revealed my future." The navigator shrugged sheepishly. "I was young then and didn't believe it . . . like you. But the palm fronds confirmed it. Don't worry. They will be saved. I know that for sure."

"How? They're in a plane that's out of control, heading away from land."

"There's a floating island. I don't know the name of this island or its *wofanu*. Perhaps it is a *pookof*." Tangaroa nodded to Mau.

"The *pookof* are sea creatures that live around certain islands. They always stay in one spot. A navigator can know where he is by learning the animals for each island." Mau recited his lesson.

The dying man smiled. He had planted the seed of the *etak* well. His work was done. Only the gods would know if Mau would have the *itang*—the talk of light, with its wisdom—to save their traditions.

"I was going to take some of your blood to make the cure, but you're too sick." Christopher rambled on, not hearing. Floundering, adrift without buoys, he was sinking again. Without Yael to anchor him he was lost. He barely felt the navigator as he pulled him closer. Numbly he watched the crusted hand pat his shoulder. The fingers hooked into talons that seized his arm with surprising strength. The pain rinsed his thoughts. Now the old man's eyes bored into him.

"I can save them. I know the way. Even your woman with the pale eyes."

How did he know that? Maddox wondered.

"Sausafay, do you want that?"

"Yes, yes. But . . ."

"There is a cost." Tangaroa's eyes narrowed shrewdly. "Are you willing to pay it?"

"Yes."

"Good. Send the boy outside. This is between men."

Tangaroa looked at length at Mau. He would not see him again in this world. "Go, Mau. Remember what you have learned. Now you must follow the *wofanu* of your heart."

Mau started to speak, but Tangaroa turned his face to the wall.

CHAPTER

—— 17 ——

U.S. Navy Nuclear Carrier Carl Vinson, *CVN-70,*
CVW-15, Mid-Pacific

"Get the Hawkeye back up. I want it refueled and on station
in twenty minutes." Admiral Turner jabbed his finger into
the plated window that overlooked the flight deck four
stories below. His left hand squashed a telephone handset
into his ear. The finger waved in circles as he talked with the
air boss on the deck above in Primary Flight Control.

Turner had taken the unprecedented step of walking up
from his flag bridge to the navigation bridge. The captain of
the *Vinson* lay below in sick bay, recovering from appendici-
tis. So Turner did what came naturally to him—he assumed
command and stepped on a few more toes and navy
traditions. Dark pools of sweat stained the armpits and back
of his short-sleeved khaki shirt and blackened the sweat-
band of the blue baseball hat he'd jammed over his crew cut,
but Turner was happy. Perhaps settled more than happy.
Truck Turner was busy, and that pleased him.

The air boss shouted into his phone, the words carrying
down the stairs to the navigation bridge as he'd intended,
and the E2-C Miniwacs extended its General Electric AN/
APN-171 radar dome and waited as the deck crew swarmed

over the plane. Seven stories above them the air boss vented his wrath, and the multicolored ants scrambled.

Color-coded vests and shirts identified the jobs of the men on the flight deck. Purple-shirted "grapes" dragged fueling hoses to the thirsty tanks of the Hawkeye while fire protection men in red helmets, life vests, and jerseys watched from their yellow fire truck. Aircraft maintenance brown shirts crawled over the plane, checking fasteners and the landing carriage.

Bad luck, Turner cursed to himself. It was bad luck to have half of his Hawkeyes down with needed repairs. Normally the *Vinson* had four E-2Cs attached with its air wing. One was down with its hundred-hour overhaul; another needed an engine change. That left him with two, each flying four-hour missions. That left Turner with only one eye in the sky. Bad luck.

Below, the Hawkeye's three-man radar system crew emerged from four hours in a black hole staring at radar and computer screens. Blind as their namesakes, the moles, the three men huddled on the sunlit flight deck with their helmet visors tapped down over light-sensitive eyes. Three blind mice. About them death waited. One misstep, one wrong move meant death. Death in the form of a whirling propeller, the yawning maw of a jet intake, or a slashing aircraft wing. A white-shirted safety officer led the moles to safety, arms on shoulders, like blind men crossing a street. Another string of moles, the relief crew, passed in a second line of blind men.

Turner's heart went out to them. Every cruise lost a dozen men. Those were the statistics. Brave men all, not figures on a computer printout to him, but men with faces and families. Most of his men were under twenty-five. This tour he hadn't lost a single man. Each night he prayed for that to continue.

JP-5 fuel splashed from a loose hose into the hot diesel engine of a mule as it cranked its generator to start an F-14

Tomcat. The low yellow tractor that resembled a cigarette carton with four wheels and a black nonskid top burst into flames. The mule driver bailed out of the cutout notch where he steered. The back of his blue life vest trailed smoke. Instantaneously a safety officer knocked the man to the deck. A fireman sprayed both of them with foam. A rapid-intervention fire vehicle, identical to the burning mule except for its white paint job and red-striped skirt, raced over. More retardant foam blanketed the tractor. The first safety officer signaled all clear: The fire was out.

The entire navigation bridge exhaled. Cheated death once again, Truck Turner thought, sighing. He'd learned that phrase from a weathered bosun. How often had he used that saying? How long would it last?

Steam billowed from the track of the starboard bow catapult meters away from the fire as the catapult crew directed a Grumman EA-6B Prowler into launch position. Oblivious to the nearby accident, the green shirts moved the electronic countermeasure and tactical warfare Prowler to hookup. Blast deflector shields rose from the deck behind the plane. The green shirts followed beneath the plane in their awkward bent-kneed crouch, attaching the catapult to the nose gear. In front of the EA-6B the cat officer watched the hookup. The green shirts signaled thumbs up and crouched beneath the plane's wings. The Prowler powered its jets to one hundred percent. Its pilot saluted. The yellow-shirted cat officer dropped to his knees and touched the deck in a sweeping movement as he ducked to avoid the knife edge of the wing. Off the edge of the flight deck in a control pit, the shooter waited with both hands held over his head. As the cat officer signaled the shooter brought both hands down to slap the dual launch buttons. One deck below, lights flashed a go to the catapult controller.

Superheated steam fired the catapult, and the Prowler lurched forward from zero to 160 knots in 165 feet. In two seconds the plane cleared the bow. Jet thunder, fiery heat, and a white plume of catapult steam rolled over the deck crew. Already the men were moving the next plane into position.

All four catapults were launching. Admiral Turner was clearing the *Vinson*. Belowdecks, the catapult crew searched for a pinhole leak in the steam system of the number two catapult with a broom. The straw broom encountered the invisible superheated steam and burst into flames. The leak was plugged. The launches continued. It was rush hour on the most dangerous street in the world.

Turner wondered what his men dreamed about. Working so close to death, did they dream of it? He did. He lived with a recurring nightmare: the *Vinson* staggering under a catastrophic explosion, smoke billowing, flames engulfing the flight deck, the scuppers awash in blood.

He blinked away his fears. The number one and number four catapults launched simultaneously. Two Tomcats, a hundred feet separating their wingtips, roared off to Kaneoe.

The Hawkeye coughed to life. The four-bladed propellers turned lazily, picking up speed until their yellow tips blended into warning circles. The E-2C used carbon fiber blades instead of steel to avoid Doppler effect interference with its sensitive radar. Like an obedient pterodactyl with tucked wings, the metal giant crept after the yellow shirt who directed it into position. The wings unfolded as it lumbered along. A salute, a burst of steam, and the airborne early warning plane rose into the sky to its station.

Admiral Turner turned as a red-faced commander entered the navigation bridge. Huffing and puffing from his race up three flights from the meteorological room on the 06 level, the chief aerographer carried a rolled chart under his arm.

"Jim," Turner greeted the weather forecaster.

"Admiral. I'm afraid I've got some bad news, sir." Commander Jim Vobrowski spread his chart over the navigation table, incurring the ire of the ship's navigator. "Sorry." Vobrowski nudged the man out of his place. The navigator retreated, grumbling about the insolence of the service corps and the sanctity of line officers. The meteorologist missed the performance as he scanned his flow chart.

Turner watched, bemused. "Trouble, Jim?" He scanned the horizon. Blue skies surrounded the *Vinson*. Not a cloud in the sky.

Commander James E. Vobrowski was one of hundreds of specialized experts who contributed to the success of the modern supercarrier. Sequestered on the 06 level with the other swamis who lived with a mystic belief in their UHF, radar, and ultrasecret satellite communications, the ship's weatherman was viewed by many of the line officers as just another witch doctor. But Turner respected his opinion.

"Here, Admiral." Vobrowski's finger poked at a series of converging ripples on his map. "There's a convergence heading this way. Moving fast. Swinging along this low." The fingers traced to another set of lines. "That'll make it turn around to hit us in the face."

"East?" Turner frowned. The usual weather patterns came from the west.

"Yes, sir."

"How bad is this, Jim?"

Vobrowski shook his head. "Bad, sir. Gale force winds. I'd estimate a force 8 on the Beaufort Scale. A major tropical storm. Thirty-four- to forty-knot winds."

Turner gazed at the weather map. More bad luck. The lines pointed like a dagger at his bow. Normally he'd change course. "When will it hit? And how long do you think it'll last?"

"Be here in three, maybe four hours. How long will it last?" Vobrowski wiped his glasses on his shirttail. The ship's navigator shook his head: not regulation. Vobrowski replaced his glasses and tucked in his shirt, but the blouse billowed over his spare tire. His right eye squinted as he calculated. "Maybe six hours, sir."

"Jesus Christ!"

Vobrowski jumped back.

"The Chinese used to kill the bearer of bad news, Jim." The navigator chuckled.

"It's going to hit us smack in the nose," Turner continued. "Right before dark. I've got to hold this bearing to intercept that TransOceanic flight. Art, what's the ETA for that plane?"

The navigator bent over his radar scope. "They've cut back on power, Admiral. Current airspeed is 190 knots." The officer corrected for the freshening winds. He blanched as his computer provided the estimated time of arrival. "Four hours, sir. Right in the middle of the storm."

"Good thing you're not Chinese, either, Art," Vobrowski added.

A tortuous vein swelled down the middle of Admiral Turner's forehead. His jaw muscles rippled. "How the hell am I going to run a search and rescue in a storm with twenty-foot waves, Jim?"

"Twenty-three, sir."

Turner shook his head. He'd seen smaller planes smack into waves when they'd ditched in the South China Sea on Yankee Station. Waves and troughs were as yielding as concrete. The result was always the same. The planes broke apart.

"There isn't going to be anyone to rescue, is there, sir?"

CHAPTER

——— 18 ———

TransOceanic Airlines Flight 805

Greg Whitley struggled to hold his plane together. By playing with the throttles and the wing flaps he defined the limits of control. A threatening vibration shook the 747 if he tried to increase engine thrust. The vibration had developed in the last hour. Greg worried that it came from the aft pressure bulkhead. That pressure wall was all that stood between the plane's cabin pressure of six thousand feet and the lower pressure of twenty thousand feet above sea level that existed on the outer side of the bulkhead. Inches of metal held back the vacuum of the blue sky. If it blew, the integrity of the hull would be lost. The floor supporting the passenger space from the cargo hold would collapse. That could buckle the control cables running in the cabin roof. No cables to the wing flaps, no cables to the ailerons, no control. The end. Whitley prayed that the bulkhead would hold.

The plane continued to yaw to starboard, away from Hawaii. Too heavy a hand to correct the yaw almost led to a fatal spin. Greg thought about dropping to a lower altitude to relieve the pressure on the bulkhead, to escape the fatal jet stream that forced him away from land, but he had no way to climb again. Slowing the plane led to its wings wobbling uncontrollably.

His course was simple. Too fast and he blew apart. Too slow and he'd career into the ocean. Whitley had one shot at a safe descent. So he flew on prayers and a bulkhead, heading for the carrier *Carl Vinson*. There he'd do his best to set his 747 in the water.

"TOA 805. This is Red-eye Hummer. Do you copy?" The headset crackled.

"Go ahead, Hummer." Whitley felt his spirits lift. He recognized the E-2C Miniwacs.

"Flight 805. We're on Zulu Station. How're you doing?"

"So-so, Hummer. Don't see you on our radar. What's your location?"

"Two hundred eighty nautical miles straight ahead of you. We're eyeballing you for *Vinson*."

"Roger." Greg recognized the Hawkeye was beyond the curvature of the earth and thus outside the 747's radar— but well within the reach of the E-2's Randtron rotodome. "Good to hear that, Hummer. Was feeling a bit lonely up here."

"We got you, 805. Switch to channel two, you're breaking up."

"Roger. That better?"

"Affirmative, 805. You've got lots of friends up here. We'll talk you home."

Home! Whitley fought back tears. "Thanks, Hummer. Where is 70?"

"You a brown shoe, 805?"

"Roger that. Did my share of touch-and-gos on the old *Vinson*."

"All right. This'll be a second homecoming. She's a little less than seven hundred miles as the crow flies. You can't miss her. We'll see to that."

"Thanks, Hummer. But I've got restricted maneuverability. One, two degrees at most."

"No sweat, 805. We're relaying your position to the *Vinson*. They're coming to you. All you've got to do is stay in the air."

"Great, Red-eye. Look forward to seeing the 70 in three hours."

"Negative, 805. Make that four hours, repeat four hours."

"Four?"

"Affirmative, 805. Storm front approaching. You'll be picking up forty-knot headwinds in about two more hours."

Four hours! The words chilled Whitley to the bone. He checked his log. One hour after sunset! He was going to be landing in the dark.

Wake Island Naval Station, Pacific Ocean

"I got it! I got it!"

Henry Clay Gifford squinted into the slanting sunlight. Powdery needles of volcanic dust stabbed into his face from the rotors of the Sea Stallion. Light and cinders created a corona backlighting the RH-53D. Charging through this maelstrom was Christopher Maddox.

"Admiral, I've got it!" Maddox sprinted through the dust, careful to stay within the white lines that marked the path to *Aesop*. Marine sharpshooters followed his run through rifle scopes. Here as elsewhere Gifford had taken steps to isolate his contaminated team. Christopher ran with two canvas rucksacks waving over his head. He swung the bags. "This is it!"

Gifford stepped out of the waist hatch. Maddox slid to a halt, out of breath. "The serum?" the admiral questioned.

"Yes, sir! A whole fucking ton of it. Enough to treat all of us and every infected tourist in the Pacific," Maddox babbled between sucking breaths.

Gifford raised a quizzical eyebrow.

"Well, at least enough for us and the entire TOA flight."

"I thought you said you couldn't take that much without endangering—"

"Yeah." The grin disappeared from Christopher's face. A puzzled look followed. "I can't explain it, Admiral, but he . . . this old man, the navigator, was expecting me. Something about his telling the future with palm leaves. It's weird. Crazy. But he knew about us . . . and the TOA flight. And he was dying."

"Dying?"

"Yeah, but he waited for me." Maddox lowered the canvas bags. Carefully, almost reverently, he clutched the satchels to his chest. His eyes wandered over these precious objects, shifting to the horizon in the direction of Taongi Atoll before returning to rest again on the counterterrorist director.

Gifford saw a changed man. A strange light burned in the face of this man. Henry Clay marked the change. Something inside him knew Maddox was no longer questionable, no longer a weak link.

"So help me God, Admiral. He said he was guarding this." Maddox thrust the bags toward Gifford. "He said he was holding this treasure until I could take it. That it was his responsibility. For the world." Maddox cradled the sacks. "Then he died, and I took his entire blood volume. I've got it here."

Gifford watched the shaken physician climb into the bowels of *Aesop*. He sensed there was more to the story. "What else did he say, son?"

Maddox turned to look back at the sky. "He gave me his responsibility, too." The words whispered back from the plane as Christopher disappeared.

U.S. Navy Nuclear Carrier Carl Vinson, *CVN-70, CVW-15, Mid-Pacific*

An F-14 Tomcat, the last plane capable of leaving CVN-70, rocketed down the waist catapult, dipped its wings slightly as it caught the wind, and roared off to Hawaii. Immediately Truck Turner and the air boss headed for the flight deck. The assistant air boss, the mini-boss, followed the exodus from the flight control radar stations.

A gust of wind over the bow caught the admiral's hat as the two men stepped over the knee-knocker of the O-2 watertight door onto the flight deck. It sailed over the side. Eighty feet below the cap struck the rolling waves before the ship's wake plowed it beneath the water.

"Goddamnit," Turner swore.

A red-shirted ordnance man sprang from his perch on a stack of Harpoon antiship missiles, disdainful of the fact that his makeshift seat consisted of thousands of pounds of high explosives—enough to obliterate him and sink his carrier. "Take my cover, Admiral." The boy whipped out his greasy baseball cap and thrust it upon Turner.

"Why, thank you, Seibert. I seem to have lost mine." Turner unfolded the cap and wedged it tightly on his head. Oil-smudged letters proclaimed the *Carl Vinson*'s numbers, CVN-70. Turner shook the startled sailor's hand.

"Yes, sir. Thank you, sir!" The boy scampered away, wondering how the admiral knew his name.

Turner wiped his grease-stained hand on his pants.

The wind picked up. Cumulonimbus clouds, dark and threatening, filled the horizon. Tufts of white spray, the nautical white horses, sprang from the tops of growing waves. Steam clouds trailed straight aft from the four smoking catapults. Turner felt the deck rise ponderously as 81,600 tons moved through the sea.

Truck surveyed the flight deck. Without aircraft it looked naked, vulnerable—the look it wore while docked for refurbishing. Turner hated that exposed feeling.

"The roof looks bare, sir." The air boss voiced his commanding officer's concerns.

"Yup." Turner viewed the four and a half acres of deck. It was 1,092 feet long, 252 feet wide, and covered with two inches of armor plate; the flight deck normally held half of the air wing's ninety-five aircraft.

Around them the rainbow warriors continued their assignments. Brown and green shirts crossed the nonskid surface with backs bent beneath loads of heavy chain. Yellow shirts wove through the clouds of catapult steam, criss-crossing the deck in the low-slung MD-3A diesel tow trucks. Already a work party of green-, yellow-, and red-dressed men marched down the deck behind a row of push brooms. A white-vested safety officer led the party in the time-honored tradition of swabbing the deck. Bobbing behind the brooms, the group resembled flamingos.

Tillie, the NS-50 aircraft crane, observed the activity with its usual stoicism. More yellow shirts chained the crane and its neighbor—the Oshkosh fire truck—to stanchions and deck cleats. A row of yellow tractors grew alongside the ship's island. The safety nets and catwalks along the sides of the deck were filled with men.

The flight deck cleared. Truck Turner stood at the center of a vast metal field as it knifed through the ocean at thirty knots. Forward, the four white lines of the catapult tracts beckoned. Aft, a similar number of wire cables of the recovery system stretched across the deck. Tire scuff marks, grease, fuel spills, and nonskid paint decorated random sections. Jet fuel and diesel fumes choked the air.

Turner loved every inch of his ship. Every rivet, every metal plate and painted bolt. And he loved his men.

His chief of staff hurried over. A clipboard with papers danced under his arm.

"Let's hear the figures, Frank."

"Aye, aye, sir." The captain tried to control the blowing papers. "All flyable ships of the air wing have been bingoed to the beach."

"Good. What does that leave us?"

"Twenty-three ships in the hangar bay. Sixteen down with hundred-hour checks, four with engine overhauls, and three Prowlers for retrofitting of their APQs." The captain mentioned the multimode Norden APQ-148 radar with its ability to provide multiple identification, tracking, and mapping solutions.

"Personnel?"

"Three hundred thirty-six of the air wing's 2,865 men. Mostly deck crew and maintenance."

"Good. And the ship's men?"

"There's 3,122, sir. Thirty-one on leave. Two Medevacs, including Jerry." The chief of staff paused for effect after mentioning the *Vinson*'s captain. Intensely loyal, he felt his superior should have passed this buck to the ship's executive officer and left with his air wing. None of Turner's staff agreed with his risky decision.

"So noted, Frank." Turner glared over his sunglasses.

"Aw, Admiral. We're just trying to protect you. . . ."

"I appreciate it, Frank. But I don't deserve to wear these two heavy stripes if I'm afraid of a hot potato."

"Not a hot potato, sir. A turd."

"Whatever, Frank. Are we ready?"

"Yes, sir. The ship's secured for the storm. We're ready to go to biological warfare status and seal off the ship's spaces. We'll lower all four elevators and use them and the sponsons to recover the passengers after the . . . after the . . ."

"Go ahead, say it."

The chief of staff measured the mounting waves. "Okay, after the crash. It's going to be rough on our men in the

217

whale boats. All seventy of the Marines volunteered for boat or shark duty. Oh, with your permission, sir, we could use your Chris Craft."

"You got it." Turner picked at a scab on his neck. He'd cut himself shaving this morning, the first time in years. Put away your doubts, he counseled himself. "Frank, give me your opinion on the losses from a 747 hitting these waves."

"Admiral, I think most of our boats will be coming back empty."

Aesop, *Wake Island Naval Station, Pacific Ocean*

"I suppose I couldn't blame you if you used the largest needle you had." Henry Clay Gifford pressed the cotton swab against the puncture wound in the crook of his arm.

Christopher Maddox just smiled. Tangaroa's serum contained a higher antibody titer than he'd imagined possible. Making an antiserum had been easy. Gifford had been the last. Surprisingly, Jackson jumped more than Owen from his injection—a fact that delighted the computer programmer. The two buddies were now comparing excuses.

"You big wimp. I saw you flinch."

"Fucking-A, I flinched. And it's no wonder. Cooped up in this plane with nobody to shoot. And no poontang, either. It's a miracle I can even stand muster. This would've dropped a lesser Marine."

A warm kiss caressed Christopher's neck. Cinnamon and cloves wafted past him. He turned to look up at Yael. She'd plaited her hair and changed into fresh khaki shorts. Leaning over him, she let him gaze wonderingly down the front of her partly buttoned blouse.

"Everybody's poontang titer is low," Jackson commented.

Laughter filled *Aesop* for the first time in as long as anyone could remember.

"God, I may live to be a father after all," Asher crowed, rubbing the puncture site in his arm. "Hannah's due anytime. Oh, I haven't even given any thought to a name for the baby."

"May Lee." Jackson astonished them all. "I've always been partial to that name."

"Why, Jackson?" Yael asked.

"She was a double-jointed bar girl in Saigon," the Marine answered honestly.

"Well, yes." Yael shot a desperate look at Asher as laughter erupted once more.

"It's a good name," the Marine replied, miffed that his suggestion wasn't taken seriously. "And she was good, too." He lost control and joined the mirth.

Maddox turned back to his array of flasks. Amber lights glowed on the electrophoresis machine as it separated the various fractions of the islander's serum. Ten minutes left, the doctor thought. Ten more minutes and I'll have enough serum for all of them. Every last one. He rechecked the antibody levels by mixing a drop of his antiserum with venom from the deadly virus. Immediately the mix agglutinated into an opaque mass. Excellent, he thought; he couldn't wish for a better reaction. If any infected passengers produced venom, the injected antiserum would destroy the poison with customized antibodies.

Now that he knew Fuchs's method of gene splicing, Maddox guessed the venom virus carried enough antigenic proteins on the surface of its shell that the islander's antibodies would recognize it and attack the virus itself before it could infect the body's cells. To test his theory, Chris added a solution of fluorescent-tagged antibodies to the common protein shell of the virus. Next he transferred a few precious drops of Tangaroa's serum onto a microscope slide. Finally he added the labeled virus.

Christopher took a deep breath as he switched on the

microscope's ultraviolet light. If he guessed right, the Marshall Islander's antibodies would already be attacking the virus, snatching the killer into clumps of damaged protein that would never be capable of entering the body's cells. Thus damaged, the venom virus would be recognized by the body's immune system and vacuumed into oblivion. Maddox clenched his shaking fingers and whispered a silent prayer. The furrowed face of Tangaroa floated in his mind. Chris exhaled as he looked into the microscope.

Tiny clusters flared in pinpoints of fluorescent blue and green across the field. It was working. Rosettes of antibodies and viruses collided as he watched. Thousands of invisible particles battled into perceptible packages tagged with the fluorescent markers. The mad German's handiwork would never get a chance to merge its invidious genetic material with mankind. Tangaroa was right. He would save the world.

How ironic, he thought. All the combined weight of modern science failed to provide a solution. Yet somehow, some tenuous thread had woven a trail that led him to a single man on a flyspeck island in the Pacific. That man was the key. Fortuitous circumstances? Perhaps. But how had Tangaroa known? How had he?

Yael slipped into the chair next to him. She searched his troubled face. "Are you thinking bad thoughts?"

"No. Just remembering John Donne's line: 'No man is an island.'" He smiled brightly. "We have a busy life ahead of us."

"Yes." She hugged him.

Gifford returned from the cockpit. Curtis Owen trotted behind. Neither was smiling.

"What's wrong?" Yael was perceptive as always.

Gifford shook his head. "Storm's coming."

"Storm?" Christopher's smile faded.

"A bad one. Right at the rendezvous point. The 747's going to ditch in big waves."

"What does that mean?" Maddox looked from face to face.

"They're not gonna make it, Doc." Jackson said the obvious.

"But they've got to! I . . . I've got the cure." Maddox tapped his vials. "It's all here. Enough for all of them."

Silence greeted him.

"Don't you understand? They can all be saved. All of them."

"I understand, Doctor." Admiral Gifford slumped onto a bench. "I understand too well. We've come a long way and overcome our obstacles, but it's beyond our control. You and Yael are to be commended for—"

"Screw the medals!"

"Easy, Doc." Jackson's hand found his shoulder.

"No, you take it easy!" Christopher pushed the hand away. "We . . . we can't just give up. Not after all—"

Gifford tired of this. "It's over. They're going to crash in the sea." A part of his mind, the analytical side, noted that this was one way to prevent the spread of the virus. His work would be done. But deep inside he saw 272 faces, all different, all with families—children, husbands, wives. And he thought of his wife.

"You don't care, is that it? Kill 'em all. A neat solution." Maddox stopped. A fleeting look of pain in the admiral's eyes stopped him. The physician shook his head. "I'm sorry. I didn't mean that."

"Isn't there an island near them?" Asher hoped there were no pregnant women on board. He thought of his Hannah.

"Nothing in their direct line of flight." Owen unrolled his chart. A red line marking the path of the ill-fated flight streaked into an empty blue expanse. An indigo line converged with the plane's path. The *Carl Vinson* moved to witness the disaster. "They've got no controls. All they can do is fly in a straight line. It'd have to be a floating island. One that could come to them."

"What?" Maddox jerked upright.

"Huh?"

"What did you just say?"

"I said they've got no controls."

"No. No. You said floating island."

"So?"

"Floating island! That's what Tangaroa said. I remember it now. He said the plane would be saved. That it would land on a floating island."

"There's no such thing," Gifford started to reply.

"Floating island. The aircraft carrier." Maddox jumped to his feet, snatching the map from Owen. *"Let them land on the* Carl Vinson!"

"That's impossible. This is a Boeing 747, Doctor." Curtis reached for his map.

But Henry Clay Gifford stopped him. "Could it be done, Owen? Get to your computer. Get me the specs of a 747."

Seconds later the group clustered around Owen's bank of CRTs. Overhead a blue screen held the wire-frame outline of the flagship of the Boeing Aircraft Company. Below it were the physical dimensions of the nuclear carrier *Carl Vinson* poured onto a green screen.

"Wingspan?" Gifford ticked off a list of questions.

"Is one hundred ninety-five feet 8 inches."

"Width of the *Vinson*'s flight deck?"

"Is 257 feet."

"TOA Flight 805's a 747SP, the short version, right?"

"Yes, sir—184 feet 9 inches long versus 231 feet 10 inches for the standard 747."

Curtis Owen's fingers tapped across his keyboard. The wire-frame airplane disappeared from the upper CRT. Dramatically, it reappeared flying in from the edge of the green monitor. It landed on the scale image of CVN 70. Clearly the plane fit on the flight deck.

"Smooth, little guy." Jackson twisted his knuckle into the back of the programmer's head.

"Admiral"—Owen shot the Marine an aggravated look—"the 747 lands at 150 knots, same as the carrier's jets."

"What about landing weight?"

"Ah, 450,000 pounds."

"Jesus Christ. A Tomcat weighs around 40,000 pounds empty."

"Actually 39,762 empty," the computer analyst corrected.

"What's the heaviest plane that lands on a carrier, Jackson?"

"A-3, Skywarrior, sir."

"EA-3B Skywarrior." Owen brought up the specifications of the twin-engine ELINT craft. "Maximum 78,000 pounds on takeoff, 41,193 on landing."

"Ten times that weight." Gifford cursed his limited knowledge of carriers. "Well, the decks will take the load. It's the arresting gear that's iffy. Otherwise the plane will roll right on off the bow of the carrier." Gifford knew the 747 wouldn't be able to stop in the 1,084-foot length of the flight deck by itself.

"We've got to try, Admiral," Maddox implored. "It's their only chance."

"Beef up the arresting wires, sir?" Even Jackson felt the excitement.

"Jackson, is that COD still out there?"

The Marine disappeared out the waist hatch only to reappear seconds later. Obviously he'd double-timed around the nose of *Aesop* to check the planes on the landing strip. "Aye, aye, Skipper. She's parked out there. One shiny Greyhound just homesick for her carrier."

"Great. Owen, get them on the horn. Tell them to refuel. Maddox, get your serum together. We're making a visit to the *Carl Vinson.*"

CHAPTER

19

U.S. Navy Nuclear Carrier Carl Vinson, CVN-70, CVW-15, Mid-Pacific

"COMCONTER arriving," the ship's MA-1 paging system blared. A bosun's whistle piped the notes for a vice-admiral. An honor guard of Marines rushed by.

"COMCONTER? Commander counterterrorism? Shit! Gifford!" The Vinson's XO shot a panicked look at Admiral Turner. "He's here? How'd he get here?"

Turner wiped the grease from his hands and cast a final glance about the hangar deck. Located two floors below the flight deck, the cavernous hall dwarfed the two men. Yellow tractors and crates of missiles and parts cluttered the space. Squatting with folded wings, Tomcats, Prowlers, and Intruders waited as droves of workers preened them. A skeletonized Sea Stallion, recovering from its surgery, rested against the starboard bulkhead. Next to it sailors lashed down an E-2C Hawkeye with its Frisbee radar dome.

A cold gray light from tunnel-sized cutouts in the sides of the ship slanted through the hangar haze. These sponsons and outer elevator openings allowed access to the hangar and ship replenishment. Beyond them roiled heavy seas.

Turner braced his right hand against a bulkhead as the *Vinson* shouldered a wave. He looked up to see his palm pressed into the generous breast of a naked poster girl that decorated the gray-painted metal. Turner snatched his hand away. A greasy palm print covered the breast. Smirking to himself, he withdrew a pen and scrawled "Turner was here" next to his print.

"Nice touch," the executive officer noted. "But Admiral Gifford's topside."

Turner watched the fidgeting officer. Nervous in the service—the phrase came to mind. Had he been the same way, pushing for that broad gold strip on his sleeve? Relax, he wanted to say. Relax, it's not that big of a deal. A thousand years from now it won't much matter whether Henry Clay Gifford had to wait for me. But he didn't.

The navy was built on tradition. Not keeping one's superior officer waiting ranked just under the tenth commandment. So he nodded and followed the XO up the ladders to the flight deck.

Leaden sky poured over the outside deck, matching the color of the navy paint that covered the four and a half acres of steel. The rainbow warriors were at work again preparing for the landing. The two men arrived just in time to see the Grumman Greyhound's twin boom tail wafting off the bow of the carrier.

Missed the hook, Turner surmised. "See, John?" He pointed to the circling plane. "The gods sometimes smile on tardy sailors. We'll be on time after all to meet Admiral Gifford. You'll still look good."

The executive officer started to protest, but Turner darted away across the deck toward the stern. There he dropped into a catwalk, continuing his loping gait aft to the landing control station. The landing signal officer nodded to the admiral. Above his head he held the "pickle" in his right hand. His left hand pressed his headset to his ear.

"Missed the hook, eh?"

"No, sir. No bolter," the LSO shouted over the wind. "Was coming in too low. Had to give him the wave-off." The man shook the electronic switch in his hand for emphasis. The switch, referred to as the pickle, controlled a set of warning lights mounted at the stern. Green lights notified the landing pilot of good alignment; flashing the pickle, however, aborted the landing with red warning lights.

"He must be nervous." Turner grinned. "He's got Admiral Henry Clay Gifford on board."

The LCO's head bobbed sympathetically. "Yessir. With all due respect, sir, that guy makes me nervous. I hear Admiral Gifford's a real head-biter. Scuttlebutt has it he's here to kick ass and take names, sir." The commander watched his superior out of the corner of his regulation Ray-Ban sunglasses while keeping his eye on the carrier on-board delivery plane as it settled into a final approach.

"Only my ass, commander," Turner replied. Truck was too long at sea in the Big Canoe Club to marvel at how the deck crew always knew about top secret things before anyone else. "And he can have it. . . ." He saw the LCO's eyebrows raise over the rims of his glasses.

"Shit. He's heading for a ramp strike again!" The pickle wavered in the air. The C-2A rolled in the gusting wind, nose up, tail down, wings tipping wildly like an albatross. "Excuse me, sir. Have to calm this boy down." The LSO modulated his voice into an even tone that could have coaxed a barefoot tap dancer over broken glass. "Bring her up ten degrees, mister."

The plane lifted.

"Right for lineup," the controller snapped. "Come on down. The groove's waiting. Nice and easy."

Miraculously, the Greyhound stabilized as it fell out of the sky at 150 knots to hit the plate deck. Screeching tires smoked as they spun on impact, and the landing gear crashed down. Protesting machinery squealed and clanked. An unknowing observer would have called it a crash landing

—in fact, it was a controlled crash. Hungry tailhooks rasped along the deck scattering a trail of sparks as they sought the number three arresting wire. The hooks found the wire, bit onto the cable, and held. The Grumman jerked to a stop. Beneath the deck hydraulics tightened the cable, pulling the airplane backward. The wire dropped out of the hooks. Spitting out the wire, it was called. Tamed now, the massive gray aircraft docilely followed a yellow shirt's waving hands until a blue shirt connected his tow bar to the nose gear and tractored the Greyhound to a parking space on the empty quarterdeck. Green shirts chained the airship to pad eyes on the deck.

The ship's XO joined Turner in time to see the tail ramp drop open and Gifford's party disembark. The commander's mouth dropped open also. "Son of a bitch" hissed past his teeth. Cheers and whistles erupted from the deck crew as Yael emerged. Admiral Turner greeted this strange party.

"Truck." Gifford thrust his hand out to his old classmate.

"Welcome aboard, sir."

"Thank you, Truck. Happy to be aboard."

"If you'd let us know, we'd have prepared a more fitting reception committee. . . ."

"Didn't have the time. May I present my team?" Gifford introduced his ragtag army. The XO never got his mouth closed until he led the two doctors, the Marine, the Israeli, and the programmer to the admiral's sea cabin.

Turner followed Henry Clay as he walked toward the bow of the carrier. Gifford waved away a string of junior officers. When they were alone Gifford turned. "Do you want the good news first or the bad news?"

Turner sighed. "Good, I suppose."

"Okay. My medical colleagues, Drs. Maddox and Ivanov, have made enough antiserum to cover every passenger on flight 805. We can stop this madness right here. No risk to your command if isolation procedures are continued until all the passengers are vaccinated."

Turner pointed to the growing waves breaking over the bow. Salt spray stung their eyes. Off the starboard bow the sky blackened in stark contrast to the low-set sun on the eastern horizon. Already white horses sprang from the crests of the swells. "Henry, look around. What do you see?" Turner forgot protocol.

"A storm, Truck," Gifford snapped. "I may spend most of my time sailing a desk, but I'm still a deep-water sailor."

"Then you know that Boeing is going to break up the minute it hits these swells. You won't need your vaccine. Is that your bad news?"

"Not at all, Admiral Turner. The bad news—for you—is that I have a direct presidential order for you to make all possible effort to recover TransOceanic Flight 805 on CVN-70, the *Carl Vinson.*" Gifford paused for effect, enjoying the sight of the color draining from Turner's face. He admitted to himself that he was still a gold-plated bastard, and he enjoyed it.

"You bastard!" Truck said it. "You just want to pass the buck!" The little man hopped around in fury.

"I'm going to help you." Henry Clay beamed his best crocodile smile. No crocodile tears, he mused; that would be too much. The smile was just the right touch. He wanted Truck Turner mad, fighting mad. The little man was at his best then.

"That's crazy! It can't be done."

Gifford shoved a sheaf of printouts at him. Owen's hasty report contained all the vital statistics on the *Vinson* and the Boeing 747SP. Henry Clay glanced at his watch. "I suggest we get cracking. We've got less than ninety minutes."

"Goddamnit, you're serious. You're fucking serious. This is no joke."

"No joke, Truck."

Turner shielded the luffing papers from the wind as he flipped pages, checking and cross-checking the data. A weight seemed to lift from his shoulders to be carried away with the gusts. "Son of a bitch. It looks possible on paper. I think it might work."

"It's got to work. Two hundred and seventy-two lives are at stake."

"If that 747 crashes and turns my ship into an inferno, we're talking thousands dead."

"Ten to one odds, Truck. Better than my usual ones. Besides, you face that risk every time you launch and recover planes. I don't have to remind you of that. Each cruise the statisticians pencil off one to two dozen men. Good men, but dead ones all the same. We live with that every day. A broken arrester cable cutting a deck hand in half. A cold shot on a catapult launch, a dead flight crew. And God knows the bets are off with a crash or a runaway piece of ordnance. How many died on the *Forrestal,* Truck, nearly three hundred? Forty-seven in the gun turret of the *Ohio.* Death sits on the shoulder of every deep-water sailor."

"I haven't lost a single man this cruise."

"Then you've been damn lucky."

"For the record, I have to protest the endangering of my ship and men in the strongest possible terms."

"So noted."

"Good. Then let's get going." Turner sprinted toward the gunmetal island that rose from the starboard expanse of the flight deck.

Gifford followed at his usual shambling pace, a stride he carried with him from the green hills of Tennessee. He never hurried these days. He'd found that death would always wait for you. Gifford paused under the shadow of the iron island. The SPY-1 fixed-array Aegis radar and the masts of the SPA-49 three-dimensional radar sprouted with the spars and pylons of the *Vinson's* electronic systems to grace the superstructure. An image passed briefly before his mind. The array reminded him of crosses atop a headstone, set in a freshly plowed and massive grave.

TransOceanic Airlines Flight 805

Greg Whitley worked his way down the aisle. He wanted to check the aft bulkhead for himself, so for the first time since the collision he relinquished the controls of his wounded craft to the copilot and left the cockpit. Running his hand over the metal barrier that held back disaster, he whispered another silent prayer of thanks to the Boeing engineers. Then he noticed a trace of metal dust on his fingertips. Tiny flecks sparkled under his flashlight. He pressed his ear to the wall. A disturbing sound greeted him. Faint, muffled by the engines and the roar of rushing air, it was nevertheless sufficient to send shivers down his back. A low groaning sounded as if the injured plane was suffering from its wounds. He had to listen closely to make sure he wasn't imagining the sound. There it was again, coming as the rising winds buffeted the Boeing. Whitley felt the partition buckle against his face. The bulkhead was flexing. Shorn of its normal structural support, without a tail to buttress it, the bulkhead twisted with the air forces. A sharp snap announced the failure of a rivet. The unnatural movement meant metal fatigue. The barrier was failing.

Hold together, Whitley begged. Hold together until I get you down. He collected himself before heading forward. Pausing at the aft galley, Whitley stopped for a cup of coffee. The flight attendants were busy piling the food cart with the tiny liquor bottles that are the bedrock of all airlines.

"Looks like the party started without me."

The senior attendant, a black woman with traces of gray in her hair, smiled as she craned her neck to check her charges. "This is the last of the booze, Captain."

"How's everyone doing?"

"Okay, I guess. This is my first crash, so I don't have anything to compare it with."

"Mine, too." He managed a smile.

The woman burst into tears. She dabbed her eyes with a wad of cocktail napkins. "I'm sorry. It's just that . . . I just realized I won't be there for my son's graduation. Did I tell you he's going to graduate this year?"

Whitley nodded. She'd told them all, many times. A single parent, she'd worked hard to send him through engineering school. "How about the passengers, Grace?" he gently prodded.

"Oh, yes." She crumpled the napkins into a tighter ball. "About half are drinking everything they can get their hands on. The other half suddenly got religion and won't touch a drop. A couple are angry. Everybody's scared, Captain. But they've got faith in you."

Great, he thought. I wish I had more of that myself.

"Will we be all right, Captain? Do we have a chance?"

"Grace, I could use some coffee. And maybe a sandwich?" Suddenly he realized he was hungry.

"Got lots of that. Nobody wants to be wide awake, and they're surely not eating. Not even the peanuts." She giggled nervously. She turned serious. "You didn't answer my question."

"Grace, my stomach's never been wrong. If it's hungry, things will be all right."

"You wouldn't bullshit an old lady?"

"Grace, you have my word on it. I give you my personal guarantee you'll see your son get his diploma."

She hugged him. "God bless you."

Whitley turned away with his coffee and sandwich before she discovered his own dubiety. Hastily he retreated to the cockpit, scarcely witnessing the penetrating eyes and patting hands that hit his back.

U.S. Navy Nuclear Carrier Carl Vinson, CVN-70, CVW-15, Mid-Pacific

"Permission to speak, sir." The yellow-shirted giant seemed to fill the flag plot by himself. Turner had moved the operation to the plotting room on the flag bridge. His sea cabin was too small, and the ship's captain's at port stateroom, while spacious, was decks below, too remote from the flight deck and the air boss.

"Speak, O'Brien." Turner acknowledged the chief master chief. Carrying the highest rating for a noncommissioned officer, the yellow giant had thirty years of carrier service dating back to the wooden-decked carriers. Chief master chief Aloysius O'Brien was the acknowledged expert on carrier flight decks.

"As you know, sir, this is my last cruise. I'm scheduled to retire in four days."

"Go on, Chief." The admiral planned a retirement party for their legend.

"Well, in thirty years—mostly good years, too—I ain't never heard nothing as stupid as this. I'd like to thank the admiral for this final screwing over."

"Fucking-A," Jackson grunted in admiration. This chief was one tough mother. A look from Gifford silenced him.

"I assume that approbation is directed at me, Chief"— Gifford stepped forward—"as I ordered this operation."

"I don't know nothing about no approbation, sir. But if the shoe fits, then wear it. I don't want to be remembered as the deck chief who thought his carrier was O'Hare Airport." Thirty years was thirty years. Chief O'Brien had earned his hash marks same as this vice-admiral who threatened his ship.

"I'm not bullshitting you, Chief. I think it can be done.

232

Besides, it's the only chance those passengers have. Sure, it may become a cluster fuck." Gifford paused for the dramatic effect of Jackson's vocabulary to set in. That Marine had a way with words, the spy-catcher reflected. "But we're trained to die fighting and killing our enemy. Why shouldn't we be prepared to die to save our friends? Now, I know you're short, Chief; so if you want out of this, you've got my permission."

"I ain't asking that, Admiral. Nobody heard me ask. Besides, you couldn't pull this off without me."

"Good. So what's really on your mind?"

O'Brien addressed Admiral Turner. "Admiral, you say the landing weight of this 747 is 450,000 pounds—about ten times the weight of a Whale." O'Brien used the nickname of the EA-3B Skywarrior, the heaviest plane on the *Vinson*.

Turner nodded. "He should have burned off all his fuel before he lands."

"Well, sir, the arresting cables only have a safety factor of four, maybe five times max built into them. And the number two and three wires have close to a hundred traps on them. They need to have the center sections changed."

"How long will that take?" Gifford asked.

"Twenty minutes, Admiral. I already got my crew working on it." O'Brien looked at the brass clock mounted on the bulkhead. "Should be done in ten more minutes." His face clouded.

"Problem?" Turner noted the concern.

"Admiral, when that baby hits those wires, the first three wires are going to snap like rotten rope. I seen too many men cut in half by flailing wires. I don't want to see that happen to my last crew."

All the men in that crowded room knew that fifty thousand pounds was the maximum designed into the system— even by adjusting the sheaves and blocks that threaded the wire cable below decks to the huge arresting engines that absorbed the impact of the landing planes. Snapping wires could kill in the blink of an eye.

"I don't want nobody topside but me and the LSO, sir. I can handle the system myself. Don't need no green shirts either. Keep them off the catwalks, too, until after the plane halts or goes over the side. That's if it don't 'mishap' and fireball into the island. And if I eat a wire, think of all the retirement pay the navy will save."

"Granted. Anything else?"

"Yes, sir. To stop that mother we're going to need everything plus our jockstraps. I'd recommend raising the crash barricade between the three and four wires." O'Brien tapped the blueprint of the *Vinson*'s flight deck. His grease-caked finger thumbed the location of the reinforced nylon net that could be strung from retractable arms set into the deck. "And I'd string our spare safety net forward of the island."

"How would you do that, Chief?" Gifford was glad this man was here.

"Use Tillie, sir."

"Tillie?" Asher looked puzzled.

"Tillie, Mr. Lod." Turner pointed out the cabin portlight to a gangly crane located beneath them and aft of the superstructure. Painted yellow like all the diesel tractors, its boom overlooked the deck with an exalted air. "She's capable of lifting any aircraft on this ship."

"But not a 747," Asher added to cover his astonishment. Behind Tillie, the Grumman Greyhound that he'd arrived on was disappearing down an elevator with wings folded.

"No." The Chief glared down at this foreigner. "But she'll hold another safety net secured forward of the island. That'll give us six barriers. That might give us the edge. And one last thing."

"Yes, Chief?" Turner knew the request was only a formality. Chief O'Brien would do it anyway.

"Sir"—the yellow mass drew up to full height—"I was on the *Forrestal* when she had her mishap. I'd suggest you place the tractors around the island, sort of like a barricade. And put the fire trucks forward of the island to protect them.

That way they'll still be there if they're needed for a fire. I learned that lesson the hard way. And keep the gawkers and picture takers belowdecks. Less of them'll get killed."

"Sounds good, Chief. Better get on it."

"Aye, aye, sir." O'Brien touched his baseball cap and shouldered his way out of the cabin.

"Good man, O'Brien." Gifford watched the saffron mountain recede.

"They're all good men here," Turner responded. He turned to the air boss. "Tom, how far is the bird?"

"Just got an update from the miniboss, sir. Two hundred nautical miles and closing off our bow. We'll need to turn into the wind and make a high-speed run when she starts her landing pattern. With the forty-knot winds over the bow and ship speed of thirty knots, the apparent wind should be about seventy knots."

"If he comes in at 150 knots, then his landing speed will be eighty knots, right, Tom?" Gifford asked.

"Yes, sir. O'Brien's men are cribbing up the arresting wires to six feet. If the 747 can come in nose up, the wires should miss his nose gear and hit his main landing gear above the wheels. The computer data states they'll withstand the stress. The Boeing has four sets of four wheels each under the fuselage."

"How about a guidance system to bring him in?"

"SPN-43 radar to control him during his landing pattern." The air boss scratched his crewcut. "You know that the pilot—Whitley's his name—was a carrier pilot?"

Gifford nodded. "Flew A-6s."

The air boss grimaced. "Intruders are easy to land. Good visibility with those forward seats and the big cockpit bubble. Wish he had some experience with Whales."

"No such luck."

The air boss shrugged. "I pulled his navy flight record. This Whitley was a competent pilot. Good head work. Nothing flashy. Too bad he's in a Boeing 747, because he's familiar with the Fresnel system."

"Fresnel system?" This time Owen appeared puzzled.

The air boss looked down at the seated programmer. Unaccustomed to questions from unknowns, he prepared to lash away at this interruption. Happily, he made the connection between this bookish-looking character and the vice-admiral standing next to him. "Ah, yes." The air boss recovered with lightning speed. "Mr. . . ."

"Owen," Admiral Gifford answered, confirming the air boss's worst fears.

"Yes, Mr. Owen. The Fresnel system is a landing-light control that aligns the airplane's position relative to the carrier and projects it onto a wide screen for the pilot's visual reference. A large yellow ball of light shows up next to another row of lights. Green row—right on. Just keep your yellow light level with the green row. Red is too low. The pilot adjusts his plane relative to the yellow ball. Dangerously low in the approach and the yellow light changes to red. Red is dead. We call it flying the meatball. All navy carrier-base planes have the system."

"And the 747 doesn't?" Owen enjoyed his mysterious rank.

"Absolutely not."

"Does this landing system utilize a laser projection system?"

"Yes."

Owen turned to Gifford. "Sir, the 747 has a landing light mounted on the nose wheel assembly as well as lights on the wings. When I was in the air force we experimented with a similar landing system. Aiming the laser at the nose light, we might be able to get it to bounce back onto the ship's reference panel."

"You think you could?" The air boss saw the possibility, and it excited him.

"Worth a try." Owen shrugged. "Can I look at the Fresnel system, Admiral?"

"Sounds good to me, Curtis. Go for it. Asher, you and the good doctors had better brief the medical department."

The room emptied. Jackson, receptive as ever, positioned himself outside the sea cabin. A quietness settled over the gray-painted room.

"Almost wish our navy wasn't dry," Gifford quipped. "Some Kentucky sipping whiskey would sure be good right about now."

"Wild Turkey, if I recall, Henry."

"Truck, I'm touched that you remember." Gifford looked around. "Ever notice how it always gets quiet before a big blow?"

"This is the part I hate the most."

"When this is over, Truck—however it works out—I'd be proud to buy you a round of Wild Turkey."

"You owe me a whole bottle, Henry."

"It'd be my pleasure." The smooth southern tones belied the emotions that filled the cabin. The old school chums had patched up their differences. Now only the mission mattered. "Come on." Gifford's arm rested on his friend's shoulder. "Let's give Whitley the good news. He doesn't have to land in the ocean."

"You didn't tell him he's about to be the first pilot to try to land a Boeing 747 on an aircraft carrier?"

"Hell, no. Didn't want to make him nervous."

"You are a brass-plated son of a bitch."

"That I am, Truck. That I am."

CHAPTER

20

TransOceanic Airlines Flight 805

"God, Captain. I feel responsible for all this. If I hadn't been up here . . . if I hadn't fallen over your back, you might have evaded that plane." Ames Cotter wrung his hands, aghast at the prospect of having caused this accident.

"Forget it, Doc."

"I can't. I . . ." Doctor Cotter continued until a flight attendant stuck her head through the flight deck door.

"Doctor, they need you back there. Your patient seems worse."

Cotter hurried off.

"Ann." Whitley stopped the attendant. "Thanks for getting him out of here. How's she doing?"

"Not good."

"And the rest of the passengers?"

"Better than you'd expect, considering our circumstances."

"TOA Flight 805. Come in, TOA 805. Do you read me?" The radio voice was different from the Hawkeye that kept up a constant patter. Mainly for their morale, Whitley imagined.

"That you, Admiral Gifford?" Whitley caught the Tennessean accent.

"Yes, sir, Greg. How's it going?"

"Okay, but the aft pressure bulkhead is ready to blow at any minute."

"Roger that. You're 160 nautical miles west of *Vinson.* She's got you on her radar. You should be picking her up on yours now."

The copilot hunched forward and tapped the green blip on his radar screen. Off to one side the E-2 AWACS represented a smaller dot of light. Otherwise the screen was empty.

"Roger, Admiral. We've got CVA-70 due east."

"Good. We compute your airspeed at 170 knots."

"Roger. She gets squirrely below 170. Much faster and the bulkhead'll go for sure."

"Okay, Greg. The *Vinson* is closing on you at thirty-two knots. Head winds are forty knots. That puts your ETA about thirty minutes from now. In fifteen minutes the *Vinson* will turn into the wind and line up directly with your flight path. Follow that on your radar. She'll light up her deck. When you see that, start your gradual descent. *Vinson* will adjust to retrieve you on Mom's 270."

"What?"

"We're going to recover you on the *Vinson.* The seas are too rough to ditch."

The copilot and flight engineer exchanged puzzled looks. Whitley stared at the speaker, unable to believe his ears. "Ah, Admiral, you do know this is a Boeing 747, don't you?"

"Roger, Greg. It can be done. It's classified, so don't let word get around, but the navy's been doing it," Gifford lied.

"When was this, Admiral?"

"Recently, son. I'm not at liberty to discuss all the details."

"With all due respect, sir, I think you're full of shit."

"It doesn't matter what you believe, Captain Whitley.

The seas are mounting to thirty-foot waves. You've flown into the middle of a storm. Try to ditch in this rough water and you'll break apart like an overripe melon. Set this baby down on the *Vinson* and nobody even gets his feet wet."

Surges of relief mixed with doubt set Whitley awash. Could they do this? It was unbelievable.

"Well, I need your answer now." Gifford sensed the opening and pressed home his attack. A fleeting moment of self-doubt surfaced. You'd better be right, it whispered. Yes, he answered it. Yes, goddamnit, I'd better be right. And you, you slimy piece of shit, will be there to remind me if I'm wrong. The mistrust slipped back into the recesses of his mind to wait. "The *Carl Vinson* is prepared to recover your ship, but they need to begin maneuvering into position, since you've got limited controls. The air boss is standing by with the LSO. Of course, if you'd prefer to ditch, I'd like to know so I can grab some shuteye. It's been a long day for me, too."

"Are you fucking with me?" Whitley swore, but he kept his microphone button off. "What is this? Is this guy crazy?"

"Easy, Greg," the copilot cautioned. "Look, he's an admiral, isn't he? Maybe he knows something we don't. After all, it's been five years since you got out of the navy."

"What do you think?" Whitley asked his navigator.

"Count me out of this decision, Captain. I'm air force. I don't know a thing about carriers. But those waves look bad." The man pointed out the window to the waves that fractured the darkening sea. Errant rays from the setting sun broke through the clouds to catch the whitecaps and set them afire, creating a scene reminiscent of a flaming cauldron. The storm was creating its own hell.

"All right, Admiral. I'm listening." Whitley didn't want to ditch.

"Good. I'm going to put the air boss on."

"Captain Whitley." The matter-of-fact voice of the *Vinson*'s air controller entered the flight crew's headphones.

"I need to know your flight status and the degree of maneuverability of the plane."

"About ten degrees pitch, nose up, nose down. No yaw. No roll."

"You've tried flying with the throttles?"

"Roger. Won't work. Too much'll put us into a spin."

"Roger that. Looks like Mom will have to line you up for the groove."

"Yes, sir. I've only got one try. Once I commit to landing and start my descent, I can't pull up for another go-round." Whitley pushed the desperation from his thoughts. No wave-offs.

"You just follow my instructions and you'll add another nice pass to your record."

Whitley remembered his carrier landings. A nice pass was the highest accolade. It also meant a safe landing. Too high, you missed the arresting wires and became a bolter. Too low and you smashed to pieces against the armored stern of the carrier—that was a ramp strike. Off the center line of the canted deck and you died in a fireball—the navy labeled that a mishap. Do it right and you survived; anything else and you died.

"Hold on, Whitley." The air boss's voice was muffled as he turned to issue a command. "You just keep coming. We've rigged up a Fresnel landing system for you so you should feel right at home. Do you still remember how to fly the meatball?"

"Aye, aye. You don't forget that. But how is it going to work?"

"We'll bounce lasers off your nose and wing lights. That requires lowering your landing gear a little early. Can you handle that?"

"We'll see. Hope it doesn't produce too much drag."

"Good. Another thing. I'm going to bring you down on the number one wire. We need 'em all to stop you. It's imperative, repeat imperative, that you keep your nose wheel up. Otherwise you're liable to slam into the deck. Got that?"

"Roger. Do you think it'll work?" Whitley had to ask.

"Captain, if you do exactly what I say and remember your carrier training, I'll get you down. That's my job."

"But do you think the traps will stop this plane once we get down?"

"Son"—Gifford came on the line—"Admiral Turner will stop your plane even if he has to use his teeth."

"I hope to God you're right, Admiral."

The air boss returned. "Twenty minutes to go, Whitley. Better have your crew secure for a crash landing. Begin your descent now. Come down to eight thousand feet. I'm going to light up the deck. You should see us in another ten minutes. Sing out when you do, then I'll transfer you to the LSO for him to talk you in."

"Roger, *Vinson*. Will do." Whitley punched the flight attendant call button.

Grace appeared, looking more worn. "The passengers are becoming frayed, Captain. A couple are really drunk. Somebody got hold of some Valium—he's passing it out. It's this waiting and uncertainty."

"Well, tell 'em the waiting's over, Grace. We'll be landing in twenty minutes."

"That's a bad joke, Captain."

"No joke. We're going to land on the USS *Carl Vinson*, one of our nuclear carriers in the Pacific."

Grace looked at the others for confirmation. The copilot and the flight engineer nodded grimly. She closed her gaping mouth. Years of training took over. "Prepare for a crash landing?"

"Right, Grace. Collect all eyeglasses, pens, pencils. Anything that can become a dangerous missile. We're going to stop faster than anything you'd imagine possible." He thought for a minute, parsing his memories of carrier landings. "And we need to modify the basic knee-hugger."

He referred to the safety technique of bending over to clasp one's knees during a crash landing. "Instruct the passengers to place their feet up against the back of the seat in front of them. Then head down and grasp the legs. When we land, tell them to push against that seat back with their legs. As hard as they can."

"And kiss their asses good-bye," the flight engineer added.

Grace shot him a withering look. "That was tasteless. How will they know when to kick with their legs?"

Whitley curled his lip into a ghastly smile. "They'll know, Grace, when their faces feel like they're leaping forward to the first-class lavatory. And the caps pop off their teeth. Believe me, they'll know."

"I can't tell them that."

"I'll hit the no smoking button, Grace," the engineer volunteered, "just before we touch down."

"Good. You've redeemed yourself." She straightened her blouse and ran her hand over her hair. A tear moistened her eye, but she wiped it away quickly. "We'll have the cabin ready, Captain." The answer was impassive. Her eyes, clear and penetrating now, searched out each of their faces. "Good luck." The words came slowly. She was gone before they could reply.

"There she is! *Vinson* dead ahead!" the copilot shouted.

U.S. Navy Nuclear Carrier Carl Vinson, CVN-70

"Got her on visual." The LSO passed his starlight binoculars to Admiral Turner. "Directly off the stern. Range ten miles and closing." He tapped his earphones. "Bearing ninety-five degrees magnetic."

"I see him." Turner located the greenish dot on the electronically enhanced screen. Five degrees off the stern. He added ten degrees for the canted deck. "Come right fifteen degrees," he barked into his headset. That would line them up with the Boeing.

"Right rudder fifteen degrees, aye." The XO passed the command to the yeoman at the helm.

"Coming right to course 285, aye." The seaman laid on the small steering wheel in the navigation bridge. The command translated below decks to steering control. With a finger flick of the wheel, ninety-one and a half tons of steel pushed into a new course.

Truck dropped the glasses and peered into the swirling blackness. His unaided eyes saw only the roiling vortex. Turner shivered as salt spray lashed the two men in the landing control station. Both men shouted over the wind.

"Tell him to drop his gear and turn on his landing lights. We need to focus the laser," the LSO hollered into his boom mike. Beside him Curtis Owen and three specialists tuned the laser landing system on the speck.

Tiny pinpoints of light flared in the night scopes. "He's got his lights on," Curtis yelled into the LCO's ear as his fingers rolled the built-in trackball, sending coordinates into the landing control. A portable keyboard interfaced with the Fresnel's computer balanced on his soaked knees. The computer beeped. "Got him! Got him!"

"Laser lock! Tracking!" A technician took over the landing controls. "LSO, we've got him on the meatball." His finger pointed to a rain-spattered monitor, a duplicate setup that mirrored the massive projection system hung off the stern of the carrier.

The men crowded around the screen. A yellow ball wavered high above a row of green lights. The ball was centered over the string of greens. The screen occupied an inset facing the ship's stern to enable the LSO to watch his landing charges with one eye on the Fresnel landing screen.

The LSO picked up his pickle switch with his right hand and lifted it over his head. The others stepped back. It was his show now.

"You won't need that." Turner pointed to the pickle. "He's only got one shot at landing."

"I know, Admiral, but I'd feel naked without it. Force of habit, I guess."

The Fresnel screen went blank.

"Goddamnit! What's the matter?"

"Sorry, LSO. Wiring got disconnected." Two sailors dived to their knees to adjust the cables entering the black box.

The meatball with its green companions flared onto the screen.

"Good. Keep it going. TOA, TOA, this is LSO, *Vinson*. Do you read me?"

"Roger, LSO," the headpiece crackled. "Picked you up on visual a minute ago. Now we're back in the clouds. But you look good on radar."

"I've got you, TOA. You're too high. Bring her down another twelve hundred feet."

"Roger."

The yellow sphere descended to settle in line with the green balls.

"Hold it, TOA. That's good. You're right in the groove. Hold it there."

"Roger, will try. There's some turbulence at this level."

"Doing good. Doing good. Keep her steady."

Admiral Turner tore his eyes away from the screen to look down the length of his ship. A vast highway shimmered in the night. Guidance lights set into the deck embellished the platform like a movie marquee. Strobes fired away at unnamed clouds and sheets of rain, spiraling red warning lights threw ruby loops against the darkness, and amber bulbs lined the safety nets.

What a sight, he thought. Unbelievable. Better than any movie. If there was a Russian sub tailing them, they would get sunburn through their periscope. Turner followed the broad white stripes painted down the deck. The parallel lines beckoned into the blackness like road paint to the River Styx.

A red-trimmed MD-3A diesel whizzed past, its white streak the only movement on this steel wasteland. True to his word, Chief O'Brien had drawn the tractors in a protective circle about the island. Now he was moving the fire trucks behind the barricade. The yellow giant was everywhere, cursing, kicking, cajoling with a ferocity that grew with the storm. He skidded up beside the landing control astride a tractor.

O'Brien squinted off the stern. "How many minutes, sir?"

"Ten, maybe twelve."

"We're ready for her, Admiral. Tillie's in place." He gestured to the extra safety net draped from the lifting crane. "Don't think she likes it. Tillie thinks she's too good to catch a runaway plane." O'Brien guffawed at his humor, then hawked a glob of phlegm onto the deck. It obliterated a set of padeyes. "Direct hit."

"Chief, may I ask you a personal question?" Admiral Gifford spoke for the first time. He'd kept out of the way and, since he had nothing to add, kept silent. Now, as he watched this yellow dynamo of grease and diesel fumes, he had to ask.

"Shoot, sir." O'Brien eyed him reservedly. Top brass made all navy chiefs suspicious. Admirals naturally interfered with the chief petty officers' running of their navy. Everyone knew that. The more gold they carried on their shoulders, the more they needed adult guidance.

"Do you ever bathe, Chief?"

"Not at sea, sir. It interferes with my ambience." O'Brien saluted smartly as he accelerated away to the island.

"Ask a stupid question, get a stupid answer," Henry Clay said.

"We'd better head to the battle aid station, Henry,"

Turner suggested. "It's armored, and I've had the communications boys set it up as a forward command post."

The two men sprinted across the rolling deck just as flight 805 broke out of the clouds.

Below decks, Christopher and Yael stole a moment for themselves. She'd found him rechecking his precious vials of antiserum for the fourth time. Gently she led him by the hand to a secluded corner. He followed, confused until her lips sought his.

"Wait, wait," he mumbled into her mouth. "I've got to—"

"Enough," she scolded him. "You've done all you can. We are ready. The rest is up to God. Now we must wait and pray."

"You're right. You're always right." He squeezed her against him. Several corpsmen cast envious glances as they hurried past. "I wonder if we could borrow a bunk from some sailor." His fingers crept over her blouse.

"Excuse me, Doctor." It was the ship's surgeon. He wore a baggy white chemical warfare suit that gave him the resemblance of the Pillsbury Doughboy. "Sorry to interrupt, but they want you to do a walk-through from here to the flight deck. To check on the isolation of the spaces."

"I don't know anything about isolating ship's spaces," Maddox protested, reluctant to release Yael.

"I know that," the surgeon persisted. "We'd all rather do what you're doing now. But I've got my orders."

"I'll go with you." Yael smiled at him. He looked like a small boy who'd just dropped his ice cream cone. "Soon this will be over. Maybe we can get some fresh air. It's so stuffy in here."

They walked hand in hand through the maze of metal corridors, guided by the red tape arrows and lighted battle lanterns that marked the way. There was no other exit. Watertight doors sealed all other passages. The *Vinson* was secured at general quarters. Climbing the steps, they came to the battle aid station. People filled the space beyond its design.

"Dr. Ivanov and Dr. Maddox." Gifford looked up from a screen. "Out for an evening stroll?"

"Our part's complete, Admiral. The ship's physicians and corpsmen have the vaccine. The route down to sick bay is sealed if they come through here. All the medical personnel have rubberized Tyvek anticontamination suits."

"Good. You and Dr. Ivanov had better go below. The shit'll hit the fan in about ten minutes." Gifford turned back to Admiral Turner. That officer connected his headset to a power pack that allowed him mobility.

"I'm going forward of the island with O'Brien, Henry. Got a better view outside. You watch the show from here." Turner stepped over the watertight sill and hopped aboard the chief's fire truck before Gifford could protest. The flat diesel rumbled off.

Gifford turned back to the radar scope and the infrared TV that followed the Boeing's approach. He failed to see the two physicians slip out onto the flight deck.

"God Almighty! There she is!" Captain Whitley shouted as the clouds parted at three thousand feet. The *Carl Vinson* glistened in the black water. A diamond in the rough, their only hope seemed minuscule. Bravely its strobes and deck lights flashed through unfolding veils of rain.

"She looks so small," his copilot said, voicing his fears.

"Yeah, less than six times our length. But it'll have to do. What's our airspeed?"

"It's 155 knots."

Whitley's mind replayed his carrier experience, but he could find no useful information. Nothing on the Boeing 747's massive flight deck remotely resembled the crammed cockpit of an A-6 Intruder. The yoke, the pedals, the look and feel of everything was different. This marvel of modern technology from the Boeing Company could take off, fly, and land by itself using its sophisticated flight computers. Unhappily, he had no way of programming the plane to land on a moving aircraft carrier. It was up to him, he realized, and his past training was useless.

"On visual. One and a half miles out. Twenty-eight hundred feet. You're in the groove. Airspeed one-five-five knots," the LCO's voice intruded, pulling him back to reality. "Cut back to 150 knots."

"Can't do it just yet. She gets too squirrely at 150. I'm going to wait until we close to within one thousand feet before cutting back."

"Roger, imperative you land at 150. Do you copy?"

"I understand. Listen, a 747 can get its stall speed down to 120, maybe 110 knots, but this baby's got no tail. I can't keep her in the air below 150."

"Shit. Okay, one mile out. You should see the meatball anytime."

"There it is. I see it! By God, I see it!" Greg exclaimed.

The *Vinson* grew before them. The squared-off stern of the carrier expanded into his window. A wide horizontal cutout in the flat steel where AIM tested jet engines smiled slyly at him as if to say: I'm reinforced with four-inch steel plate to protect me from pilot error, from "mishaps."

Whitley saw that the skipper was pouring on the coals to help him land. Foamy wake boiled behind the *Vinson*, spreading out into phosphorescent streamers that glowed across the dark sea, riding the waves into oblivion. The faster the carrier moved into the wind, the less disparity in speed when he touched down. He prayed for the impossible—a ship that could sail at 150 knots. Then he could hover over the deck, cut off his engines, and simply fall onto the ship. No such luck.

"Half mile out," the LSO droned.

The ship grew into more detail amid the low clouds. Whitley remembered it all: the tiered island, rising from starboard and sprouting pylons and radar arrays like a schizophrenic's Erector Set; the retractable antennae spreading from the ship's sides like insect feelers; the catwalks surrounding the flight deck with its jumble of fire hoses and equipment contrasting with the emptiness of the deck. And off the port side, just forward of the stern, the Fresnel landing system shimmered at him. Jutting out on its own shelf, the movie screen-sized display flashed a yellow meatball wavering a hairsbreadth above a row of green lights.

Flying the meatball again. He could hardly believe it.

"One thousand feet out," the headphone barked, "155 knots. Too fast! Cut back to 150."

"Cutting back now." Whitley eased back on the four throttles, all the while mesmerized by the landing display. The ghostly circles of light danced in his mind. The airspeed indicator settled at 150 knots. The plane wobbled unsteadily.

A gust of wind slapped the Boeing down.

The meatball dropped below the green row. Simultaneously the green lights changed to yellow and then to red warning lights as the 747 plunged to a collision course on a line below the *Vinson*'s flight deck.

"Too low, TOA! Pull up! Pull up!" The LSO hit his pickle switch instinctively. The entire display changed to flashing red lights.

Whitley pulled back hard on the yoke. Nothing happened.

"Pull up, TOA! You're too low!"

"I can't!" Whitley threw his weight against the controls. "It won't respond. It won't come up!"

The flashing lights screamed a wordless warning. The flight engineer punched the no smoking button. The opening in the *Vinson*'s stern threatened to swallow them.

Ramp strike. The vision flared in Whitley's mind. Fear crystallized the images before him, sharpening the details. The deck of the carrier swelled upward. White-painted shackles to the four arresting wires crossed the painted lines to converge at the bow. A gigantic number seventy was inscribed on the foredeck. His eyes caught even rows of padeye fasteners inset across the expanse of nonskid coating —each a tiny cross, all precisely aligned like graves in a cemetery.

We're going to crash into the stern! Ramp strike! Ramp strike! his mind screamed. He strained against the steering column. "Can't pull her up," Whitley groaned over his effort.

Admiral Turner braced against the fire truck. Alone except for Chief O'Brien, he watched in horror from the kraal of tractors.

The blue-and-green painted nose of the 747 swelled menacingly off the stern. Sleek and polished, the commercial airliner roared while it overtook the *Vinson*. Turner's headset monitored the desperate conversation.

"My God, he's too low!" Turner cursed. "All engines stop!" he screamed into his microphone.

"All engines stop, aye," came the instantaneous reply.

Energy from the two Westinghouse A4W nuclear reactors to the four geared steam turbines drove four massive propellers at 280,000 shaft horsepower, moving the keel over thirty knots. On Turner's command, exhaust valves bypassed steam away from the turbine shafts. The blades stopped.

Turner toppled backward as the *Carl Vinson* slowed to twenty-five knots.

Two things happened. TOA 805 overshot its line of death as the relative speed and distance from the aircraft carrier dropped. Its nose crossed the stern. All four sets of landing wheel trucks, designed to touch down in sequence, struck the *Vinson*'s deck inches from the end of the runway. Smoking rubber trailed behind the tires as they bit into the nonskid. The nose wheel, last to contact, broke off on impact. Slowing the ship had allowed the plane to reach the flight deck. But now the Boeing hit the first arresting wire at five knots faster than expected.

Number one's three-inch wire rope caught the forward landing gear above the tires. Designed with a maximum safety factor of four times the heaviest navy plane, the wire was snapped by the gigantic 747 like sewing thread. With an earsplitting twang the cable parted as its monumental blocks and sheaves sent tortured vibrations throughout the body of the ship.

Sparks, aluminum chunks, and burning titanium fragments flew into the night. Wire ends whipsawed across the deck with lightning speed, igniting the fuel-soaked flight deck into blazing streaks.

The Boeing bullied its way through the number two and three arresting wires in similar fashion. More sound and fury filled the night. Broken wires lashed across an empty deck, seeking and destroying equipment but no humans. Chief O'Brien's plan was saving lives.

Within the cockpit, Captain Whitley and his crew surged forward as the plane decelerated. He and his copilot jammed their feet against the brake pedals. Helplessly they watched their plane fighting to break loose. Whitley threw his engines into reverse. Headphones ripped from their heads and shattered against the windows. The flight engineer's seatbelt snapped, and he flew into the back of the copilot's seat. Knocked unconscious, the force held him in midair against the seat back. More metallic dust, pencils, and water droplets from the ruptured air conditioning lines rolled in a cloud over the men.

The starboard landing gear collapsed as the arresting wires sheared through the wheel struts. Like splintered bone protruding from an amputated stump, the twisted metal ends gouged a furrow in the armored deck. Flight 805 slewed to the right, the starboard wing pointing at the carrier's island like a medieval lance.

The nylon crash barrier, raised from the deck on its retractable arms, caught the 747 and wrapped across the plane's nose before tearing away. Uncurtained and out of control, the Boeing skidded across the deck. Only the fourth arresting wire and the second barricade held by Tillie remained. Beyond, the dark sea beckoned.

Christopher and Yael had strolled along the starboard catwalk as they sought a moment alone. The incoming 747 caught them by surprise. Both froze as the Boeing struck the flight deck.

"Run," he urged her as they scrambled back toward the combat aid station.

"Chris, it's closed!"

The reinforced metal door was sealed. General quarters required it be locked until further orders. Shrapnel from the plane struck the door.

"Look out!" Chris knocked her to the catwalk deck as the fractured number two cable lashed over their heads.

The cable cut into the side of a utility crane. Amid a shower of sparks the wounded piece of machinery toppled into the catwalk. Hot metal slivers rained over their backs while they dodged the crashing lift.

"Yael, the safety nets! It's our only chance!"

"I'm caught!" Yael struggled with her shirt. A hook from a reel of fire hose held the fabric.

Maddox pulled her free.

They dived into the wire baskets just as the crane obliterated the spot where they had been. Suspended from pipe framing over the side of the carrier, they dangled in the air. Thin mesh held them eighty feet above the waterline. Phosphorescent lights along the ship's wake reached upward, and spray from the waves soaked them.

A shadow passed overhead. The Boeing's wingtip crossed them to drive into the side of the *Vinson*'s superstructure. The wing sank into the armored island at the 07 level, four stories above the flight deck. The attack carried away the pilot landing aid television camera and its entire turret. The Boeing's wing sheared off with a sickening snap, redirecting the airliner back down the center of the landing strip.

The wingtip hung for a moment, embedded in the side of the island, before the ship's roll tore it loose. It crashed across the deck to plunge over the side, dragging its severed cables and hydraulic lines overboard.

The falling lines carried away the tubular supports for the safety netting. The nets collapsed.

"Chris!"

Maddox watched Yael roll over the side of the basket. His hand shot out, locking on her wrist as she fell. Her momentum pulled him along. His left hand raked over the metal netting as they slid down the flapping mesh. Below the patient sea waited.

His fingers locked around a wire loop.

Together the two of them fluttered in midair. Battered by the storm, they twisted while his fingers held on. As the *Vinson* moved through ten-second-long side-to-side rolls Chris and Yael were flattened against the side of the ship only to be cast out into the air as the carrier heeled.

"Chris, let me go!"

"No!"

"Please! Save yourself!" she pleaded with him. A forty-foot wave snatched at her feet, threatening to carry her away. Its force swung her aft, yet Maddox held on.

"I'm not letting go," he snarled through clenched teeth. "Not this time."

"Let go!" She fought him, her free hand flailing at the air, desperately trying to save the man she loved even though it meant losing her own life.

"No. Not ever!" His right hand tightened its death hold on her wrist.

The wire rope sawed into the fingers of his other hand as they swayed in the storm.

* * *

Topside, Admiral Turner scrambled to his feet. He and Chief O'Brien watched the 747 fighting to escape the traps they'd set for her. The Boeing was winning.

"Hold her, you mother," the chief petty officer ordered his rigging.

The plane struck the fourth wire. The wire held, and the airplane slowed as the arresting hydraulics played out against this 450,000-pound catch. Then the center section, worn and not replaced after one hundred traps, failed. First one strand, then another parted under the load. The cable unraveled with a shot. Freed, TOA 805 surged forward.

"Come on, Tillie!" O'Brien shouted. He was pounding Admiral Turner's shoulder.

The NS-50 aircraft crane held her ground against the onrushing behemoth. Holding the spare crash barrier, it waited like a matador. The 747 collided with the remaining obstacle.

Weakened, its energy bled off by the preceding traps, the Boeing slid into the netting. Almost as if in slow motion, the crane and the plane battled. Tillie gave inch by inch, but the runaway plane was weakening.

"She's doing it! She's fucking doing it!" O'Brien nearly choked on his plug of tobacco.

The Boeing slowed to a crawl.

Just then a rogue wave hit the carrier's starboard quarter. The massive wall of water lifted the *Vinson* aft of the island. The bow dug into a breaking wave that broached the flight deck. Bulling its way into the leading wave, the carrier heeled twenty degrees to port. Port shoulder into the wave, the flight deck tipped perilously.

The Boeing's nose swung away from the center line as it slid toward the edge of the flight deck. Tillie, locked in place, held her net, but the airplane headed away across the beam of the barrier. Without a starboard wing or landing gear to catch on the netting, the Boeing pivoted above the barricade to point over the ship's side.

* * *

Inside the cockpit Greg Whitley watched in horror as the flight deck slipped away. His hands gripped a useless yoke while his feet, under constant pressure, threatened to meld with the brake pedals. Black ocean encroached beneath his window, replacing the steel deck with alarming swiftness. The plane's nose swung further.

"We're going over the side!" he moaned.

"Holy Mary, Mother of God, pray for us now in our moment of need. . . ." the plane's copilot recited continuously. "Holy Mary, Mother of God . . ." The words droned on, mixing with an eerie grating of metal.

The bulbous nose of the 747 crossed the edge, and its wide body followed to sway above disaster.

"She's breaking off to port!" Turner screamed over the wind. "Going over the edge!"

"You fat-bodied bitch, you're not doing that to me!" O'Brien's hand released the hand brake on his diesel tractor. The red-and-white-rimmed truck leapt forward. It stood barely three feet off the deck yet carried enough foam to cover a burning navy fighter.

"Get off, that's an order!" Admiral Turner shouted into the chief's ear as he jerked the man's yellow vest.

The startled noncom tumbled out of the rolling MD-3A. O'Brien hit the deck and pitched onto his back in time to see the diesel-powered tractor speed off with Admiral Turner in his seat. "Goddamnit, come back . . . sir!" he swore into the storm.

Skidding across the heeling deck, Turner aimed the tractor at the underbelly of the swaying 747. His foot smashed down on the accelerator. The red and white missile sped for the threatened Boeing.

Another roll lifted the plane's remaining wing above the catwalk; then the whole aircraft started to slide, nose first, over the edge. Legs thrashing like an overturned land crab, Chief O'Brien righted himself and scrambled to his knees.

The sight of the foundering plane greeted him. The chief crossed himself.

The plane slipped over the rim of the flight deck.

Turner and the speeding tractor rocketed off the landing deck, hurtling through the air to wedge between the catwalk and the underside of the 747's wing just as the airfoil slammed down. The roll of the flight deck crushed the tractor beneath the wing. The shattered vehicle wedged between the Boeing and a heavy crane mounted on the catwalk. Pinioned, the plane ceased its fall.

Collision alarms and klaxon horns shattered the night as antlike lines of rescuers streamed across the flight deck to catch passengers as they tumbled down inboard escape shutes. The Tyvek-suited crewmen led dazed passengers away to isolation. Some travelers wept, a few complained, but most moved, slack-jawed and uncomprehending, in the arms of their alienlike deliverers.

Captain Whitley was the last to leave his plane. He stood aside as two corpsmen eased Sally Ericson onto a stretcher. The senior medical officer, a general surgeon, knelt beside the stretcher. He examined her and looked up into the haggard face of Dr. Ames Cotter.

"She's dead, sir."

"Yes." He sighed. "I know." Head down, Cotter shuffled behind the litter as it moved away.

Admiral Gifford and his steadfast shadow, Jackson, ran to the site. The two men worked their way around the massive plane. Already damage-control parties were hosing down the flames on the deck and lashing cables to the Boeing. Tillie strode off carrying a twisted plate like a praying mantis balancing a leaf.

"Goddamn, sir. It's down. And almost in one piece. I never would have believed it."

"It is unbelievable, Jackson. Where's Truck? He'll get another star for tonight's work if I have to give him mine." Gifford searched the crowded deck. A grin spread across his face. "And I owe him a bottle of Wild Turkey. Look, there's Chief O'Brien. He ought to be proud of himself. O'Brien, where's Admiral Turner? I thought he was with you."

"Under there, sir." O'Brien stood in the shadow of the nose, head bowed as he gazed at the carcass of his fire truck. A pool of blood mixed with diesel fuel from the tractor's ruptured fuel tank. Lifeblood of man and machine bled onto the nonskid. The blood shifted, running toward his scuffed deck boots as the ship heeled. O'Brien stepped back to avoid the flow.

Henry Clay's grin faded. "What happened?"

"He took my goddamn tractor and jammed it under this mother's belly to keep it from dumping into the drink. Pulled me out and just took off." O'Brien shook his head. "But he wasn't fast enough to get himself out, sir." The chief straightened up, saluted the wreck, and stormed off, yelling at a repair crew that fell close enough across his bow to see the tears in his eyes.

"This had damn well better be worth it," Gifford railed at the night. "He was a good man, and he didn't deserve to die like this. Fanatics and science—the combination always adds up to terrible mischief." The admiral's hand slapped against the belly of the 747. "Dr. Maddox's antiserum better be all he says it is."

Jackson's eyes widened. "The docs! They were outside when we went to GQ. I never saw them come back. They must've been on the deck when the Boeing came down."

"Damnation! Start a search!"

In the darkness of the superstructure the objects of the admiral's concern dangled in the shadows, desperately fighting for their lives. Wave after wave struck Yael. Her body spun, and Christopher's grip again hammered against the ship. Blow after blow weakened his hold on her, each injury chipping away at his strength while his mind fought to bolster his failing tendons. He willed his hand to fuse with her wrist. Sweat covered his face and neck, mixing with the salt spray and rain as he battled his body's weakness as well as the storm. Eyes locked on her eyes, he struggled to keep his dreadful memories suppressed. His body had failed him before, in the long-dead past, when he stood outside a flaming cockpit and watched his wife burn. He would not let that happen again. He would not, he screamed inside.

But his body wouldn't listen. A final bone-jarring strike deadened his nerves, the numbed fingers unraveled, and his love slipped out of his grasp.

"Yael!" he screamed, watching her face disappear into the blackness. "Yael!" Every fiber, every molecule and cell of his being burst in anguish. "Not again! Not this time!"

He let go and dropped after her. As he fell his good hand hit something soft. Instinctively he clutched it.

The eighty-foot drop into the trough of the waves lasted two lifetimes. Falling, he marked the bobbing head of his lover as she was swept away in the wake. Dark hair in a darker sea, only the water's phosphorescence outlined her.

Icy water stung him. Pressure crushed his chest, forcing air from his lungs as he knifed underwater. His ears popped. His lungs burned. After an eternity his descent slowed until he reversed his plunge and kicked outward. Air—his whole body screamed for air.

But which way was up? Blackness encased him in its deadly cocoon. The twisting fall had disoriented him. He looked about: Sable walls surrounded him. He might as well have had his eyes shut. He saw something. Overhead a flash illuminated the surface even though no moon or stars shone in the midst of this storm. He swam to the light.

Then a familiar sensation layered terror atop his determination. He was about to seize! The scarred locus of his oxygen-deprived brain started to respond as it had in the past. He would seize and drown. And Yael would be lost. No, no, his mind cried amid its pre-epileptic aura. He bit down hard into his tongue, striving to keep conscious by using the pain.

Adrift in the chilling darkness, Yael struggled to keep her

head above water. Spray choked her nostrils. A wave carried her up, offering a glimpse of sailing lights, illuminated masts, and flashing strobes . . . all tantalizingly beyond her reach. The *Carl Vinson* plowed away into the storm. The lights dwindled.

Panic assailed her. She wanted to scream, to thrash the water, to lose control. Stop, a part of her shouted: Live! Live, and there is always hope. Always hope, her grandfather's phrase. His kindly face grew in her mind, his finger pointing to nowhere, admonishing her that she held precious genetic material for future generations. That was the big picture, he said; never forget your genes. She laughed. Her genes were all wet.

That private joke warmed her. Christopher's face came to mind. She desperately wanted to live, to see him again. And he was safe. She was treading water, riding the waves while her mind inventoried her situation. Craning her neck, she searched for the ship. Pinpoint lights appeared, only to be shuttered by cresting waves. The *Vinson* was beyond reach.

Another swell thrust her toward the sky. A flash of light winked off to her right. She paddled in that direction.

Jackson bent over the fragments of the landing aid television camera snared in the tattered safety nets. His eyes followed the scars in the nonskid that led over the side. The collapsed frame, flapping netting—all met his gaze. A white object hung from the basket . . . Yael's tennis shoe. Instinctively the Marine sounded the man overboard alarm.

Yael swam to the flashing cloud. Each surge dangled the beacon before her, only to hide it in the following trough. So she played its deadly game of hide-and-seek, marking its location when she could and struggling on that bearing. As she came near she recognized it as a strobe flashing in its own cloud of mist. She reached out.

Her hand touched hair. A human head bobbed facedown in the water. A hand clutched a life vest. Fastened to the inflated collar, a water-activated Firefly strobe cheerfully fired away, battling the darkness. Its light had guided her. She rolled the face out of the water.

It was Chris.

CHAPTER

——— 21 ———

U.S. Navy Nuclear Carrier Carl Vinson, *Mid-Pacific*

"I can't launch a SAR chopper, Admiral!" the XO protested. "The SH-3s are all below decks in the hangar. That 747 is blocking the main elevators. And the port elevator is fouled by debris from the Boeing's wing. I just can't get them up!"

"I've got two of my people out there! I want them found!"

"We're working on it, sir."

"How long?"

"It'll take three hours to jack up the plane and tow it off the elevators."

"Three hours!"

"Please, Admiral, we're doing the best we can. This storm is making the salvage more difficult."

"We don't have three hours. They'll die of hypothermia by then, if they don't drown first!" Gifford scowled at the veins popping over the commander's forehead. His thumb jerked contemptuously at the plane. "Push the fucker over the side."

Chief O'Brien agreed.

The XO choked. "Admiral, that plane costs millions! You can't do that!"

Jackson's hand moved to the .45 automatic strapped to his side. The XO noted his movement. O'Brien rubbed his mouth on a greasy sleeve in anticipation.

The XO straightened. "I would have to have written orders. . . ."

"Jackson?"

"Aye, aye, sir." The Marine whipped out a notepad from the leg pocket next to his Colt .45, enjoying the commander's jump as his hand passed over the pistol.

PUSH THE FUCKING PLANE OVER THE SIDE, Henry Clay wrote in huge block letters. He signed it Gifford, VADM, and handed it to the XO.

"I hope that order is plain enough, Commander."

The XO grimaced. "Push the fucking plane over the side, Chief."

"Aye, aye, Commander." O'Brien stormed off to punish the plane that had killed his commanding officer.

Yael stared at the unresponsive face of her lover. His eyes were closed, the face pallid in the flickering strobe. Why wasn't he safe on the carrier? Had he followed her? Was he dead? Her mind reeled. She shook off her fears and her questions. His skin was icy to the touch, but so was hers in this water. She cradled him, keeping his head above the waves, treading water. With the next flash of the strobe she forced his eyelids open.

His pupils reacted to the stabbing light! He was alive. But he wasn't breathing.

Prying the life jacket from his grip, she slipped it on while cinching the straps. Next she tilted Chris's head, pinched his nose with her fingers, and fastened her mouth over his. She gave three sharp breaths.

Nothing happened.

Stifling her dread, she blew again, all the while shielding

him against her. Air escaped passively from his lungs. More air, she would give him more air. She inhaled a mouthful of water and choked. Sobbing, she tried again, refusing to give up. Three more deep breaths passed her life force, willing him to live.

Maddox twitched. A weak cough followed. Sea water and phlegm spewed out of his mouth.

"Chris, Chris," she alternately cried and laughed while he gulped lungfuls of air. "You're alive." She repeated the words over and over.

"Eat this!" Chief O'Brien snarled as he rammed Tillie into the side of the Boeing. Like a vindictive Lilliputian swarming over the remains of a fallen giant, the chief petty officer directed the NS-50 aircraft crane in a furious attack on the 747. Each strike inched the behemoth closer to the edge.

A final stab and the aircraft's nose swung over the water. O'Brien dropped to the deck beside his crane. He released a single wire cable from its padeye and watched the Boeing slip away. Tortured metal screeched into the night as the Boeing 747 resumed its path to a watery grave, a path that had been interrupted less than an hour before. As a final, defiant act the remorseless machine carried along the crushed remains of the fire tractor, and with it the body of Admiral Clement Turner. Hissing, it sank beneath the waves with its grisly keepsakes.

"It'll be another two hours, Admiral," O'Brien apologized. He hated to bring that news, but the XO was hiding back up in the navigation bridge, fearful of bearing bad messages.

"What's the trouble now, Chief?" Gifford voiced his rising frustration. He braced against the roll of the flight dock, watching the damage-control crews cutting with their welding torches. The flashing arc welders sent mushrooming clouds of incandescence, mixed with sheets of rain and fog, spinning into the darkness. The repair crew jerked around in the stroboscopic lighting like unruly puppets. Gifford's watch flickered with the light. Forty-eight minutes! His missing doctors had been in the water at least forty-five minutes.

"Sir, that 747 cut across the elevators. It bent the edges of the elevator platform so it's jammed. The boys are cutting it free now." O'Brien jerked his thumb at the cutting torches. "But they say two more hours . . . max." The chief's voice carried a softer tone that was the closest he ever came to apologizing.

"How long can they last in this water?"

Curtis Owen had been sent down to sick bay to find the answer. He'd located a medical officer in the midst of inoculating the isolated passengers and had just returned with the information. "Three hours, Admiral."

Gifford wiped the spray from his face. His hand automatically brushed across his shirt, but that, too, was soaked. Like Owen and Jackson, he was drenched by the storm.

Jackson offered a camouflaged handkerchief. That also was sopping.

"Camouflage?" Gifford raised a dripping eyebrow as he accepted the wet cloth. "You never cease to amaze me, Jackson."

Jackson grinned. "Semper Fi, Admiral."

Henry Clay turned away to gaze into the ebony wall off the stern. His mind easily imagined Maddox and the girl bobbing out there alone, abandoned. He sighed. It'd been a long week. They'd all come so far together, and now to end like this . . .

"I used to think it was easier in the field. But I was wrong. When you lose someone in an operation that you're flying from your desk, they're only typewritten names on some computer printout. It's harder when you know their faces. You never quite get them out of your head, do you? They may fade with the years, but they're always there, aren't they?"

"Aye, aye, Skipper." Jackson carried his share of ghosts.

Gifford desperately wanted Chris and Yael to live. His world would never be right without their being together. He'd gotten them into this, and he wanted to get them out. Sure, he'd made all the right decisions, and his judgments had stopped the venom virus. His analytical sense told him that. But that no longer mattered. He wanted them safe.

He was a soft old man after all. But he needed this. And he had only one ace left to play. "Jackson, promise me one thing."

"Skipper?"

"Promise me when the H-3 is ready to go, you'll go along, and you'll bring them back."

"I'm supposed to be saving you," Christopher mumbled between chattering teeth. He coughed out another wad of blood-tinged sea water. His skin looked ghastly in the flashing light from the life-jacket strobe.

"You did, darling. You brought the life jacket, don't you remember? It's keeping us both afloat." Yael struggled with her own shivering. She pulled Maddox closer, and they quivered together.

The cold water leached all feeling from her hands, so she entwined her fingers in his shirt to keep from losing her hold. Over the last hour the shivering had become involuntary and more intense. In spite of floating with their legs and arms crossed and held against their bodies to reduce heat loss, the water was winning. She knew they were becoming hypothermic. Soon they would lose consciousness; then their hearts would stop.

"Did I?" he sounded confused.

"Yes, darling. You saved me."

"Yael." He shifted in her grasp to bring his face closer to hers

"Yes, Chris," she answered patiently. After he'd regained consciousness he'd insisted on her wearing his jacket as well as the life vest. The extra layers provided her with more insulation, but he was paying a terrible price for his chauvinism. Clearly he was cooling more rapidly than she was.

"I'm sorry I let go of you."

"You did the best you could. Don't talk. Try to save your strength."

"I let you down. . . ." His words were faint, barely audible, although his lips were next to her ear. "Let you down," he repeated. "You and Tangaroa . . ." His words trailed off into silence, and he spoke no more.

For what seemed an eternity Yael clasped him against her body, trying to share her waning warmth. She managed to keep his head above the swirling waves. The night crawled on endlessly, and with it the storm. Yael prayed, but the sea had no ears. And the storm had no pity.

She thought of her grandfather. Silently she hummed a song he'd taught her as a child. She felt less alone after that. She remembered another song, but the words escaped her.

The cold was better now. She actually felt warm all over. Warm and tired, very tired. She closed her eyes. The warmth increased. She was back in Israel, on the beach, the warm beach. It was night, but the sun was rising. A noisy sun.

The sun was shining stronger now, bright, warm, chasing the night away. It moved directly overhead. The sun hovered above them.

The water splashed nearby. Wind beat the sea into a froth around them. Yael's lethargic eyes fluttered. She really wasn't interested. Something was moving toward her. She opened her eyes wider and smiled.

Someone was swimming into her dream. That person swam to them amid the wind-whipped swells. As he came closer she recognized his face. It was Jackson.

CHAPTER

22

Taongi Atoll, Marshall Islands, Mid-Pacific

The first traces of morning seeped above the ocean's rim. It was that magical time when night surrenders to day, enacting another power transfer eons old before a patient sea. The old guard shuffled off. A distant squall dumped its slanting rain across the horizon and departed, taking its waxen clouds beyond the growing influence of lavender and saffron light. The wind slackened to light airs, the seas calmed, and silence reigned across this coral atoll. It was a time of endurance. And as always, a time of change.

Coconut crabs scuttled about on their way to safety in the shadows. Night birds sailed away. To followers of Rousseau, this was nature in its purist form; but those casual observers would overlook the swirl in a tidal pool as a mantis shrimp captured a reef fish and a newborn bird was pulled from his nest by a tree crab. Nature as always cared little for labels, being cognizant of one supreme truth: Man belongs to nature, not nature to man.

Out of the shadows stepped Mau. The boy limped across the sand, dragging his deformed foot, and waded into the surf. At waist depth he stopped. Overhead the morning stars

268

watched. Mau wiped his hands on his *thu*. The waves lapped at his tattered T-shirt. Slowly he pulled the shirt over his head. The fabric parted with the strain. A few threads dropped into the sea, and a squirrel fish struck at them. Disappointed, the fish spat out the strands and swam off.

Mau folded the cloth reverently. Beneath the shirt he wore the cowrie shell amulet of Tangaroa, mark of the navigator. Starlight fired the polished shells. His fingers caressed the shirt, the last vestige of his long-vanished father. His right hand rose to the amulet on his chest. In his short life Mau had lost two fathers.

Carefully he placed the shirt atop an outgoing wave. The cloth raft hesitated briefly, then rode the surge out to sea. Mau watched the shirt until it was only a white speck in the darkened waters. Breathing deeply, he turned to the brightest star on the horizon and raised his arms.

"I sit on Satawal, I go rising Mailap to Truk, I sit on Truk, I go setting Mailap on Satawal . . ." Softly, hesitantly at first, he recited the *wofanu*.

The stars watched silently.

Mau's voice grew. He recounted another *wofanu*. Now the liturgy of island sightings poured out. Emptied, he stood trembling in the breakers.

Beyond the stars he heard the grumbling chuckle of Tangaroa.

"*Atirro*, old navigator." The boy bowed low to the light of the Flying Fish. Somehow he knew his mentor sat in the sky with the old gods. Tears flowed freely down his cheeks as he broke into the *itang*, the talk of light, repeating a student's farewell to his teacher:

> "I reach ahead, I reach behind.
> Will you still hold me,
> After my voyage?"

Henry Clay Gifford watched Mau leave the beach. He, too, had risen before the dawn to make peace with the spirits. At the water's edge the admiral produced a bottle of Wild Turkey.

"The sun's not over the yardarm yet, Truck, but I guess we can break that old navy tradition. I've broken so many, one more won't matter."

Gifford broke open the bottle and took a long drink. The liquor burned a path down the back of his throat. Gifford coughed to quench the fire. He held the bottle at arm's length.

"I promised you this Wild Turkey, Truck." Gifford poured the contents into the ocean. The sea accepted the libation without change. "I never envisioned it would be like this, but neither one of us should be too surprised. The coins of our payment include death and dishonor. Death for you. Dishonor for me—this time maybe you're the lucky one."

He bowed his head and began the prayer for all seamen lost at sea.

"Godless heathen! Devil's spawn! Get out!" Fiery words shattered the solitude. Gifford interrupted his service.

A flutter of unsettled terns marked the direction of the disturbance. A giggling naked woman darted out of the bushes to dodge across the beach toward the forest. Close behind ran Jackson, clutching his pants in one hand and the woman's pareo in the other. He tossed the dress to the girl as he skidded to a halt by his commander. The nubile thing scampered away like a forest deer. Jackson quickly secured his trousers.

"Sins of the flesh!" Reverend Castle thundered as he wheezed up the path. Even in the dim light his face glowed crimson, and his chest heaved from exertion. "Were you two involved in this act of fornication?" Castle shook a heavy Bible at the two men while his head swiveled about for the girl.

"No, Reverend," Gifford countered, producing a small, worn Bible of his own. "We were holding a service for one of our men lost at sea."

Jackson bowed his head.

Castle shot a suspicious look at the Marine. His eyes raked the man. Surprisingly, Jackson's fatigues looked neat, and the man showed no signs of exertion.

Jackson crossed himself.

"Would you care to join in the service, Reverend?" Gifford asked.

The minister shook his head. "No time, thank you. I'm hot on the trail of God's work."

With that the reverend churned across the sand in search of a sinner. A confused Gifford watched Castle's rumpled coat plunge into the bushes.

Gifford shook his head. "I guess stamping out sex has priority over memorials. Even for good men," the admiral added bitterly. "By the way, Jackson, when did you become Catholic?"

"Methodist, sir. At least, that's what I was baptized as."

"What was that crossing all about?"

"Seemed like a nice touch—for the benefit of the reverend, sir. Even though he's a Methodist, too."

"Don't get too dramatic on me, Jackson. I couldn't stand that. One needs some constant standards in life."

"No, sir. Damn, I almost forgot." Jackson extracted a crumpled paper from his pocket. "I was looking for the admiral when I got . . . er, distracted." Jackson stared wistfully at the forest where the girl had vanished. "Cipher from the pres." He thrust the wad into Gifford's hand with a broad grin. "For your eyes only."

"And of course you know what's in it, eh?"

The Marine's head bobbed happily.

Henry Clay unrolled the message and read out loud: "'Outstanding job. You are a credit to your country. All the world marvels at how we stopped this terrorist threat to humanity.'" Gifford paused. "We? It seems the president and I are heroes." His voice dripped with irony.

Gifford recrumpled the message and ground it into the

wet sand with his shoe. "He didn't even mention you, Jackson."

"That's good, sir. Don't want those brass hats knowing I exist."

Once more movement caught the admiral's eye. A couple moved arm in arm toward him. They stopped to kiss, enjoying the predawn serenity as well as each other.

Shadows from the palm and *kiawe* trees cloaked the lovers as they paused at the edge of the sand.

Henry Clay caught himself sighing. An inner part of him wished for better things. He stifled this weakness.

The girl wore a Polynesian pareo draped to reveal long legs. The moon threw off its cloud wraps to cast its beams upon the lovers. The waning moonlight was especially kind to the girl. It enveloped her ebony hair and kindled her eyes. Unlike the other women of Taongi, she had violet eyes.

Yael kissed Christopher Maddox with all the fire and passion she had used to hold him only hours before in the ocean storm.

Gifford called to them, "Better not let the right Reverend Castle see you holding hands!"

The couple strolled to him.

"But we're married, Admiral." Yael smiled dreamily. "Thank you again for that lovely ceremony." Her smile beamed even in the twilight. She released her hold on Christopher long enough to plant a kiss on the admiral's cheek.

"That's not permitted either. Kissing a superior officer. What happened to the Israeli Defense Force that I knew?" Gifford covered his embarrassment.

"We still show no mercy," Yael said, laughing.

"I think puritanical issues will be the least of Reverend Castle's problems." Maddox gathered her in his arms. "Dr. Cotter was up all night reorganizing the clinic. He was swearing a blue streak over the lack of sterile precautions and sex education. Said the prenatal clinic was a disgrace. Right now he's gunning for Castle."

Gifford scratched a mosquito bite on his neck. "That *was* one of my better ideas, enlisting Dr. Cotter to run the medical clinic on Taongi. Lord knows he needed something to do, and this place could use an obstetrician."

"He almost jumped at the idea when you pointed out there were no lawyers within eighty thousand square miles," Maddox added, laughing.

"Marrying you two was another brainstorm. Got you off my back, and onto yours . . . so to speak."

Yael sighed. "It's so beautiful here. So peaceful. It's a perfect place to have a honeymoon. It's sad I have to go back to Israel. Admiral, do you think you could arrange a visa for Chris?"

"No," Gifford replied flatly. "Commander Maddox still has important research to finish on sea snake antidotes. I don't ever want this sort of thing to happen again. You understand that work would be classified. He's in the U.S. Navy, and you're in the Israeli Army. Of course, you have dual citizenship, but you're still under orders from Israeli Command."

Her face saddened, and tears brimmed in her eyes.

Gifford struggled to control a Cheshire cat grin. "Are you familiar with the Marshall Islands Marine Research Center? They specialize in sea snake study."

She shook her head.

"I'm surprised, Captain Ivanov, because you've been sleeping with the Research Center himself."

Both Chris and Yael looked puzzled.

"On my recommendation," the admiral continued, "the department has authorized Commander Maddox to work here on Taongi. And you, Yael, have been assigned to work with him—courtesy of the Israeli Defense Force. Your orders will be forthcoming. And I've got to figure how to hide this line item in the budget."

"How can we thank you, Admiral?" Maddox shook first his hand, then Jackson's. "Now I can keep an eye on Mau like I promised Tangaroa. He's an orphan, so now we're his

273

family. Cotter's got a friend of his—an orthopedic surgeon who loves to sail—lined up to fix the boy's clubfoot."

"It's the least I could do," Gifford shrugged. "I asked you to do some pretty hard things this week, and you gave more than I asked. Hell, consider this a wedding present."

"I'm still not clear how you found us in the middle of that storm," Maddox said.

Gifford grinned a second time. "Owen remembered that homing device was still implanted in your arm. And it was still working. Jackson just followed the signal."

"It saved my life twice." Maddox rubbed his arm respectfully. "Thank you for all you've done."

"We'll name our first son after you," Yael added.

"God, don't do that!" Gifford shuddered. "Asher's threatening to do that already. The world's not ready for another Henry Clay Gifford."

A buzzing shattered the air. Once again civilization encroached on this remote island.

The admiral studied his wristwatch. "Nine days," he noted as he turned the timer off. "Nine days ago all this started. Seems like another lifetime." His eyes settled on the horizon as he reflected on what had passed. No time for regrets, he reminded himself. "Say, Jackson, my birthday watch kept perfect time."

The Marine beamed. "Ought to, Skipper. It's the best money can buy."

"You know"—Gifford turned his wrist slowly, admiring the heavy case—"I've wondered how you could afford this on your pay. Had to be damned expensive."

"No sweat, sir. I got a special price for it."

"Special price? You didn't steal it, did you?"

"Hell, no, Skipper." Jackson chuckled. "Just the opposite. I was lighting up a smoke that night, trying to find a liquor store so I could buy you a bottle of Wild Turkey. Well, these two dudes tried to mug me in the alley."

"And?"

"Well, the three of us had a sort of discussion. One of them had this fancy watch, and he agreed to part with it."

"You didn't kill him, I hope."

"Skipper!" Jackson feigned an injured expression. "No, sir. I paid him for it, and he left with his unconscious buddy. Even got a bill of sale—all nice and legal. Got it for twenty bucks."

Henry Clay hefted the gold Rolex. "Worth every penny, Sergeant. Thank you, again."

Everyone laughed. Yael hugged Jackson and kissed Gifford again. Her lingering warmth reminded him of how sorely he missed his wife. He thought of long-forgotten plans and shattered dreams, all gone with her death. Yael and Christopher had rainbows in their eyes, as he had once had. Silently Gifford wished them the future he'd been denied.

He squared his shoulders and cleared his throat.

"Come on, Jackson. Time to go. I can hardly wait to see the paperwork on my desk."

The two warriors trudged to the waiting helicopter. As Gifford turned back to wave a real rainbow arced above the island.

Among the quarter poker machines
and cowboy bars was an ex-cop who
couldn't leave the past alone...

ROJAK'S RULE

STEVEN M. KRAUZER

Available from Pocket Books

POCKET
B O O K S

512